WINGS OF HONOR

BOOK ONE OF THE FORGOTTEN FLEET

CRAIG ANDREWS

GW00568771

ALSO BY CRAIG ANDREWS

The Machinists:

Fracture

Splinter

Martyr

Capture

Exposure (Forthcoming)

The Forgotten Fleet:

Wings of Honor

Wings of Mourning (Summer 2021)

Wings of Redemption (Fall 2021)

For Callan,
who shines brighter than any star
and lights the world for everyone around him.
Now you have a book too.

Get exclusive fan discounts and bonus content when *Wings of Mourning* and *Wings of Redemption*, Books #2 and #3 of The Forgotten Fleet go live by signing up for the Craig Andrews mailing list.

Sign up for the mailing list!

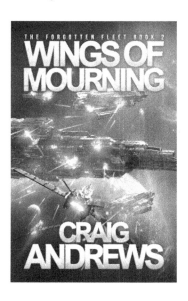

1

Coliseum, Terran Fleet Academy
  Sol System, Earth, High Orbit

CALLAN "CODA" O'NEIL SLIPPED ON HIS VIRTUAL-REALITY helmet, muffling the surrounding voices and sounds of excited anticipation. The VR's imaging display flickered to life, and the real-life image of his squadron donning their own simulation helmets on the floor of the Coliseum was replaced by a simulated first-person view of the inside of his fighter drone. Resistant to radar, lidar, and other forms of detection, the matte-black Z-18 Hornet flew silently through the digital representation of space.

This calm before the battle, the silence before the rest of his squadron plugged into the simulation and the radio chatter began, was usually one of Coda's favorite moments. But the upcoming battle was with Andrei Krylov's Shadow Squadron, and Coda's nerves and overwhelming desire to win spoiled whatever personal heaven the prebattle isolation normally provided.

Andrei Krylov, call sign "Moscow," was one of the finest drone pilots in the Terran Fleet Academy and, in Coda's opinion, its biggest prick. More importantly, Shadow Squadron was tied with Coda's own Viking Squadron for first place in the academy's standings. In addition to determining the Ace Squadron of their class, the battle would be one of the deciding factors in determining the pilots' post-graduation assignments.

Coda already knew where he would be stationed. The image of the sleek black hull of the SAS *Americas* filled his mind's eye. The battle cruiser was the flagship vessel in the Sol Fleet and home to the *Nonpareil*, the finest drone squadron the Sol Fleet had ever assembled. Coda would soon be one of them, fighting battles that weren't simulated, battles that actually meant something. He couldn't wait to rub Moscow's smug face in it.

One thing at a time, Coda told himself, dismissing the daydream. *Don't get ahead of yourself.*

"Heads-up," he said softly, and his heads-up display overlaid his view of space, providing him with important flight data and a small three-dimensional map displaying a full view of the battle. The battle map, which was relegated to the bottom right-hand corner of his vision, would soon be teeming with green and red dots indicating friendly ships and enemy fighters. For the moment, however, a white dot of the friendly capital ship cruised behind the friendly green symbol that marked his fighter.

Above the floor of the Coliseum, where Shadow and Viking Squadrons were plugged in, was a much larger version of the battle map. Nearly four stories tall and almost as deep, the battle map gave the spectators front-row seats to the upcoming incursion. Instead of the green and red dots on Coda's HUD, though, the spectators enjoyed three-dimensional, photo-real images of the fighter crafts.

There, the extensive view would shift to where the battle was thickest, like the vids of a space race moving to where the race was most interesting. A normal battle would draw most of the student body—it was a perfect opportunity to study a fellow squadron's tactics, after all—but there wouldn't be an empty seat in the house tonight. Even the faculty would attend. Not to mention representatives from Fleet Command.

Coda turned, the view in his VR helmet shifting seamlessly with him, and saw the rest of his squadron formed up beside him. Every battle simulation began this way, with the sixteen drones of the squadron stretched out in a simple line that gave each squadron leader a block of clay that they could shape into a formation of their choosing.

"All right, report in." Coda listened as all of his pilots announced they were plugged in and ready for action. When the last radioed that he was ready, Coda ordered the squadron to move into standard formation, and in practiced unison, the drones shifted into a V with Coda at its point.

He didn't intend to remain in the standard formation for long, but it gave the spectators something to see and provided his pilots with an opportunity to put their drones in action. Not that they needed the practice, of course; they'd logged thousands of hours in their drone operation bays, but Coda had long since learned that even the best pilot could hesitate during the early moments of battle. Having them shift formations before it began allowed them to get control of their nerves and avoid any serious mistakes.

"Contact!" Buster boomed suddenly.

"Copy that, Buster," Coda said. "What do we have?"

"Looks like your standard smash-and-go scenario," Buster said.

Coda glanced at his battle map, noting the newly appeared red dots marking the enemy fighters. They were two minutes out and zipping toward Coda's fighters, away from a capital ship of their own.

"Let's get some space between us and our ship." Coda keyed an intercept course and sent it to his squadron. "Seventy percent burn for sixty seconds on my mark... Mark."

Viking Squadron moved as one, angling below their previous flight path, and creating some space between them and their capital ship. The scenario's objective was simple: destroy the opposing side's capital ship and the easiest way to accomplish that was to destroy the opposing squadron then go for the capital ship itself.

The way this particular scenario had been constructed seemed to push them toward that inevitability. There was no cover, no territory to hold, nothing that would make their sensors go haywire. Not even a planet and an associated gravity well to contend with. Just empty space. The academy leadership wanted an old-fashioned duel. But Coda wasn't interested in giving them what they wanted. He was interested in winning. Thoroughly.

He wasn't planning on taking on the second-best pilot in the academy straight on, either.

"Vikings, form up in the Revised Coleman Diamond and wait for my mark."

The Coleman Diamond was a formation named after the famed pilot Commander Chadwick Coleman, a hero from the early days of the Baranyk War before drone warfare had replaced real pilots in real starfighters. Commander Coleman had used the formation in a suicidal attack on the Baranyk Fleet, the battle that had turned the tide of the war—or at least staved off imminent defeat, depending on who was telling the story.

The tactic was simple enough to understand though rarely leveraged. Unlike the starfighters of old, drones could be fielded in much greater numbers, replenished faster, and more importantly, since their pilots were tens of thousands of kilometers away, not limited by the same physical constraints the former star pilots had been.

As a result, the newer formations employed on the front were more fluid, capable of shifting strategies at a moment's notice. They more closely resembled a school of fish, changing directions on a dime, yet still coordinated, moving as one, never colliding. With that in mind, Coda hoped the formation would distract Moscow enough that he wouldn't notice the new wrinkle Coda had put on it.

Coda remained in position while thirteen drones formed a diamond behind him, its top and bottom points equal distances above and below the plane of the impending battle. Coda's wrinkle was to have the remaining two fighters throttle down to fall behind the formation then match speed before going completely dark. Their dark hulls would make them all but invisible to visual identification, and their lack of heat signatures would help hide them from computer detection.

The plan wasn't foolproof since radar or lidar could still detect the drones, and their residual heat signatures might intermittently pop up on enemy HUDs. Of course, anyone paying attention might also notice that the incoming squad was suddenly two fighters short, but that would be easy enough to miss since the fighters would go dark while the formation was coming together.

As soon as Viking Squadron completed its formation, Moscow countered it with one of his own.

"Coda, this is Buster. Are you seeing this?"

"I am," Coda said. Shadow Squadron had slipped into a spear with Moscow at its tip. "He means to punch through our diamond."

"What are we going to do?"

"We're going to let him."

"We're going to do what?"

"Three seconds before collision, break formation and form up into seven battle pairs twelve degrees positive-Z," Coda said. "That will give us a better attack angle as they break though. If they don't engage, burn hard in pursuit. If we do this right, we'll have time to break their formation before they're able to get to our capital ship."

"That's not going to give us a lot of time," Buster said. As Coda's best friend and flight leader, he was the only one who could get away with directly question Coda's orders.

"Then don't miss," Coda said. "Every shot counts. Vikings Fifteen and Sixteen, remain dark and maintain your trajectory. We're going to end this before they know what hit them."

They were committed now. Even if Coda wanted to alter strategies, they didn't have time.

"Contact in fifteen seconds." Coda shifted excitedly in his seat. All his time spent at the prestigious military academy, everything he'd worked for, every test he'd aced, and each battle he'd won culminated in this moment. Anything short of a decisive victory would be a supreme disappointment. "Ten seconds. Prepare to break formation."

At seven seconds, Coda fired a volley of digital projectiles at the incoming drone spear. He hadn't given the order, but the other ships in the formation followed his lead, firing as well. The odds of them hitting one of the incoming vessels was slim, the distances were too great, but like before, the action allowed his fighters to get the first shots out of the way.

"Five seconds," Coda said. Then three. "Break!"

The diamond shattered, breaking into seven shards of two fighters apiece, all darting above the battle plane. There was no up or down in space, but if there were, the new position would have given Coda's fighters the high ground. They blanketed Shadow Squadron's flight trajectory with cannon fire.

Moscow didn't have time to adjust course and lost four fighters as they sped through the barrage. Unfortunately, the losses weren't enough to force them into a different strategy.

Coda keyed in his pursuit and maximized thrust, burning hard. His wingman, Hound, just off his wing in the dash-two position, did the same. Panic flared in Coda's chest as Shadow Squadron showed no signs of breaking course. He keyed in on the nearest enemy fighter, thumbing the switch on his joystick, activating his missiles. A red square appeared around the target, and a second indicator, larger than the first, tracked behind it.

The target took evasive actions, trying to slip missile lock. But this is where Coda shined. He countered the target's moves almost as if he knew what the other pilot was going to do before they did it, and quickly closed the distance. As he did, he toggled the lead fighter and the Viking capital ship. A countdown appeared in the corner of his vision, counting down the time before the tip of the spear was within firing range of Viking Squadron's capital ship.

This is going to be close.

The two indicators came into alignment on the enemy target, then glowed more brightly and was accompanied by a steady tone. Coda had missile lock.

"Viking One," Coda announced. "Fox three!"

Coda launched the first of his eight AIM-220s. He didn't have visual on the missile, it was too small to register in the black, but a yellow indicator identified it on his HUD. It zipped from his fighter, streaking toward its target.

"Splash five!" Coda shouted as the enemy drone exploded in a brief flash of light. He shoved the joystick forward, avoiding the debris from the destroyed drone as another flash of light flared, and another red dot disappeared from his battle map.

Six down. Ten to go.

Five fighters remained in the haft of the spear, the rest creating a V at its head. Positive-Z, Coda and his wingman had a clear firing angle, but just as they got missile lock again the haft of the spear broke away, streaking toward its pursuers. Half of Coda's squadron was forced to take evasive action and engage the enemy.

Coda and Hound held course. *Not me. Not today, Moscow.*

He eyed the countdown to their firing range, then searched the battle map hoping to see signs of life from Vikings Fifteen and Sixteen. Viking Squadron's best chance of winning was if the two fighters could get to Shadow Squadron's capital ship before Moscow got to theirs. It was a race, and one Coda was beginning to feel less confident about winning.

Two more fighters broke away from Shadow Squadron, flipping nose to tail and plotting an intercept course with Coda and Hound. It was a maneuver only a drone could perform. At a minimum a real pilot would have blacked out under the immense strain. More likely, the inside of the cockpit would have been coated in human soup.

"Evasive maneuvers," Coda ordered, and he and his

wingman split, allowing the attacking fighters to slip between them.

"They're coming around on our tails," Hound said.

"Break off," Coda said. "Stall them. Keep them off my six. I'm staying on the leader."

"Roger."

Hound flipped, then spun and shot toward the nearest enemy fighter, opening up his cannons. Coda stayed focused on the tip of the spear, trusting his wingman would keep him safe. Moscow was at the tip of that spear. He knew it.

A glint caught his eye, something closer to a lesser darkness than to light, then was followed by another flash of light just off Moscow's wing. Coda looked back at his battle map, and all became clear. Buster, on a cleaner attack vector, had fallen into firing range. Coda could almost see Moscow calculating his chances. Could he get into missile range before Buster eliminated him and his wingman?

Not likely.

Moscow must have come to the same conclusion. He aborted their attack run, diving negative-Z below the battle plane and racing back toward the dogfight. Grinning, Coda flipped his drone, plotting a new intercept course.

In his all-or-nothing gambit Moscow had accepted catastrophic casualties and was now significantly outnumbered. Coda's squadron remained at full strength, while Moscow's was down nearly two-thirds. If Coda had been in Moscow's shoes, he would have doubled down on the attack, but the risk of losing that way, losing without firing a single shot, would have been too much for Moscow to bear. At least this way, he could save a little face in front of the room full of superiors and say he'd taken some of Viking Squadron with him.

The battle's over, Moscow. The rest is just a formality.

Moscow entered the dogfight, attacking with desperate ferocity. His pilots were on the run, most with tails, and disappearing by the second. Moscow provided aid where he could, guiding his pilots into trajectories that brought their pursuers into his firing range. It wasn't enough to turn the tide of the battle, but Moscow had drawn blood. And as each friendly indicator disappeared from his HUD, Coda grew more and more frustrated.

As the battle had played out, he'd had illusions of completing it without a single casualty. That dream had disappeared.

Coda weaved through the fray, staying on Moscow, and little by little gained on him. Then, as Moscow slipped through the edge of the dogfight, he flipped nose to tail and rocketed directly toward Coda's fighter.

He knows it's me. He knows I'm coming.

Coda settled into his seat, blinking to ensure his vision was clear. He wanted Moscow. Wanted to destroy him. Grind him into oblivion. He would only get one shot at this. If he made a mistake, Moscow would turn him to dust, and regardless of whether Viking Squadron won or not, Coda would never live it down.

Coda tightened his grip on the joystick. He and Moscow opened fire at the same time, the two ships speeding toward each other at incredible speeds. They juked and janked, tracer fire ripping passed their cockpits, somehow avoiding the incoming slugs and staying on course.

Three seconds.

Coda held course, continuing the barrage, finger held firmly on the trigger, rounds erupting from the six-barrel gatling gun to the tune of four thousand per minute. Moscow did the same.

Jerking his joystick to the side, Coda pitched his drone

into a wide aileron roll. He came out of it slightly below the battle plane expecting to have a clear shot at Moscow's underbelly. The other pilot had anticipated the maneuver. They were now on a direct collision course. Slugs slammed into each other, giving the pilots a preview of what was to come.

Coda screamed, finger still pressed against the trigger as his ammo ran out. Moscow was still—

The simulation faded to black. The image of Moscow's incoming drone dissolved in Coda's VR display.

"No!" Coda bellowed.

He yanked off his helmet and stood, his eyes immediately going to the large battle map overhead. Moscow had killed him. The thought was nearly enough to make him sick. The only thing worse than losing was losing to Andrei fucking Krylov, asshat extraordinaire. Except when his eyes found the vid screen above, it too was black.

Confused, Coda looked around to find the rest of his squad throwing their helmets aside, screaming and high-fiving those close to them. Before he could register what had happened, Buster was pulling him into a hug, slapping his back hard enough to knock the wind out of him.

"We did it!" Buster yelled into his ear. "Oh my god, we did it."

"Did what?" Coda said. "What happened?"

Buster pushed Coda away and gave him a pointed look. "What happened? We won!"

"We what?"

"I said we won!" Buster grabbed Coda by the back of his head and drew Coda's forehead to his. "Your nearly disastrous strategy actually paid off."

Coda finally allowed himself to smile. Maybe Moscow hadn't killed him after all.

"You really didn't know?" Buster asked. "What did you think happened?"

Coda didn't respond. He'd grown obsessed with Moscow and had lost sight of the larger objective. He'd completely missed it when Viking Fifteen or Sixteen—he didn't even know who had fired the winning shot—had ended the simulation and claimed victory. Then in ripping off his helmet in frustration, he'd missed the victory message that would have been displayed across his HUD.

His superiors wouldn't miss that act of arrogance and attitude unbecoming of a drone pilot. But he refused to worry about that now. He'd just beaten Andrei Krylov and Shadow Squadron, and his Vikings were the Ace Squadron of their graduating class. Everything Coda had dreamt about for the last several years was about to become a reality.

2

Viking Squadron Ready Room, Terran Fleet Academy
  Sol System, Earth, High Orbit

CHILLED CHAMPAGNE WAITED FOR THE VICTORS IN THE VIKING Squadron ready room. The pilots rushed forward, pushing and shoving their way to the bottles, ready to shake, uncork, and spray their fellow victors as though they had just won the World Series.

"Wait! Wait! Wait!" Coda screamed over the din. "Hold up a second!"

His pilots did as ordered, though they reminded him of a group of puppies, unable to sit still without trembling with excitement. They still wore their slate-gray flight suits fashioned after the ones worn by twenty-first-century fighter pilots.

Coda surveyed the room, milking the moment and testing their patience. "I just want to say a few words," he said. "When I took command of this squadron a year ago, I didn't know what we had. But I do now. We have the best damn pilots in the academy!"

Cheers erupted.

"And so does every other pilot, teacher, civilian, janitor, and commander in this place! You are the best. The best of the best. And it's been a pleasure serving as your squadron leader."

This was met with an even more enthusiastic chorus of cheers, and some of the pilots took things further, shouting their own gratitude.

"The pleasure is ours, Coda!" Buster shouted.

"You're the best!" Hound added. Coda's wingman had somehow found time to unzip his flight suit, exposing a black tank top underneath.

"Moscow ain't got nothing on you!" Hot Rod shouted.

The last one made Coda laugh, even if it was a break from decorum. He should have reprimanded the pilot, but their time was coming to an end, and he didn't want to mar an otherwise joyous moment. Besides, the ready room was a place of confidence for the pilots, a place where everyone was equal and could speak his or her mind.

"No, he doesn't," Coda said. "And Shadow Squadron ain't got nothing on you, either." He turned to Buster, who was holding an unopened bottle of champagne. "Let me see that."

His friend handed him the bottle, and Coda quickly uncorked it. He held it high so all could see. "To Viking Squadron!"

Coda took a long pull from the bottle and handed it back to Buster, who echoed the sentiment with a drink of his own then handed it to the next pilot. Around the room the bottle went, until it found its way to Hot Rod, who finished it off. Another cheer went up, then the true celebration got underway.

Sometime later, Coda found himself sitting with Buster at the back of the ready room, watching as the pilots of Viking Squadron joked and told stories, enjoying their final moments as a group. It was one of the rare moments Coda had seen his fellow pilots completely without inhibition.

They'd gone through their formal victory celebration, where Captain Hughes himself presented their victory pins, before returning to the ready room. With that behind them, they were left completely without supervision. No senior officers. No commanders. They could finally be themselves, and they weren't letting such an opportunity go to waste.

"I can't believe it's over," Buster said.

"Me, neither," Coda said. "You going to miss it?"

Buster shrugged. "Probably."

"I will," Coda said. "We really did do something special, you know?"

"Of course I do. We beat Moscow." Buster shoved Coda playfully. "I'll tell you what I'm *not* going to miss, though. I won't miss having to juggle studies with simulations. Life's about to get a lot simpler."

"You think?"

Buster leaned back in his seat, throwing a foot on the back of the chair in front of him. "Definitely."

Coda wasn't sure he agreed. Their time at the academy was coming to an end, but that only meant they would be joining the real war effort. Flying with real drone squadrons. Fighting in real battles. Stationed on battle cruisers and capital ships, not a floating school orbiting the Earth. But he didn't want to argue with his friend and spoil his mood. *Not today.*

"When do you think we'll get our orders?" Coda asked.

"You're the Squadron Leader. I was hoping you knew."

"They haven't told me anything yet."

"It's got to be soon, though, right? I mean, what else are we going to do? Sit around and jerk off all day?"

Coda laughed. Like all young men, if Buster wasn't playing with his junk, he was talking about it. The familiarity of the male banter put Coda at ease, though. "You're right. It'll probably be soon. So do me a favor."

"Of course."

"Don't think about it. Just enjoy it. Enjoy this." *Because I don't think life is going to be as simple as you think it is.*

Viking Squadron Ready Room, Terran Fleet Academy
   Sol System, Earth, High Orbit

ONCE VIKING SQUADRON HAD EMPTIED THE REMAINING champagne bottles and were feeling more than a little light in the head, they left the ready room for the final time.

Coda lingered behind, soaking up the view, committing it all to memory. At some distant point in the future, he knew he would think back on this moment and remember when and where his journey had *truly* begun. He knew that wherever his orders took him, he would be successful. He didn't have a choice. He was fighting for something greater than himself.

The ready room emptied into a wide corridor, where the floor curved upward in both directions. The Terran Fleet Academy, like all space stations designed before humanity had reverse-engineered Baranyk technology and learned to manipulate gravity, was built around a central axis with a spinning wheel providing artificial gravity. Students and pilots loitered in the corridor, reliving the recent battle. Coda stopped just outside the ready room. Moscow stood with a few members of Shadow Squadron outside a nearby doorway, their eyes intent on the Viking Squadron ready room.

They've been waiting for us.

Adrenaline pulsed through Coda's veins, making his arms and legs feel light. He knew better than to think that Moscow simply wanted to congratulate him. Coda looked down the corridor to where the rest of his squadron was already disappearing from view, too invested in their celebration to notice their squadron leader had fallen behind.

Coda briefly thought about ignoring Moscow and his thugs, acting as if he hadn't seen them, but his supreme dislike for the man won out. Besides, he wasn't one to back down from a fight. It wasn't in his blood. It was the same reason he'd sought out Moscow during the simulation.

It's also why you have several demerits on your academy record.

Coda leaned his back against the corridor wall just outside the ready room, directly across the corridor from Moscow and his six thugs. "Come to congratulate us on our victory?" Coda looked down at the Ace Squadron pin at his breast then back up at Moscow with a patronizing grin.

Moscow spat at his feet and crossed the hallway. "You know as well as I do that your *victory* was luck."

"It doesn't look that way in the standings."

Moscow stopped directly in front of Coda, his face inches from Coda's. "I had you, *O'Neil*."

In most instances, calling a pilot by something other than their call sign wasn't necessarily a form of disrespect, but Coda knew better. He saw it in the way Moscow sneered as he said Coda's last name. He was trying to connect Coda

to his father, to remind him who Joseph O'Neil had been...
and what he had done.

Burying his anger, Coda feigned nonchalance. "You
didn't have dick."

"You and me, O'Neil, let's go. One on one."

"What the hell's going on?"

Coda looked up, spotting the rest of Viking Squadron
heading back down the corridor. Buster was at their head,
his pace quick, eyes on Moscow as if expecting the other
squadron leader to do something.

"Moscow didn't get enough of Viking Squadron," Coda
said. "He wants a rematch." It wasn't exactly what Moscow
had proposed, but Coda didn't care. He didn't have any
intention of honoring the request anyway.

Moscow shot an uneasy look at the approaching mob of
Viking pilots. Even with his gang, he was outnumbered.
"That's not—"

"Thing is," Coda interrupted, turning back to Moscow,
"what's in it for me? Battling you would be like arm
wrestling a girl. If I win, who cares? I already beat you. But if
I *lose*, well, then I got beat by a girl. It's a lose-lose. You know
what I mean?"

Laughter filled the corridor. Coda smiled and made for
his squadron, turning his back to Moscow.

"You're just like him, aren't you, O'Neil?" Moscow's voice
was cold and sharp, and it cut like a knife driven into Coda's
back. "You're just like your father."

Coda froze.

"A *coward*."

Before Coda knew what he was doing, he'd spun, his
right fist rocketing through the air in a vicious right hook. It
connected cleanly with Moscow's jaw, dropping the larger
man. But Coda wasn't done. He was on top of Moscow in an

instant, one fist holding his flight suit, the other driving into Moscow's nose. Blood sprayed across Coda's pale knuckles, staining the clean metallic surface of the corridor crimson. He heard shouts and screams as someone tried to pull him away, but Coda shoved them off.

Nobody talked about his father like that. Nobody disrespected his family. Nobody could do that but him. The primal instinct buried deep inside him meant to use Andrei as an example of what happened when someone broke that unspoken rule.

When someone finally wrestled him off Moscow, Coda's eyes stung with tears, and he could barely lift his arms. Lying helpless on the floor, his face barely recognizable, Moscow groaned, moving slowly.

"We need to get out of here," Buster said. "Come on."

Buster pulled Coda away from the scene, dragging him up the corridor through the group of Viking pilots. They watched him in shock, eyes wide, mouths agape. Coda's face burned with shame. He'd lost control of his emotions and let Moscow goad him into doing something stupid.

Maybe he was right. Maybe you are *like your father.*

Buster hauled him to his private quarters. "Get inside." Buster shoved him again, and Coda fell into the small room, catching himself on the edge of his bed. His friend followed him into the room, closing the door behind him. "What the hell was that? Christ, man! What was going through that tiny-ass brain of yours?"

"He insulted my family," Coda said.

"I don't care what he did. We're twenty-four hours away from graduation and receiving our orders. Do you have any idea what you just jeopardized?"

Coda didn't know what to say. He couldn't believe the sudden turn of events. An hour ago, he'd been primed to become one of the newest recruits on a ship on the front, and now he was... what? He had no idea what the future held in store now.

"I know your family name doesn't have the best... *reputation*," Buster continued, "and Moscow can be a royal ass. But you can't go around hitting everyone who insults your family's honor."

"You don't understand—"

"No, Coda. I do. Your father disgraced himself and everyone he's ever known. And you've taken it upon yourself to undo that."

Coda opened his mouth to speak, but the words died on his tongue.

"You see," Buster said. "I understand more than you think, and I respect the hell out of you for it. But you're not going to do any good if you're kicked out of the academy."

Coda found the edge of his bed and took a seat. He ran a hand over his closely cropped hair. "You don't think it'll come to that, do you?"

"You beat him pretty bloody." Buster crossed the small room, grabbed the only other seat, and dragged it in front of Coda. "But no, I don't think they'll kick you out. You're too damn good. Besides, what do they think will happen when they put five hundred soldiers together in a metal container floating through space and tell them to battle one another? And it wasn't like Andrei didn't deserve it. He had you up against the wall. Had his boys with him. What you did to him was self-defense."

Buster's version of the story wasn't entirely accurate, but it was close enough to the truth that it gave Coda hope.

"Thank you," Coda said.

"No problem."

"No. I mean it."

Coda had spent so much time planning for his future that he hadn't thought about who would be in it, and for the first time, he realized Buster probably wouldn't be a part of it. Meeting his friend's gaze, he saw that Buster had come to the same conclusion a long time ago.

No wonder he's so angry. I took away what was supposed to be his final happy moments with his squad mates.

"Go on back," Coda said. "Find the guys. Celebrate. Tell them I'll join them when I can."

"I'm not leaving you here, Coda."

"I'll be fine. They'll be worried, and I don't want to ruin their night. Please, go."

"You sure?"

But Coda didn't get a chance to answer. There was a knock at his door. Then a moment later, it opened, and two officers stepped inside.

"Ensign O'Neil," the first officer said, "come with us. Captain Hughes demands your presence."

The cold hands of despair strangled Coda's remaining hope. If Captain Hughes, Commander of the Terran Fleet Academy, wanted to see him, he was in more trouble than he'd realized.

4

Captain Hughes's Office, Terran Fleet Academy
Sol System, Earth, High Orbit

"Tell me, Ensign," Captain Gary Hughes said, "do you consider yourself a special kind of stupid?"

If Coda hadn't been standing at attention, his eyes on the wall behind his commanding officer, he might have stirred under the weight of Captain Hughes's gaze. Even sitting behind his desk, he was nearly as tall as Coda.

"No, sir."

"No?" Captain Hughes feigned surprise. "Then tell me how someone can be dumb enough to beat up one of their fellow students on the same day they were supposed to graduate."

"It was a temporary lapse in judgment, sir."

"A temporary lapse in judgment." Captain Hughes chewed on the words. He stood from behind his desk, his broad, two-meter frame towering over Coda. Space stations weren't built for men like Captain Hughes, whose clean-shaven head nearly touched the stainless-steel ceiling. Combine that with his square face, and he looked every bit like the career military man he was. "A temporary lapse in judgment."

The amusement in his voice terrified Coda more than anything else about the situation. Good things rarely followed a superior's laughter.

Captain Hughes rounded the desk and took a seat on its edge, crossing his arms. His cold eyes didn't match the amusement in his voice. "Tell me, Ensign, do you consider yourself an honest man?"

"Yes, sir."

"How about someone who takes responsibility for their mistakes?"

"I... I think so, sir."

"Then I'm confused, Ensign. Because from my perspective, striking Ensign Krylov once, maybe even twice, would have constituted a 'temporary lapse in judgment.' But three times? Four? Having to be dragged away by your fellow wingmen? That doesn't strike me as temporary. So either you're lying to me, *or* you're refusing to accept responsibility for your actions. So which is it? Are you lying or acting like a child?"

"Sir?"

"I asked if you're dishonest or immature."

"It was a mistake, sir. One I was goaded into."

"Ah, so it's the latter."

"Excuse me, sir?"

"I said it's the latter," Captain Hughes repeated. "Actions of a *boy*. An inability to accept responsibility. Not too surprising, given your family situation."

Coda's eyes slipped from the rear wall, finding Captain Hughes's.

"You have a weak spot, Ensign. One your enemies will exploit if you don't take better care of hiding it."

"With all due respect, sir, I don't see how I can hide my family *situation*. Our name is known throughout the galaxy, and it isn't thought of kindly."

"No, it's not, but that doesn't mean you have to wear it as a badge of shame. It drives you, Ensign. I can see that. But it also holds you back. Three times, you've been in this office, and all for the same reason: because you can't keep your anger in check. All because you thought defending your family honor was more important than defending the human race."

"Sir, that's not—"

"Another lapse in judgment?" Captain Hughes asked, raising any eyebrow. "Arguing with your commanding officer?"

"I'm sorry, sir."

"You're a damn fine pilot, son—nobody will debate that. Squadron Leader of the Ace Squadron of your graduating class, you should have your pick of commissions. Unfortunately, I can't recommend you for deployment. Not until you've learned to control your anger."

Coda's head spun. *This can't be happening.* It was his worst nightmare—beyond his worst nightmare.

"Permission to speak freely, sir?"

"Granted."

"You're making a mistake, sir." Coda kept his voice cool, devoid of all emotion. If getting angry had jeopardized everything he'd worked for, he wasn't about to make that mistake again. "I am a very good pilot, one of the best in my class, and from what I understand, there's a shortage of those skills on the front."

"That's where you're mistaken, Ensign. You're one of

over one hundred fifty pilots in a single graduating class from a single academy. There are others like it. Pilots, we have, Ensign. Drones, on the other hand... So maybe if you were in a more demanding field like advanced manufacturing or robotic engineering, something where you had to use that tiny brain of yours, I might be more lenient."

"This isn't just any academy, though, sir. This is the Terran Fleet Academy. The best of the best. And I'm in command of its top squadron. Surely that counts for something."

"It does," Captain Hughes said. "Which is why you're being allowed to graduate. You'll be stationed either in the Orbital Defense Force or on one of the smaller vessels deeper in the black. But you won't be on the front."

"All because of a little fistfight, sir?" Coda couldn't believe what he was hearing. The Terran Fleet Academy was a *military* institution. Violence wasn't just encouraged; it was taught.

"Because you clearly don't understand what it takes to be a part of a squadron. When you're in battle, a real battle, your fellow wingmen need to have absolute trust in you. There's no room for grudges. There's no room for ego. And there sure as hell isn't room for pilots who aren't capable of learning from their mistakes."

The jumble of emotions inside Coda was nearly enough to break him. Anger, frustration, devastation, confusion—he could barely tell them apart. They mixed with the fear he'd already felt, causing sweat to drip down his back and his eyes to water. He attempted to blink the emotion away, but it was too much. Captain Hughes was right. Controlling emotions was a requirement for any great pilot. And Coda just didn't have it.

But buried deeper was something that kept Coda standing, kept him from lashing out, from giving up. Determination.

He was Callan *O'Neil*. The cards had been stacked against him his entire life. He'd been through worse, faced stiffer odds, and still been accepted to the most prestigious flight academy in the Sol Fleet. This was only a setback, and one he refused to accept. He would fight. He would succeed. And when he won, he would smile at Andrei, Captain Hughes, and anyone else who had tried to stand in his way. He would make fools out of *all* of them.

"Let me remind you, son," Captain Hughes continued, his voice taking on a more somber tone. "We are at war with an enemy more terrifying than you can imagine. They have the advantage in technology. They have the advantage of numbers. And they've had us on the defensive for longer than you've been alive. We're the only thing that stands between them and the destruction of the human race. They don't give a damn about your family history or personal grudges. Do I make myself clear?"

"Yes, sir," Coda said.

"Good," Captain Hughes said. "Because if you're to stay in the drone fleet, you will begin your career elsewhere."

Coda blinked. "*If*, sir?"

Captain Hughes uncrossed his arms and stood with a sigh. "You're being given a choice, Ensign."

"Between what, sir?" Coda tried to temper the hope blooming in his chest.

Captain Hughes didn't respond, though. Instead, the door opened behind Coda, and another man strode in. He was shorter than the captain by a few centimeters though still thickly built, with ebony skin and closely cropped black hair peppered with white. Lines creased his forehead and the edges of his mouth, drawing Coda's eye to his brown eyes and full lips.

Coda struggled not to stare. The man in front of him was straight out of military legend. He'd killed more Baranyk than any other known pilot and was someone Coda had studied and tried to emulate during his time at the academy. Commander Chadwick Coleman.

"Ensign," Commander Coleman said. "You know who I am?"

"Yes, sir. It's an honor, sir."

"Spare it, Ensign," Commander Coleman said. "There's no time for flattery. I have a number of these to get through, so I'll be brief. I'm putting together a special squadron, and I want you to compete for a spot in it."

"Sir, I—"

"Before you give me your answer, Ensign, there are a few things you need to understand. There are no guarantees. You'll have to earn your place. And by 'special,' I mean top secret. Nobody can know who or what's involved. Understood?"

"Yes, sir."

"And it'll be dangerous. Far more dangerous than anything you've experienced, maybe even more dangerous than being on the front itself. But I'm offering you a chance to fly, Ensign."

"How many other pilots will be in the squadron, sir?"

"A few."

"Any I know, sir?"

"Perhaps."

"And who might I expect, sir?"

"Other pilots like yourself, Ensign. Pilots who have shown a knack for flying but might not have all the qualities Captain Hughes is looking for."

"How long will the deployment last, sir?"

"That depends on how successful we are."

Despite the commander's elusive answers, Coda wanted to say yes on the spot. Very few pilots had the chance to fly under the great Commander Coleman. But he had one last question. One that was essential to his longer-term goals.

"Will I get to kill Baranyk, sir?"

A smile parted Commander Coleman's face, exposing teeth as white as porcelain. "You might, Ensign. You very well might."

For the first time since beating Shadow Squadron, Coda felt like smiling. "Then sign me up, sir."

Commander Coleman pulled a tablet from the inside of his uniform and held it before Coda. "Just need your prints, Ensign."

Coda should have been more nervous than he was, but he placed the palm of his hand against the tablet, allowing it to scan and record his prints. Little green boxes similar to his targeting-guidance system appeared around his finger-tips, then when the tablet had taken a proper scan, they flashed, indicating a successful scan.

"Welcome to the training program, Ensign," Commander Coleman said. "Or should I say Lieutenant?"

Coda let himself smile. He wouldn't be promoted a full lieutenant yet, of course, merely a lieutenant junior grade, but it was a start, and it was certainly more than he'd expected only a few minutes before. "Thank you, sir."

"Don't thank me yet, Lieutenant. Grab any personal belongings you have and meet me in Shuttle Bay Three at sixteen hundred, ready to ship out."

"Yes, sir." Coda saluted and spun on his heels, dismissed.

"And, Lieutenant..."

Coda stopped in the doorway.

"You should know I flew with your father. He was a good man and a hell of a pilot. If you're half of what he was, I expect great things out of you."

For the first time in forever, Coda was speechless. He couldn't remember the last time someone had spoken kindly of his father, let alone compared Coda to him and meant it as a compliment. Eyes brimming with tears, and not knowing what else to do, he nodded to Commander Coleman then exited Captain Hughes's office.

———

"Ah, shit," Buster said as he entered Coda's quarters and saw Coda's personal belongings strewn about his bed. "That bad?"

"No," Coda said. "Not at all. Well, that's not true. Captain Hughes *did* rail into me for fifteen minutes and tell me that I wouldn't be joining any of the ships on the front, but then..." Coda paused, trying to figure out how he could tell his friend what had happened. "Then, well... it's classified, but it's really exciting."

"That's good," Buster said, sounding relieved but sharing none of the excitement Coda felt. "I think. What can you tell me about it?"

"Not much. Mostly that I won't be serving my time on a third-rate ship patrolling the belt or something."

"Glad to hear it." Buster took a seat, watching Coda place the rest of his personal belongings in his bag. There was something off about him.

"You okay?"

"Me? Of course." Buster smiled, but the expression didn't reach his eyes.

"You're full of it. What's up?"

"It's nothing, Coda. Really."

"Damn it, Buster, we've trained together for months. I can tell something's wrong."

"That's just it. We've trained with each other for months. You and me. Us and Viking Squadron. We're the Ace Squadron, and you're shipping out with barely a goodbye."

"It's the nature of the beast, Buster. But trust me, this is better than the alternative."

"I guess."

"It is." He zipped up his bag and set it aside. "Commander… the other officer said he had a few other meetings. I think he's recruiting other pilots. If you haven't been invited yet, I'm sure you will be."

"Why?" Buster asked. "Why me?"

"Because we were the Ace Squadron, and you played an integral part in that."

Buster laughed. It was livelier this time. More real. "I just kept your ass out of trouble."

"Which is a difficult job," Coda said. "Obviously."

"Obviously. What time do you ship out?"

"Sixteen hundred."

Buster looked up at the clock inset in the wall above the door. "Better get a move on it then."

Coda grabbed his bag and slapped Buster on the shoulder. "I'll see you on the ship."

"What if you don't?"

Coda didn't want to think about it. "Then you're going to kill a lot of bugs on the front."

"What do I tell the squad?"

"Tell them I'm doing something exciting and not to worry. They'll hear about it soon."

Buster nodded. "I will." He crossed the distance between them and pulled Coda into a tight hug. "Take care of yourself, Coda."

Coda hugged Buster back, slapping his friend hard on the back. "You too, man."

When the embrace ended, Buster smacked him on the arm. "And stay out of trouble. You're not going to have me looking after you."

Coda laughed. "I'll try. Probably fail, but I'll try."

"All right."

Coda nodded a final time, and not wanting to extend the moment out any longer, he left his quarters and best friend behind, headed toward the true unknown.

5

Docking Umbilical, Terran Fleet Academy
  Sol System, Earth, High Orbit

Coda floated through the docking umbilical connecting the academy to Commander Coleman's transport ship. Away from the spinning operational facilities of the rest of the space station, he didn't experience the simulated gravity felt elsewhere, instead relished the seldom-felt, disorienting zero-g experience. He and the rest of the academy pilots operated their drones in three-dimensional space, but those were simulations, and while simulations could train the mind how to think, they couldn't train the body how to react. As a result, his body wanted to panick, unsure whether it was floating, falling, or flying.

The umbilical was mostly transparent, giving Coda a breathtaking view of the Earth below. Two years had passed since he'd left, leaving behind everyone he'd ever known or loved. He and his mother hadn't separated on great terms—

Coda had seen to that when he'd applied for the Terran Fleet Academy against her wishes.

"I lost my husband to the war," she had said, tears streaming down her face. "I won't lose my only son too."

But lost him, she had. And her words continued to haunt him. His actions had driven a wedge between them, and she hadn't been there for his graduation from basic. She hadn't responded to his letter informing her that he'd been accepted into the prestigious Terran Fleet Academy. And she wouldn't have been at his academy graduation, either. It was as if he were already dead to her.

Looking down at the beautiful planet below, Coda realized why he'd been so quick to say yes to Commander Coleman. There was nothing left for him on Earth. Nothing in those blue oceans, sandy beaches, green forests, or snow-peaked mountains. Nothing but a mother who didn't want anything to do with him and a past he desperately wanted to rewrite.

The transport ship had a traditional winged design that resembled NASA's original space shuttle and was large enough to seat twenty or thirty passengers and crew. Able to fly in atmospheric conditions and land planetside in an emergency, the ship was truly meant for space travel with metallic walkways, rounded edges and corners, and a seating design that would make a terrestrian nauseous.

The ship's crew greeted him at the air lock, took his bag, and led him to his seat—a formfitting gel seat with a five-point harness meant to keep him in place and protect him during hard burns and excessive G's. He floated into position and latched the lap belt, keeping his eyes focused on the air lock.

Jose "Uno" Hernandez, Raptor Squadron's top pilot, was the first to arrive. He looked surprised when he saw Coda, but he masked it quickly and took his seat across the aisle from Coda.

"Coming with us, huh?" Coda asked. "I was starting to think I was the only one."

"Not today," Uno said. "I'm surprised to see you, though. Thought you'd be going to the front."

Word of Coda's demise apparently hadn't spread throughout the rest of the academy yet. That was one of the benefits of shipping out prior to graduation, he supposed.

"I couldn't pass up the opportunity to fly with a legend," Coda said.

Uno grinned. "Me, neither."

"Any idea where we're headed?"

Uno shook his head. "You?"

"Nope. I'm in the dark too."

"Well, I'm not going to lie, Coda. I feel better knowing you're going too."

Coda nodded. He'd spoken with Uno on only a few occasions, but the Raptor pilot had always struck him as someone he could get along with. He was also damn good at what he did, and if Uno was the caliber of pilot Commander Coleman was after, then he was truly building something special.

More pilots trickled in after Uno, fifteen in all, including David "Squawks" Anderson and Benjamin "Noodle" Campbell. After joining Coda and Uno, the other two pilots chatted amicably, doing their best to hide their anxious anticipation.

Coda kept one eye on the air lock, hoping to see Buster, but as the minutes ticked by and the transport began to fill up, his hopes dimmed. When Commander Coleman arrived, he did have another student in tow, but it wasn't the one Coda was hoping for.

"You've got to be kidding me," Coda mumbled.

Moscow floated behind the commander, sneering as he surveyed the shuttle's occupants. He'd been cleaned up since his fight with Coda but still sported a split lip and swollen eyes that were beginning to purple. A pair of butterfly bandages crossed his right cheek, and another held together a cut above his left eye. If Moscow was embarrassed by his injuries, he didn't show it. Instead, his sneer turned into something more sinister when he spotted Coda.

"What is he doing here?" Uno asked as Moscow found a seat and strapped in.

"Bringing some talent to this sorry-ass group," Moscow said, apparently having heard the remark. "Isn't that right, O'Neil?"

Coda ignored him and took some sadistic pleasure in hearing how Moscow's injuries made his words come out with a slight lisp. Commander Coleman floated down the aisle toward the front of the ship. Once there, he anchored his feet in a pair of handholds and peered over the gathered pilots.

"Welcome aboard," Commander Coleman said. "The Sol Fleet doesn't often show its appreciation for its service members—there are ceremonies and awards for that sort of thing. But as I look over you now, I want you to know that *I* appreciate you taking this risk and joining me. I know you have a lot of questions, and I promise you, answers are coming. But in the spirit of military efficiency, we'll wait until the rest of the squad has arrived."

Commander Coleman gave them a small grin, drawing a few nervous laughs.

"But when you look around this shuttle and see the quality of pilots we've assembled, I hope you agree we're beginning something special. I can't tell you what that is yet, but I can tell you where we'll go to begin our journey."

Coda perked up. Only a few hours had passed since his discussion with Commander Coleman, but already he felt like a man drowning in a sea of questions, grasping for answers.

"We fly to Jumpgate Sol Four, where we'll hyperjump to Proxima Centauri B, and rendezvous with the SAS *Jamestown* and the rest of your squadron. There, you'll get your answers and begin your training. So buckle up and get comfortable. We'll be at the jumpgate in four hours."

CODA COULD IMAGINE WORSE THINGS THAN BEING STRAPPED into the gel seat of a transport vessel for four hours but not many. Unlike the battle cruisers and capital ships that made up the bulk of the Sol Fleet, transport vessels weren't equipped with much in the way of entertainment or facilities. They ate terrible food, shat in something closer to a bag than a toilet, and were forced to entertain themselves. That mostly meant conversation and simple games, and Coda, leery of Moscow, had to force himself to partake in any of it.

He knew it was an important bonding time for the squadron: friendships would be made, alliances solidified, and old rivalries made worse by adding new players. In typical Moscow fashion, he was already making new friends and turning them against Coda. He could feel their eyes, hear their laughter and caught more than one glance in his direction.

Coda tried to ignore it and focus on the group he was engaged with, but it was easier said than done.

"So something I'm trying to figure out," Squawks said, speaking fast and loose in something that resembled a verbal swagger, "is how you all earn your call signs? I mean some make sense, right? Squawks—I talk a lot. Squawk, squawk, squawk. Makes sense. Uno—first, I thought it was cause you only had one nut or something, but then you shot me down with one shot. Boom. Dead. Uno. Makes sense. But then you got Noodle." Squawks gestured toward the thin pilot. "I have a few guesses, but tell us, what's your story. Someone just razzing you or what?"

Noodle's pale faced colored. There were two kinds of call signs: those that were earned and those that were given. The ones that were earned were generally forms of respect like Uno, but the ones that were given were an altogether different story.

Some could be innocuous, little more than simple jokes. Buster had given a new pilot in Viking Squadron the call sign "Crash" due to his early propensity to, well, crash. But others could be downright insulting. A guy in the class ahead of Coda had been called "Sluf," which had been given to him because someone had overheard one of the female pilots calling him a "short little ugly fucker." The call sign Sluf was born, and it had stuck.

If Noodle's embarrassed reaction was any indication, his call sign had been given, not earned. "I just don't like working out," Noodle said quietly.

Squawks looked at him skeptically, then his face split into a broad smile. "Noodle. Cause you've got noodle arms?" He laughed. "That's good. Accurate too. I've seen skeletons with more muscle than you."

Noodle's face burned crimson, something he tried to

hide with a fake laugh. If Squawks noticed or cared that he'd made his squad mate uncomfortable he didn't show it.

"What about you?" Squawks said, turning his attention to Coda. "What's Coda even mean?"

Coda bit back a sarcastic comment about looking it up in the dictionary. Like Noodle, he wasn't comfortable talking about his call sign. His hadn't been given *or* earned. He'd come up with it himself and convinced the other pilots to call him by it—not an easy feat since that wasn't how things were supposed to work.

"I don't want to talk about it," Coda said.

"C'mon, man. We're supposed to be getting to know each other."

"Another time."

"You're no fun."

Deceleration began thirty minutes before the transport ship docked with the jumpgate. The ship flipped on its axis so that the thrust of the engines pointed *away* from the direction they were traveling, and as if to remind them why their seats were made from a soft gel material, the pilots were shaken, battered, and bruised for the duration.

Jumpgates were a modern marvel—the first faster-than-light travel conceived by the human race. The how and the why were closely guarded secrets, and while its science well above Coda's pay grade, he did understand it on a crude, fundamental level.

The jumpgate itself was like a giant gun that the transport ship would be loaded into, though instead of being shot across space, the ship was shot *through* it, arriving almost instantaneously at its destination. The jumpgate had limits on how far it could send them, of course, just as the ships equipped with EmDrives had similar, albeit much larger, limitations. However, Alpha Centauri, only 4.367 light-years away, was well within jumpgate capabilities.

As the transport vessel slid down the chamber of the jumpgate, Coda found himself growing increasingly uneasy. He had never given much thought to how he would die—he'd always assumed it would be somewhere on the front as his battle cruiser went down in a hail of gunfire—but he thought about it now. He could almost hear the news reporter on the vids.

"Lieutenant Callan 'Coda' O'Neil and fourteen other Terran Academy graduates, along with the heroic Nighthawk pilot, Commander Chadwick Coleman, are confirmed dead after a jumpgate malfunction."

The reporter would keep her tone somber, her lips slightly downturned in mock sadness before she sent the program to a commercial break. It would be another tragic chapter in the O'Neil family story and one that would bring his father's mistakes back to the forefront of public consciousness.

Coda did his best to hide his growing unease. Jump travel was, after all, a common form of travel these days, especially among the Sol Fleet. The front was uncomprehendingly far away and only accessible via the jumpgates, so fearing it was useless. But fear, like all emotion, was an irrational beast, and no matter how much Coda attempted to talk himself through it, his back still grew wet with sweat, his hands clammy and trembling, his breath shallow.

The loading procedure took several minutes, but once complete, the power-up process began. Blue bands of energy like a tempest of pure electricity stretched throughout the interior of the jumpgate, shining bright enough to wash out the backdrop of distant stars.

The ship began to vibrate. It wasn't painful or nearly as violent as the acceleration and deceleration burns. Instead, Coda felt as if he and everything around him were brimming with energy, trembling with adrenaline-infused anticipation. Then, without any word from the ship's pilot, the length of the ship appeared to *stretch*, the seat in front of Coda seemingly pulling away from him. When he reached out to touch it, his fingers brushed against the back of the gel cushion, and his arm looked as if it had stretched too.

The sensation was beyond disorienting, and he fought with everything he had not to vomit. Then, just as before and without warning, the world snapped back into perspective, and everything around him returned to normal. Even without being able to confirm it, Coda knew they had arrived in the Alpha Centauri System.

6

Hangar Deck, SAS Jamestown
    Alpha Centauri System, Proxima B, High Orbit

LESS THAN A FULL DAY AFTER HAVING HIS FUTURE RIPPED AWAY
from him, Coda found himself and the rest of the select
group of pilots from the Terran Fleet Academy on the
hangar deck of the SAS *Jamestown*. Commander Coleman
stood in front of a squadron of Hornets.

Coda fell into parade rest with the rest of the squadron,
watching his commander but wishing more than anything
that he could run his hands along the dark exterior of the
drones, feel the contours of its smooth body, trace its fuselage with his fingers. Seeing the ships felt like seeing an old
girlfriend. Buried emotions swelled to the surface.

"Welcome aboard the SAS *Jamestown*," Commander
Coleman said. "This is Hangar Bay 7B. We'll be spending
much of our time here, but right now, follow me." He spun
on his heels and strode across the hangar through a set of
double doors that hissed open as he approached.

They entered into a light-gray corridor lit with series of artificial lights set into the wall near the floor and ceiling. Having spent a year and a half in the wheel of the academy's space station, it was odd seeing the corridor stretch out straight in front of him. The SAS *Jamestown* was one of the oldest ships in the fleet equipped with artificial gravity, and the lack of curve somehow made everything appear both bigger and farther away.

The *Jamestown* was a warship through and through, the evidence plain for all to see. The corners of the walls were rounded and coated with a compound that was soft to the touch, and spread throughout the corridors were various handholds to grab should the ship shake or spin in the heat of battle.

Coda found himself smiling as a sense of satisfaction welled up inside him. He couldn't help feeling as if he'd made it. He was aboard a warship. The opportunity for glory rested at his feet.

Commander Coleman led them into an area of the ship that was less busy. "These will be your quarters," Commander Coleman said. "These four barracks sleep twenty-five a piece. The rest of the squadron will be arriving shortly. In the meantime, the facilities are that direction." He pointed down the corridor back the way they had come. "So, take a shower, get in a workout, do whatever you need to do to mentally prepare yourself for what comes next."

"The rest of the squadron?" someone asked.

"Yes," Commander Coleman said. "You didn't think you were the only pilots vying for a spot in this squadron, did you?"

The pilot who asked the question, Autumn "Whiskey" Jones, stirred under the commander's patronizing gaze.

"There aren't even enough pilots here to fill out a

squadron, let alone build one," Commander Coleman said. "Yes, other pilots will be joining us. A lot more, in fact. I said each of these barracks sleeps twenty-five, and we have four of them, so even the worst student here should be able to figure out that means one hundred pilots. You number only fourteen. So you can expect to see a lot of new faces. Now get ready—your briefing begins in two hours."

Commander Coleman disappeared down the corridor, and the pilots began filing into the various barracks. Coda noted which barracks Moscow entered and avoided it.

"Bunk together?" Uno asked Coda and the two other pilots who had enjoyed the flight with them.

"Sure." Coda pointed toward the nearest barracks, the one farthest from Moscow's. "This work?"

"Doubt any of them are different," Squawks said. "And it's closest to the crapper, so it works for me."

When nobody voiced disapproval, Coda stepped inside. Like the rest of the ship, the barracks was long and narrow, with bunks stacked two high and inset into the wall on either side of the room. At the foot of each bed was a vid screen, and each was provided with a privacy shade that could block out light and muffle unwanted noise. It was a step down from his private quarters at the academy, but as far as sleeping arrangements went, he'd heard of worse.

"Back or front?" Coda asked. "Less privacy up front, but it has its advantages too."

"Like what?" Noodle asked.

"You're the first people the commander sees when he enters, and the last he sees when he leaves," Uno said. "And squadron leaders are traditionally near the door. I vote the front."

"Oh god," Squawks said. "I didn't know you were a kiss

ass. We can't be friends." He smiled as he said it, clearly making sure Uno understood it was a joke.

"So… you vote rear?" Coda asked.

"Oh no," Squawks said. "I vote front too. Too hard to sneak my drunken rendezvous through an entire barracks of sexually pent-up twenty-something-year-old men, you know?"

"Do you always talk this much?" Uno asked.

"Call sign's 'Squawks,' remember?"

"Great."

"It's settled then," Coda said. "We bunk at the front."

The group dispersed, each grabbing the bunk nearest them. That left Coda with the bottom bunk two bunks deep into the room. Uno grabbed the bunk above him, with Squawks and Noodle across from him.

Coda quickly surveyed his new space, pushing a hand against the gel mattress. It felt like standard military issue, which meant it was only a few centimeters thick and barely softer than concrete. He opened the two drawers under the mattress and a locker with a handprint security system, finding each of them empty.

We'll probably get our flight gear when the rest of the squadron arrives.

Coda slipped away from the barracks alone, took a shower in the communal facility, changed back into his clothes, and returned to his bunk, where he pulled the privacy shade closed. Something Commander Coleman had said had been gnawing at him since they'd arrived. He'd said more pilots would be joining them, a lot more, and that the squadron would soon number one hundred.

Squadrons in the academy were on the small side, numbering only sixteen in all, but on the front, squadrons numbered an even twenty-four. Commander Coleman had said he was building a squadron. Not a wing. And not a group. If one hundred other pilots were vying for a position within its ranks, that meant more than seventy-five would wash out.

He's going to whittle us down, Coda thought. *Only take the best of the best.*

Coda's previous feelings of accomplishment vanished, immediately replaced by an anxious pit in his stomach. The odds were stacked against him. Again. And something told him this would be his toughest challenge yet.

He gritted his teeth, his resolve hardening. He would meet the challenges head-on, and he would succeed. He didn't have a choice.

7

Ready Room, SAS Jamestown
Alpha Centauri System, Proxima B, High Orbit

THE READY ROOM OF THE SAS *JAMESTOWN* WAS EASILY TWICE the size of those back at the academy, though it lacked the polish of the newer space station. The chairs were worn, their cushions cracked, and the paint on the walls had faded with age. Commander Coleman stood behind a podium at the front of the ready room, prepared to address the pilots, who had already found their places. Behind him, a large digital display board, the only technological upgrade in the aging room, stood out like a new button on a well-worn suit.

The rest of the squadron had trickled in over the last couple hours. Always in groups of ten or twenty, they were as diverse as their dress. Like Coda and the rest from the academy, some seemed have been recruited from other flight schools, but others wore the light blues of stationed officers, insignias proudly displayed on their uniforms.

The uncomfortable pit that had been balling up in

Coda's gut blossomed into full-blown anxiety. Competing for a spot against other students was one thing, but how was he to compete with pilots who'd flown in real battles?

The others seemed to feel the same way too. Noodle and Uno wore uneasy expressions, their lips tight, eyes slightly downcast, and Squawks, for once, had nothing to say. Most of the officers ignored Coda and the rest of the academy graduates, but others weren't so kind and regarded them as if they were nothing more than fresh meat for the grinder.

"Good morning," Commander Coleman said, his voice easily carrying to the back of the room. "I stand before you, looking at a sight I never expected to see again. Take a look around, ladies and gentlemen. Take note of your fellow wingmen. You all come from different backgrounds. Some just graduated and are serving in your first deployments. Others have already been deployed and have fought on the front. Still others have made a name for yourselves through years of battle. But listen to me when I say this: in this, you are all students. Your backgrounds and any previous successes mean exactly dick. Here, you are all *nuggets*."

The lights suddenly dimmed, and the digital display behind the commander flickered to life. A chill of excitement snapped down Coda's back, and he found himself sitting forward in his seat, staring at a still image taken from battle. The sleek Hornet drones of the Sol Fleet were engaged in a massive space battle with the insectoid ships of the Baranyk.

"What I'm about to show you is a galactic secret that will not be discussed beyond these walls. Failure to comply with this order will result in *stiff* punishment." Commander Coleman stepped away from the podium, stopping in front of the first row of seats. "This is your last chance, nuggets. If any of you are having second thoughts, now is your chance to leave. You will not get another."

Coda surveyed the room, waiting for someone to take the bait. Nobody did. It appeared everyone else was like him —utterly captivated.

"All right." Commander Coleman toggled something on his tablet, and the still image behind him began to play.

The hornet drones flew in a series of tight formations, wing to wing, nose to tail, with incredible precision. They moved fluidly, attacking like a swarm of their namesakes. And there were dozens, maybe hundreds of squadrons, each assaulting the Baranyk fighters and ships with devastating efficiency.

Coda had seen similar vids in the past, but many of them were classified beyond his clearance level, and without the proper instruction, they were impossible to emulate. That was one of the things that excited him the most about fighting on the front—becoming a fighter pilot and learning the secrets behind such precise tactics.

"This was taken thirteen days ago in the Dakara System," Commander Coleman said. "Our ships had been engaged with the Baranyk Fleet for seventeen minutes when... well, see for yourselves."

The ships on the vid continued their assault. Missile trails and tracer fire filled the vacuum between the larger vessels, carving into the reinforced ship exteriors with little resistance. Smaller points of light flashed briefly then disappeared as drones and Baranyk ships exploded. The human fleet was pressing their advantage and making for the Baranyk capital ship when the drone fleet just... *stopped*.

They didn't stop in the traditional sense—there was no stopping in the vacuum of space—but all navigational movement ceased. As if the pilots had lost all navigational control, the drones continued on their course, never deviating or avoiding fire.

The Baranyk made quick work of the drones, eliminating the human fleet in moments before turning their sights on the human capital ships. As the alien fleet closed on the human vessels, Commander Coleman paused the vid, freezing the enemy fire as it hurled toward the metal constructions with violent intent. He stood silently as if encouraging questions.

"With all due respect, sir," said a pilot in the front row. "But what the hell just happened?"

"According to Fleet Intelligence, the Baranyk have developed a new weapon that knocks out all communication between our drones and the drone pilots aboard our battle cruisers."

"But that would mean..." The pilot's voice trailed off as he came to the silent conclusion.

"That our ships are sitting ducks," Commander Coleman said. "Yes, if Fleet Intelligence is correct, the Baranyk have eliminated our greatest advantage in this war."

Coda ran through the implications in his head. The Baranyk were a fierce enemy with superior firepower and a technological edge. The humans' only advantage, if they even had one, was in numbers. Maybe not human numbers but fighter numbers. And only because drones were easier to replace than pilots.

At some point after the early years of the war, when the fleet had faced catastrophic losses among its fighter wings, Fleet Command had realized it was easier to manufacture new starfighters than it was to train new pilots, and within a year, Fleet Command had shifted away from manned starfighters to drones that could be operated from the relative safety of the heavily armored battle cruisers. The Baranyk, for all their technological advancements, hadn't adopted a similar strategy against their human enemy. *Until now.*

Of the many theories why the Baranyk hadn't altered their original tactics, the prevailing one was that the Baranyk fighters were some kind of lesser creature akin to drones themselves, something easily produced in large numbers. Still, humanity, with its vast network of colonized planets and moons, could manufacture drones faster than the Baranyk, and that had given them the advantage. If that was no longer the case, then the Baranyk had a bigger advantage than they had ever had before.

"Fortunately," Commander Coleman said, "Fleet Intelligence believes the Baranyk were reluctant to use the weapon, which explains why they didn't use it until human victory was clearly at hand, and why we haven't seen it used since."

"Why would they be reluctant to use it again, sir?" another pilot asked. "I understand them wanting to keep it a secret, but use it once, and the secret's out. What advantage do they have by not using it again?"

"Intelligence has a couple of ideas. The first is that it's some sort of new weapon, and with all new weapons come bugs. Maybe they've attempted to use it, but it hasn't worked. Another thought is that since it *is* a new weapon, not all Baranyk ships are equipped with it. In either case, Intelligence is working to counteract the weapon, and that's where you come in."

Coda felt his face contort in confusion. Fleet Intelligence harbored some of the smartest men and women the human race had to offer, and if anyone could solve the latest riddle, it was them. He was no mental slouch, but he wasn't qualified to assist in any intelligence efforts, either.

"Intelligence is working on ways to counter the device so that our ships can retain communication or ways to boost the strength of our signal so that the drones are unaffected when the enemy attempts to use their weapon. But that's not for us to worry about. That's not our mission. We're the backup plan. Hell, we're the backup plan to the backup plan. The redundancy in case everything Intelligence comes up with fails. We're another kind of experiment."

"And what kind of experiment is that, sir?" The words were out of Coda's mouth before he knew it. Squawks and Noodle looked at him, their mouths agape, leaning away as if attempting to distance themselves from him.

"The best kind, Coda. The kind that'll put all of you into the cockpits of real starfighters. The kind that will allow you to become real pilots, just as I was."

Commander Coleman's words cut to Coda's very core. *He wants me to be a pilot. Not a drone pilot—a fighter pilot. Just like my father.* Coda never would have thought it possible. Hell, since the advent of drone warfare, it *hadn't* been possible. Now suddenly placed on the same treacherous path as his father, Coda's doubts resurfaced.

His blood runs through my veins. What if I'm just as weak? What if I fail? What if I cause death and destruction just as he did?

It was almost unimaginable. If Coda failed, the O'Neils would never have a place among the military again. They would be disgraced. Discarded. Hated. Coda tried not to think about the riots in his hometown, about the vile threats and vandals terrorizing what little peace his mother still had.

I can't do it. I won't. I can't risk it.

Even if he avoided the traps of his father, Fleet Intelligence wanted to put Coda and ninety-nine other rookies into the cockpit of a death machine. Casualties among fighter pilots had been the highest among all Fleet personnel and for good reason. The extreme conditions pilots faced in a starfighter were as dangerous as anything the Baranyk could throw at them. Even with inertial dampeners and other systems meant to lessen the strain, the physical toll alone had accounted for nearly ten percent of all fighter deaths, and many of the pilots who had survived suffered lifelong ailments. Flying a starfighter was akin to looking into the face of death itself.

But...

Some of the most renowned military figures had been pilots. It was no coincidence that Coda had recognized Commander Coleman on sight. He could have done the same with a handful of other legendary pilots. Of everyone he looked up to, of all the prestigious drone pilots fighting on the front, he knew their call signs and had maybe even seen a picture or interview with them once or twice, but none of them were as recognized as those original starfighter pilots. If Coda's goal was restoring honor to the family name, what better chance would he have?

I have too much riding on this.

It was almost poetic, in a sense. He'd dreamed about righting his father's wrongs, and now he had an opportunity to do it from the same cockpit.

Can I really turn that down?

Coda found himself nodding. Nodding in excitement. Nodding in agreement. Ready to get started.

"I see a lot of nervous faces," Commander Coleman said slowly. "And rightfully so. I'm not going to sugarcoat it. This isn't going to be easy. Chances are some of you won't survive.

Statistics say that five of you will stroke out before you ever see battle. And even then, the cards are stacked against you. In my day, a pilot spent six weeks at Advanced Preflight Instruction, then six *months* at Primary Flight School, and another eighteen weeks at Advanced Flight Training. We have twenty-six weeks."

Nervous whispers filtered throughout the room.

"The odds are slim," Commander Coleman continued. "I understand that. Fleet Intelligence understands that. Which is why there are one hundred candidates in this room. Out of all of you, only twenty-four will make the squadron. The rest of you will receive new orders. But unlike you, I understood the challenges and expectations when I accepted this post. I understood the odds and the limitations of our timeline. But I also understood what was at stake. There's a very real chance that Fleet Intelligence will fail in their attempt to counteract the Baranyk weapon, and if that happens, we are the *only* thing that stands in the way of our fleet's total destruction."

Commander Coleman paused, letting the words sink in. He knew, just as Coda did, that when it was put like that, when they were faced with the ugly, terrible, terrifying truth that their fleet's destruction meant the eradication of the human race, nobody would quit. They were all here for reason, and they would give it their all or die trying.

"Look around, nuggets. The men and women in this room are the best and brightest fighter minds in the fleet. I personally picked every single one of you, because if there's anyone who can learn to fly a starfighter under these conditions, it's you. We will become the most fearsome squadron in the Sol Fleet. Now grab some food and some sleep, because we begin FAM Phase tomorrow at oh six hundred. Dismissed."

8

Corridor, SAS Jamestown
Alpha Centauri System, Proxima B, High Orbit

CODA WAS SO DEEP IN THOUGHT AS HE LEFT THE READY ROOM that he didn't hear Moscow fall into step behind him. Uno and Squawks were at his side, talking animatedly about how they were going to kick Baranyk ass, when Moscow's voice cut through the corridor.

"Gonna be a pilot like your old man, huh, O'Neil?"

Coda's body tightened at Moscow's words, but he continued forward, acting as if he hadn't heard him. He felt his friends' eyes on him, but they took his lead, letting the taunt go unanswered.

"Seeing as your old man went rogue and killed his wingmen," Moscow continued, "I'm not sure I like that very much."

Coda let out a long, slow breath, silently repeating Captain Hughes's words over and over again. *You don't learn from your mistakes. You don't learn from your mistakes. You don't learn from your mistakes.* Letting Moscow goad him into another fight wasn't a mistake he would make again. He wouldn't give Moscow the satisfaction.

"You hear me, O'Neil?" he said even more loudly. "You going to kill us like your old man killed his wingmen?"

Coda's resolve broke. He turned to face his tormenter.

"What do you say—"

"Stow it, Lieutenant!"

Every pilot inside the corridor froze, their eyes falling on Commander Coleman, who had just exited the ready room.

"Do you have an issue with who I assembled for this squadron?" Commander Coleman asked, advancing on Moscow.

The other rookie looked genuinely terrified. His eyes darted to the small gang he had assembled, but each of his new friends gave him a wide berth. He was on his own, and he knew it.

"I asked you a question, Lieutenant!"

"No, sir."

"Then you will cease all talk of Lieutenant O'Neil's family. Do you understand?"

"Understood, sir."

"Are you sure, Lieutenant?" Commander Coleman closed the remaining distance between him and Moscow in a single step, bringing his face inches from the other pilot's. The larger officer made Moscow look like a child by comparison.

"Crystal, sir."

"Good." Commander Coleman surveyed the corridor, looking at Moscow's gang and the others who were milling around. "Anyone else?" When nobody answered, Commander Coleman returned his attention back to Moscow. "Get to your barracks."

"Yes, sir." Moscow turned and started down the corridor. He didn't say anything to Coda as he passed, but his eyes burned with anger and embarrassment. *This isn't over,* they seemed to say. *Not by a long shot.*

As Coda turned toward the barracks, Commander Coleman's gaze settled on him. The Commander's expression was unreadable, and as the moment drew longer, Coda grew increasingly uncomfortable. Turning his back on the commander felt inappropriate, especially since he had just come to Coda's defense. Fortunately, Commander Coleman nodded at him then continued down the corridor in the opposite direction, sparing Coda from further scrutiny.

"Come on," someone said to him, and Coda found himself being pushed toward the barracks.

Back in the privacy of their quarters, Coda's new friends huddled around him.

"What the hell was that all about?" Squawks asked. "I mean, I knew you and Moscow didn't like each other, but damn."

Coda shrugged, not sure how much he wanted to talk about it.

"Seriously," Squawks pressed. "What just happened?"

"Nothing," Coda said quietly.

"Didn't look like nothing."

"It's... complicated," Coda said.

Squawks opened his mouth to say more, but Uno laid a hand on his shoulder. "Lay off him. He obviously doesn't want to talk about it."

"No," Coda said. "It's fine. Me and Andrei have been rivals since our first day at the academy. I don't know why, but we never got along. Actually, I'm pretty sure he hated me since day one. And it only got worse when we got our own squadrons. Anyway, when Commander Coleman recruited me, he told me that he had flown with my father. That he was a good man. I guess hearing Moscow bad-mouth him pissed the commander off as much as it did me."

Coda's friends shared an uneasy look. Joseph O'Neil wasn't someone people usually talked about, and when they did, they certainly didn't praise him. Calling a known war criminal a "good man" just didn't happen—especially from a superior officer.

"The commander flew with your father?" Uno asked tentatively.

Coda nodded.

"Did he say when?" Squawks asked. "I mean, was he there when... you know..."

"When he allowed the Baranyk to wipe out his entire squadron?" Coda asked bitterly. "He didn't say. But I got the impression that they knew each other pretty well. They might have even been friends."

Squawks whistled his surprise.

"Are you going to talk to him about it?" Uno asked. "You know, so you know for sure."

"No."

Another awkward silence, made worse by the other pilots' reluctance to meet his eye, fell over the group. Coda wanted to say something, but he didn't know what. He hated talking about his father, because when he did, things got awkward... and he lost friends.

"Look," Coda said, "I know you've all thought about it, so if we're going to fly together, you deserve to know. Yes, my father is a war criminal. Maybe even a traitor. And his wingmen died because of it. But my father's mistakes were his own. Not mine. And for as long as we fly together, I promise I will do everything in my power to be the best wingman I can be."

"You don't have to say that, Coda," Uno said.

"Yes, I do," Coda said. "It's important to me. And I need all of you to understand that, okay?"

He was met with a series of small nods.

"We're going to kick some serious Baranyk ass, aren't we?" Squawks said, his playful bluster shattering what remained of the awkward moment.

"Hell yeah." Coda was grateful for the new subject and gave Squawks a knowing smile. He reminded him of Buster, who'd had a rare ability to say the right thing at the right time, protecting Coda with words when he resorted to fists.

Uno hooted his own battle cry, and the rest of them followed. Before Coda knew it, they were smiling and laughing again, their nerves and concerns disappearing. Coda took part in all of it, silently noting that for the first time since he could remember, nobody cared who he was or where he came from. In that moment, Coda and his small group of friends were ready for whatever the following day had in store.

9

Hangar Deck, SAS Jamestown
  Alpha Centauri System, Proxima B, High Orbit

THE NEXT MORNING, THE PILOTS FORMED UP IN FRONT OF Commander Coleman on Hangar Deck 7B. The Commander stood in front of a squadron of X-23 Nighthawks; the single-manned starfighters were larger than the Z-18 Hornet drones the pilots were more familiar with, sporting a sleek design with angled wings, four rear thrusters, and a narrow cockpit. Matte black and ornamented with a full armament of missiles and a nose-mounted cannon, the Nighthawks looked every bit like the big brother to the Hornets that Coda had imagined them to be.

"Welcome to FAM Phase," Commander Coleman said, "also known as the Familiarization Phase. Over the next two weeks, you will familiarize yourself with every nut, bolt, nook, and cranny of the X-23 so that when we are done, you will be able to rebuild your Nighthawk in space with nothing more than your flight suit and fingernails.

"Make no mistake, ladies and gentlemen, the next two weeks will be one of the most trying times of your lives. It will test your patience and mental endurance more than ever before. FAM Phase is not fun, but it is important, and I expect you to treat it as such. Is that understood?"

"Yes, sir!" the squadron echoed in unison.

"Good," Commander Coleman said. "There are one hundred of you and only twenty-five X-23s, so form into groups of four and find a fighter. Over the next hour, I want you to acquaint yourself with it. Run your hand along her body. Sit in her seat. Look her up and down, inside and out, then we'll begin the real fun."

Coda quickly formed a group with Squawks, Uno, and Noodle and found an X-23 that wasn't already surrounded by overly excited pilots. Squawks bounded up the ladder and climbed into the cockpit before anyone had an opportunity to argue, grinning as he took in the various gauges and screens.

Coda circled the X-23, studying its contours. The Nighthawk wasn't just bigger than the Hornet, there were subtle variations in the curve of the body and a slightly different angle to its wings. Its navigational thrusters were more numerous and spaced out more evenly to increase maneuverability.

Like the Z-18, however, the Nighthawk's matte-black exterior seemed to absorb the light of the hangar, and Coda knew from his studies that it was resistant to radar, lidar, and other forms of detection. Most of the battles on the front were fought at range with missiles, but the larger battles often devolved into close-quarter combat—

dogfighting—and the fighter's dark exterior made it difficult to spot amid the black of space.

Uno took Squawks's place in the cockpit, easily outmuscling Noodle for the next position in line. Coda didn't mind. He would get his turn, and besides, he was equally fascinated by how the fighter's hundreds of plates fit together so perfectly that the ship almost looked as though it had been carved from a solid block of metal.

When he finally took a seat in the cockpit, the childlike excitement that had consumed the others overcame him as well. Where the Hornet drones were little more than cold predators, there was something majestic about the Nighthawk. A history. A connection to every pilot who had sat in its cockpit. Beyond the luminous dials, instrument panels, buttons, switches, and triggers was the smell of sweat, blood, and human resolve. Squawks was right—the fighter *was* awesome. Coda couldn't wait to see what it could do.

Unfortunately, the commander had other ideas, and by "real fun," he had actually meant unbelievably tedious. After their session with the Nighthawks, Commander Coleman brought each of them to a private room no larger than a broom closet and had each sit on a deck-mounted metal chair in front of an embarrassingly old computer terminal.

"What is this, sir?" Coda asked, sitting down on the uncomfortable chair.

"This is your Computer Assisted Instruction," Commander Coleman said. "It will guide you through all of the technical workings of your starfighter."

Coda looked at the ancient screen skeptically. It looked like it would sooner project a grainy black-and-white image than it would anything Coda was accustomed to.

"Is there an issue, Lieutenant?"

"No, sir," Coda said. "It's just that... sir, how old is this?"

"The *Jamestown* is one of the oldest ships in the fleet, and it's not equipped with the *fancy* technology you were pampered with at the academy. If you're looking for state-of-the-art equipment, Coda, you signed up for the wrong squadron."

With that, the commander turned to leave. Coda watched him go, silently cursing himself. As far as early impressions went, he wasn't making a very good one. Turning back to the terminal, he sighed, ready to begin. There was only one problem.

"Sir!" Coda shouted as the door hissed closed. "I don't even know how to turn this thing on."

The Commander didn't return. He didn't even respond.

"Great," Coda mumbled. He looked over the terminal and, seeing no buttons or switches, touched the screen. It immediately came to life, displaying a propaganda-like image of a squadron of X-23s overlaid with a menu of options. There were seventy-five modules to choose from, and with a sigh, Coda toggled the first one, titled Program Overview.

The menu disappeared, replaced by a clean-cut private citizen who no doubt worked for the contractor who had built the X-23. The man gave a standard introduction, highlighting the Nighthawks' capabilities, top speed, and success in battle as if he were reading straight from a brochure—which he no doubt was. Contractors were every bit as concerned about securing their *next* contract as they were about fulfilling their present one, and that meant constantly touting their successes.

Ten minutes into the program overview, Coda's legs began to tingle. The metal chair was cutting off the circulation to his lower half. Worse yet, since it was bolted to the floor, he had no way to move it to a more comfortable position.

Two weeks, Coda thought. *I've got two weeks of this.* The thought filled him with dread, but failure wasn't an option. He had to get through it so he could get to the good stuff.

When the overview ended, Coda immediately moved onto the next module, and for the next two hours, he listened and took notes on an introduction to the miniature Shaw Drive equipped on the X-23. It was dry stuff, which the presenter made worse with a slow, monotone voice that catered to the lowest common denominator.

Coda's eyes burned, and at one point, he nearly fell asleep. He would have let himself if the video didn't stop periodically to give him a short quiz, making sure he was paying attention. And the longer the video played, the more difficult the quizzes got. Coda began missing questions, and the module responded by forcing him to rewatch entire sections until he passed the mid-module exam.

He felt triumphant when he finally got to the end of the first module, but the feeling quickly turned to despair when he saw the one-hundred-question test that awaited him. Despair then turned to irritation when he failed the test and was forced to retake the module from the beginning.

After a brief meltdown, he forced himself to take the module more slowly, often replaying certain parts so he could take more detailed notes and ensure he understood the content. When he came to the test again, he passed it without issue, though not with the score he would have liked. Still, passing was passing, and as the old saying went, "Cs get degrees."

That afternoon, Coda and his group of friends met in the mess hall. The room was like every other mess he'd eaten in. Stainless-steel tables and chairs lined the room and were all bolted securely to the floor. Refreshment stations serving recycled water and black coffee framed the food buffet, where cooks lethargically spooned slop onto their plates.

"What is this?" Squawks asked, staring at his tray. "Looks like you puked on my plate and called it a meal."

He wasn't far from the truth. The food, if one could call it that, was a brown paste that resembled something between meatloaf and Jell-O.

"Why can't I have some of that?" Squawks pointed at a tray of hamburgers piled on a warming tray.

"You're with the new squadron, right?" the cook asked.

"Yeah."

"Then this is what you get." The cook spooned a second helping onto Squawks's plate and gave him a sarcastic look.

"This is some horseshit," Squawks said.

"I don't think we're going to get prime rib and scallops," Coda said as the cook scooped a spoonful onto his tray. "Come on. Let's find a place to sit."

They found a table near the refreshment station and sat, poking their food as if it were a strange creature that had washed up on the beach. Noodle was the first to brave a bite. The rest of the group watched as he chewed, swallowed, and made a face Coda couldn't read.

"Well?" Squawks asked.

Noodle just shrugged. "Tastes like someone mixed some proteins, fats, vitamins, and water in a blender and called it good. It's not going to win any cooking awards, but I've had worse."

Hearing it wasn't as bad as it looked, Coda took a bite of his own and was pleasantly surprised by its lack of taste. Like Noodle, he shrugged and helped himself to more.

"If we're saving the fleet, we should at least eat like it," Squawks said, stirring his food with a disgusted expression.

"We *are* eating like it," Uno said.

"What do you mean?" Coda asked.

"Think about it," Uno said. "Flying a starfighter takes a serious toll on the body. Whatever's in here, it's more than just fat and protein."

"What are you saying? You think there's steroids or growth hormones in here or something?" Coda's appetite was disappearing by the second.

"Of course there is," Uno said. "They said there would be."

"Who did?" Squawks asked.

"The commander."

"He didn't say anything like that to me."

"Me, neither," Coda said.

"It was in the paperwork." Uno looked around the table and was met with a series of blank expressions. "I'm the only one who read the release, aren't I?"

The group nodded.

"Wow," Uno said. "You guys signed up for something without reading what would be required?"

"They said it was classified," Noodle said.

"The mission was classified," Uno said. "Not what would be required to fulfill that mission."

"What did it say?" Coda asked.

"You pretty much figured it out already. They have us on a special diet chocked-full of your standard fat and proteins but with an added helping of experimental growth hormones meant to strengthen our bodies for the stresses of space flight."

Coda slid his tray away. The word "experimental" turned

his stomach, and he was left with a mental image of himself growing a third arm.

Noodle came to a very different conclusion. "I'm going to get jacked, aren't I?"

"Sorry, Noodle," Squawks said. "He said '*experimental*,' not '*miracle.*'"

"Shut it, Squawks."

"It's okay, little guy. One of these days, you'll hit puberty."

"And one of these days, I'm going to kick your ass."

"You're welcome to try," Squawks said. "Just remember, I've got bigger muscles."

"You've got a bigger mouth too," Noodle said.

Laughter erupted around the table. Squawks took the jibe in stride, laughing the loudest of all.

"Well played," Squawks said, giving Noodle a fist bump. "There's hope for you yet."

The banter was familiar to Coda, even welcomed. Viking Squadron had bickered like family too, and Coda believed it was a true sign of camaraderie. When your wingmen made fun of you, that meant they liked you. If they ignored you... well, that was an altogether different story.

"Whether Noodle will ever fill out remains to be seen," Uno said. "But either way, I'm sure the commander will have us in the gym soon. So eat up. It might be the difference between life and death out there."

"If I don't die of boredom first." Squawks pushed his tray away. "Seriously. FAM Phase can suck it. Who knew being a pilot would be so *boring*?"

Noodle began mimicking the instructor's slow monotone voice, and everyone laughed again.

"I don't know," Uno said. "It's not that bad."

"*What?*" the other pilots said in unison.

Uno's face colored, and he kept his eyes on his tray, absently poking at the food paste with his fork. "I kind of like it. It's interesting."

"You're messed up in the head, man," Squawks said.

The conversation eventually drifted in other directions, but Coda's mind was occupied with what Uno had said. Like the pilots in Viking Squadron, those in Commander Coleman's would have their own strengths and weaknesses, and it would be vital that their squadron leader know how to use them accordingly.

Coda made a mental note of Uno's. He didn't know if he would ever be in a leadership position again, but if he was, he promised himself he would be ready.

10

Ready Room, SAS Jamestown
  Alpha Centauri System, Proxima B, High Orbit

UNO'S PREDICTION THAT THEY WOULD SPEND PLENTY OF TIME in the gym proved to be true. Apart from their mealtimes and daily briefings, it offered the only reprieve from their computer-aided training.

Coda had never been much for working out, but he took to it immediately, relishing the opportunity to get away from the droll voice of the narrator. The highly technical overview of the inner workings of the X-23's guidance system had been more than enough to turn his brain to mush, and he was growing increasingly frustrated with the process.

He was a pilot. Building a fighter wasn't his job—flying one was. Who cared how the guidance system worked as long as it did? But after making a less-than-ideal first impression, he wasn't about to voice his displeasure. Instead, he took his aggression out in the gym.

The only person who seemed to hate the gym more than

the CAI was Noodle. He complained about it as much as Squawks griped about the food.

The goal of their workouts, Commander Coleman had said, wasn't to bulk up. They weren't interested in pure strength; it would only get in the way. Instead, they were after enhanced flexibility and muscular endurance. That meant, in addition to heavy cardio and partner stretching, they focused on exercises that strengthened their cores, utilizing low weight with high reps. After the gym and the mental undertaking of the CAI, Coda went to bed exhausted, both mentally and physically.

Three days into FAM Phase, Commander Coleman posted their first progress report on the display boards of the ready room, and to Coda's great surprise, he was dead last. Every other pilot had completed more CAI modules than he had, and most had better scores. Worse yet, Moscow was in the top ten and made sure Coda knew it. The only thing that kept Coda sane was that Uno had not only finished the most but had also remarkably scored the highest on each of the evaluations.

When Coda asked him how he'd scored so high, Uno had just shrugged and repeated that he found the subject matter interesting. Unfortunately, such advice wasn't helpful, and even after reapplying himself, Coda didn't make up enough ground to dig his way out of the bottom quarter of the class by the end of the week. For the first time in his life, Coda was failing at something, and he had no idea how to fix it.

That night, during their daily briefing, Commander Coleman reviewed their progress, calling out everyone in the bottom half by name. It was public humiliation at its worst. When he got to Coda's name, Moscow snickered and muttered something to one of the nearby pilots. Coda couldn't make out what he'd said, but the outburst had drawn the commander's attention.

"What was that?" Commander Coleman asked, pausing his review.

Moscow stiffened, his smile disappearing immediately.

"I asked you a question, Lieutenant."

"Yes, sir."

"Then answer it."

"Sir," Moscow said, "I just wonder when the first cuts are going to be made. You know, when the first pilots will be sent home."

"Afraid of your competition, Lieutenant Krylov?"

"No, sir," Moscow said, apparently refusing to take the bait. "I'm more afraid of flying with pilots who can't pass a simple test, sir."

Commander Coleman chewed on the words, his face a mask of displeasure. Coda waited for him to scold Moscow, but to his surprise, the commander did the opposite. "I would be too, Moscow. That is why any pilots who haven't completed their computer-aided instruction by the end of next week will be cut from the program." He surveyed the ready room. "Hear me now, nuggets. You have seven days. Make them count."

11

Gym, SAS Jamestown
  Alpha Centauri System, Proxima B, High Orbit

UNO WAS THE FIRST PILOT TO COMPLETE HIS CAI, FINISHING four full days before the deadline, with an impressive cumulative score of ninety-six percent. The next batch of graduates came a day later, and to Coda's great frustration, Moscow was among them.

"Ninety-three percent," Moscow said when Coda passed him in the gym. "That's what I scored, O'Neil. Did you see it? You won't even make it through ninety-three percent of the material."

Coda seethed but said nothing. He strode past Moscow, making for the free weights on the other side of the gym. When he got to the bench press, he slapped a series of weights on either side of the bar and lay down into position.

"What are you doing?" Noodle asked, appearing above him. "We're not supposed to be using these weights."

Coda ignored the question—it should have been pretty damn obvious what he was doing. "Spot me."

"Coda—"

"Spot me," Coda repeated, then without waiting for a response, he lifted the bar from the bracket and lowered it onto his chest. It felt lighter than he'd expected. Fewer than two weeks into the program, his body was growing stronger and showing signs of increased muscle definition. He finished the first four reps without issue. By the fifth, the bar began to get heavy. By seven, he was noticeably slower, and by the ninth, his arms were shaking.

"One more," Noodle said, placing his hands under the bar in case Coda's arms gave out. "Come on, Coda. One more."

Feeling as though he was lifting the weight of the world itself, Coda pushed with everything he had. When the bar slammed back into place with a satisfying *clang*, he let out a triumphant scream then, breathing heavily, sat up. Noodle was grinning at him.

"Thanks," Coda said.

"You're welcome," Noodle said. "What was that all about, anyway?"

Coda just shook his head. He didn't want to be reminded of the CAI.

"How'd your session with the computer go?" Noodle asked, proving there was no getting away from it.

"Not good."

"It couldn't have been that bad."

"I've got three days left, Noodle, and I'm only seventy-five percent of the way through it. I might as well start packing."

"That's a bit dramatic."

"Yeah? And what should I be doing?"

"Well, for starters, I wouldn't be in here. There's only so

much time in the day, Coda, and you can't afford to waste any of it in here."

"I'm not sure the commander would agree."

"The commander isn't here," Noodle said. "Neither is Squawks or Uno or a bunch of other people."

Coda surveyed the room with fresh eyes. Noodle was right. Squawks and Uno were nowhere to be found, and the gym was noticeably emptier than usual.

"Where are they?" Coda asked.

Noodle raised an eyebrow as if the answer was obvious.

"Both of them?"

"Yeah."

"But Uno completed his... wait, Uno's helping him?"

"That's what you do when you need help, isn't it? You ask for it. Just like you did when you asked me to spot you."

"Can he do that?"

"Did anyone say he couldn't? Seriously, Coda, if you're not resourceful enough to figure this out, maybe you don't belong in a cockpit."

Noodle smiled as if to suggest he was joking, but there was too much truth in the statement for Coda to laugh. He hadn't thought to ask for help, partly because he didn't know he could, but also because he didn't like doing it. He'd always wanted to succeed on his own, and if that meant failing on his own too, then so be it. But if he didn't get through a quarter of the program in the next forty-eight hours, that hypothetical situation would become a very real possibility.

"So, uh, you think you could help me out?" Coda asked awkwardly.

"Me?" Noodle said. "Coda, I think you misunderstood. I'm not doing much better than you are. I'll finish, but just barely, and that's with me putting in extra work. No, you're going to have to talk to Uno or something."

"All right," Coda said. "I'll do that."

———

CODA FOUND UNO AND SQUAWKS IN ONE OF THE TRAINING rooms, huddled close to the screen. Uno was pointing at something and explaining it in simpler terms. Coda didn't recognize it, so it must have been from a later module. That was a good sign. If Squawks was closer to completing the CAI, that meant Uno would have more time to help him, wouldn't it?

"Making progress?" Coda asked from the doorway.

Uno and Squawks looked up immediately then at each other. Coda couldn't tell for sure, but Squawks appeared to be trying to decide whether to be embarrassed and concerned.

"Relax," Coda said. "Noodle said I could find you here. What module is that?"

"Fifty-seven," Uno said. "The inner workings of Shaw Drive mechanics."

Coda couldn't believe his luck. Just before heading to the gym, he'd completed module fifty-six. Squawks was literally working his way through the very course he was set to begin.

"Do you have room for one more?"

"Are you wanting to help too?" Uno asked.

"Actually, no." Coda's face grew hot. "I'm looking for a tutor if you have space for another student."

"You need help?" Uno asked, a hint of surprise in his voice.

Coda nodded. "A lot of it. I'm actually on module fifty-seven too."

"No way," Squawks asked.

"Yep."

Squawks looked at Uno and shrugged as if saying the decision was up to him.

"I don't mind," Uno said. "But there's no way for you to undock and work in here with us."

"That's fine," Coda said. "What I need is someone who helps me understand this stuff. I can figure the rest out."

"Then grab a chair," Uno said.

"Thank you," Coda said.

In a nearby room, Coda found a chair that wasn't bolted to the floor then squeezed it in next to the two pilots. The room was already tight with two and was completely crammed with three, but even as the room grew hot, nobody complained.

Uno was a born teacher. He often paused the videos, taking time to explain them in greater detail and with less technical language. He answered their questions patiently and without condescension, and even though the video took twice as long to get through, they completed the module in half the time Coda had taken to complete the previous one.

They worked late into the night, not stopping until a full two hours after the three of them were supposed to be in bed. In that time, they had wrapped up two other modules, ending on the sixtieth. With Uno's help, Squawks had completed eighty-percent of the program and had rising evaluation scores.

Armed with a tablet full of notes, his eyes bleary with exhaustion, Coda returned to his training room and fired up the computer. There was no way to fast forward through the video, so he was forced to watch it from the beginning. At first, he tried to tell himself that he would watch it again, but ten minutes into the first video, Coda was struggling to hold his eyes open. Scared he would fall asleep and lose an entire night, he pulled out his personal hand terminal and set an alarm for every ten minutes.

When he got to the exam, he was pleased to find that the questions were the same questions Squawks had answered, only in a different order. Between his familiarization with them and Uno's tutelage, Coda breezed through the evaluation, posting his best score yet.

Suddenly feeling better than he had in days, he began the next module.

12

CAI Room, SAS Jamestown
  Alpha Centauri System, Proxima B, High Orbit

FOR TWO FULL DAYS, CODA WORKED WITH UNO AND Squawks, and for two full nights, he took what he'd learned from their group study and applied it to his own evaluations. By the end of the second night, Coda wasn't worried about completing the remaining modules in time, but he was growing increasingly concerned that his test scores wouldn't be high enough to pass.

Commander Coleman had set the benchmark at a cumulative eighty percent, and while Coda was within spitting distance of that mark, the long days and nights were beginning to take their toll. In the last forty-eight hours, he hadn't managed more than thirty minutes of continuous sleep, and faced with severe sleep deprivation, he found himself making stupid mistakes—misreading questions, making basic arithmetic errors, and simply highlighting the wrong answers.

By the time he was ready to begin the final module his uptick in scores had taken a dive, and he would have to score a ninety-six on his final exam to meet the commander's benchmark.

As with nearly every other test, the questions began simple: *Identify the various components of the X-23's navigational thrusters. The X-23 leverages how many navigational thrusters for its X, Y, and Z-axis maneuvers? Unlike the Shaw Drive propulsion system, which leverages electromagnetic propulsion, the navigational thrusters used what fuel?*

Coda calmly punched in the answers for each, and it wasn't until he was a third of the way through the exam that he even needed to consult his notes.

Name the optimal compression range for the aft- and port-side nose thrusters. In the event the liquid oxygen compressor is damaged, what other system can provide emergency navigational abilities? What steps are required to bypass the compressor to make this possible?

He was halfway through the exam when he got his first question wrong. It was a ridiculous question about hydrogen composition mixes where the four possible answers varied by less than a tenth of a percent. By that point, almost an hour into the exam, his adrenaline rush of having nearly completed FAM Phase had worn off, and he made his second mistake, simply miscounting the correct number of zeroes after a decimal point. It was exactly the kind of question that pissed him off.

Who cares what the optimum hydrogen composition mix is for the navigational thrusters? That's not my job.

Captain Hughes had criticized him for not trusting others—well, he sure as hell trusted that the Deck Chief knew how to service the X-23 better than he did.

Seething, Coda queued up the next question and immediately erupted into a series of curses. Of course it was a follow-up question. It only made sense that the test was doubling down on something he obviously didn't understand. Something he didn't care about. Worse still, he had twenty-five questions to go, and if he got another question wrong, he would have to answer every other question correctly in order to score marks high enough.

His emotions getting the better of him, Coda punched in the first answer he thought might be correct, and to his welcomed surprise, the terminal flashed green.

Sometimes it was better to be lucky than good. Knowing he'd somehow dodged a self-inflicted bullet, Coda put himself through a relaxing exercise that his anger counselor at the academy had taught him. He closed his eyes and breathed in slowly through his mouth for ten seconds, held it for ten seconds, then out his nose for an equal amount of time. After five long breaths, he opened his eyes. Feeling a renewed sense of clarity, he read the next question.

The monitor flashed green with another correct answer.

Five questions later, five right answers. Then ten. Twenty. Before he knew it, he had five to go and only needed to get four correct.

Three left. Then two.

His body trembled as he read the second-to-last question. It would almost be fitting if he missed the last two questions—to come so close only to fail. That was something his father would have done.

Coda read the question three times, and his answer five more, consulting his notes every time to ensure he wasn't making a stupid mistake. Satisfied he wasn't, he held his breath and punched in the answer with a shaky hand. His eyes welled with tears as the green bracket appeared, and alone in the small room, Coda let them flow freely down his face.

I did it, he thought. *I did it.*

The words of the final question were blurry through his tears, but even then, barely able to read them, he still got it right.

WALKING INTO THE READY ROOM THAT NIGHT, CODA WAS HIT with a strange mix of excitement and dejection. The pilots milling around the auditorium seating wore grim expressions that randomly broke into smiles. Everyone in the room had lost someone they'd known to the commander's exceedingly high benchmark, and while it was tough to say goodbye, it was equally tough not to feel proud of what they had accomplished.

Coda found Uno and Squawks talking to Noodle. Unlike the rest, they wore openly relieved expressions, smiles shining through bloodshot eyes and pale faces. Their excitement only grew when they spotted Coda.

"You did it?" Uno asked.

"Ninety-eight percent!" Coda shouted triumphantly.

"I told you!" Uno slapped him on the chest and gave him a friendly shove. "I knew you could do it."

"By the skin of my teeth," Coda said. "I wouldn't have been able to do it without you. Any of you. Thank you."

Uno beamed, and the others inclined their heads in recognition. Before anyone could say anything more, the door to the ready room opened. Commander Coleman strode in.

"Attention on deck!" someone shouted, and every pilot inside the ready room snapped to attention.

"At ease," Commander Coleman said. "And find your seats."

It wasn't until everyone had sat down that Coda noticed just how empty the room was. He couldn't say who was missing, or even how many, but it was a sizable number.

Moscow, unfortunately, wasn't one of them. He met Coda's gaze and didn't look happy. His group was down a member, and Coda's unexpected success was surely salt in the wound. Shoving the thought to the back of his mind, Coda turned his attention back to Commander Coleman, who waited at the front of the room.

"For the last two weeks, you and every member of this squad have been familiarizing yourself with the inner workings of the X-23 Nighthawk. Look around. The pilots you see here are the pilots who passed."

"How many are left, sir?"

"Eighty-seven."

Eighty-seven, Coda repeated in his head. Thirteen percent of their total number had already been removed from the program. The commander had said competition was fierce, but Coda hadn't expected it to be this intense.

"FAM Phase is meant to separate the mentally strong from the weak," Commander Coleman continued. "Every pilot who sits with you tonight has displayed the mental fortitude required to pilot an X-23. Like you, they deserve to be congratulated."

Polite applause filled the room, followed by half-hearted hoots of excitement.

"Congratulations," Commander Coleman said without a hint of pride in his voice, "you have completed FAM Phase. Tomorrow, you'll begin to truly understand what it means to fly an X-23 Nighthawk."

13

Simulator, SAS Jamestown
Alpha Centauri System, Proxima B, High Orbit

THE OPERATIONAL FLIGHT TRAINER WAS ONE OF THE MOST beautifully intimidating pieces of equipment Coda had ever seen. Mounted in the center of a gyroscope was an exact working replica of the cockpit of an X-23 Nighthawk, its insides already alive with multicolored lights, screens displaying simulated flight data, gauges, switches, knobs, dials, and more.

Commander Coleman stood in front of it like a proud parent. "Welcome, nuggets, to the simulator."

A wave of awe swept through the pilots, and Coda heard more than a few hushed whispers. Smiling, Coda looked at his friends standing beside him. Squawks and Noodle were smiling too—the kind of smile that was so wide, it had to hurt. Uno, however, looked as though he was going to lose his stomach. His already-pale face had turned a sickly green color.

"Once upon a time," Commander Coleman said, "pilots trained in primitive versions of what you see in front of you. They were static, didn't move, and focused more on training pilots to understand the cockpit than the sensation of flying. That's not the case here, ladies and gentlemen."

Commander Coleman took hold of one of the outer tubes of the gyroscope and gave it a hard push. The various tubes making up the frame of the simulator began to move, and when they did, the cockpit spun with it.

"The Simulator will spin you. It'll twist you. It'll hum, throb, and shake you. And when you crash, it'll hurt. It's not flying, but it's damn close."

Coda was smiling again—he couldn't help it. The commander saw it too.

"What are you smiling at, Coda?" he barked.

"Just excited to get started, sir."

"Good," Commander Coleman said. "That's good. But the pilot with the honor of giving it its first spin is the pilot who completed their CAI first."

"Oh no," Uno whispered.

"Lieutenant Hernandez."

"No, no, no, no, no," Uno continued to whisper. His eyes took on a wild look, as if he were a spooked animal about to flee.

"Uno!" Commander Coleman snapped. "Get up here."

Uno suddenly pitched forward and lost his stomach on the dull-gray deck. The pilots standing in formation around him shied away, giving him a wide berth as he vomited again. Coda looked on in confusion, unsure of whether to laugh or console the friend who had gotten him through the computer-aided training.

Moscow's shrill laugh cut through the sound of Uno's retching.

"Knock it off!" Coda shouted, pointing a finger at Moscow, then was at Uno's side. "You all right?"

Uno turned away.

The sound of heavy bootsteps caught Coda and Uno's attention, and they looked up to find Commander Coleman making his way toward them. Uno sprang to his feet, snapping once again to attention as Commander Coleman stopped.

"Sir," Uno said. "I…"

"Don't just stand there!" Commander Coleman shouted. "Find a mop and clean it up."

"Yes, sir," Uno said.

"And while you're at it, scrub the entire deck. I can't have my Simulation Room smelling like vomit."

"Yes, sir," Uno said then, his face red and eyes bloodshot, darted out of the room.

Commander Coleman watched him leave, shaking his head. "At least he didn't piss himself."

The jibe stoked Coda's anger, but when nobody else, not even Moscow, said anything more, Coda realized what the commander had done. By speaking up first, he'd taken the opportunity away from everyone else and effectively neutralized their response. Despite his previous criticisms of the commander, Coda was growing to respect the man more and more every day.

"Coda!" Commander Coleman said. "Get up here. It looks like you get your chance after all."

"Yes, sir!" Coda said.

"Lucky bastard," Squawks mumbled as Coda left him behind.

Commander Coleman grabbed one of the still-spinning arms of the gyroscope, bringing it to a halt when the cockpit was positioned right-side up. He locked it in place by yanking a nearby lever then looked expectantly at Coda.

"Well? Climb in."

Coda looked at the cockpit, his excitement beginning to give way to nervousness. The gyroscope was nearly twice his height and, since it was spherical in design, just as deep. That meant the cockpit was well off the ground, more or less at Coda's eye level. Surely, he wasn't supposed to climb the arms of the gyroscope to get in, was he?

Commander Coleman cleared his throat, and Coda looked at him then followed his eyes to a ladder set off to the side of the simulator.

Right. Of course.

He fetched the ladder and climbed into the cockpit. It was exactly as he'd expected it to be, a complete working replica of the same X-23 cockpit he'd sat in during their first day of FAM Phase. However, resting on the seat was a VR helmet similar to the one he'd worn back at the academy.

Commander Coleman stepped through the labyrinth of arms of the gyroscope, settling in next to the cockpit. "Know what you're doing?" he asked quietly.

"I think so, sir."

"Good. Take it easy. Uno isn't the only nugget I've seen empty his stomach, though they usually wait until *after* they've flown the simulator."

"Yes, sir."

"Fire it up."

Coda reached for the switch that would ignite the X-23's thrusters then paused. He looked to the commander, suddenly unsure. Was it the right switch? He didn't want to break something or embarrass himself.

"What are you waiting for?" Commander Coleman asked, loudly enough for everyone to hear.

Coda flipped the switch, and immediately, his seat began to rumble. In that moment, the two weeks he had spent in front of the computer were worth it.

"It's something, isn't it?" Command Coleman said, his voice quiet again.

"Hell, yeah, sir."

"Nervous?"

"A little, sir."

"I'll be with you the entire time, guiding you through a series of exercises. Stay calm and take it slow. Nobody is going to be an expert their first time out. That's why we use the simulator, understand?"

"How will you see what I'm doing?" Coda asked. "It's just a VR helmet, right?"

Commander Coleman pulled his tablet from his pocket, and after a few short commands, the lights in the room dimmed and an entire wall of the room lit up. It wasn't nearly as impressive as the Coliseum at the academy, but the image on it was as clear as if Coda were floating through space himself.

"We'll see what you see, Coda. Ready?"

"Let's do it, sir."

"Strap in, then."

Coda pulled the shoulder straps down, snapping them into the buckle at his crotch, then buckled another set, completing the five-point harness.

"Good. Put your helmet on and wait for my command."

With that, the commander stepped from the center of the gyroscope, falling in line with the rest of the pilots. Coda pulled on his VR helmet; the same star-speckled sky he'd seen on the imaging wall immediately replaced his view. Except now, when he turned his head left or right, the image rotated with him. Between the rumble of the cockpit and the gentle swaying motion of the gyroscope, he was begin-ning to grow disoriented.

"Can you hear me, Coda?" Commander Coleman's voice said through the helmet's speakers.

"Loud and clear, sir." Coda heard his own voice echoing throughout the room. *So they can hear me just like I can hear the commander.*

"Good," Commander Coleman said. "This simulation is designed to give you a feel for the X-23, so we're going to go through a small flight course. Your goal is to navigate the course and fly through a series of checkpoints. For this simulation, and this simulation alone, your speed will be computer regulated, so just focus on navigation, understood?"

"Understood, sir."

"Good. Let's see what you got."

The rumble of the thrusters intensified, and Coda's HUD came alive with various pieces of navigational infor-mation indicating his speed, coordinates, and weapon counts. A small yellow arrow at the top of his vision pointed upward, and a series of numbers counted down faster than he could read them. He'd gone through similar training exercises when he'd learned to fly the Hornet, so he knew the arrow was pointing toward his first objective.

Coda pulled back on the joystick, and several things happened at once. The display image shifted, mimicking the movement of a real X-23, and with it, the entire gyro-scope rotated. Coda was thrust back into his seat then flipped upside down. When he finally got his bearings, he realized he was flying upside down and *away* from the checkpoint.

"Holy shit," Coda said breathlessly, his stomach in his throat.

"Careful, Coda," Commander Coleman said. "You do that in a real Nighthawk, and the chief will have to pull you out in a body bag."

"Yes, sir," Coda said. "She's just a little more sensitive than I'm used to."

"That she is. Be gentle with her."

"Will do, sir."

The yellow icon that pointed to his next objective was at the bottom of his imaging screen now, the numbers growing larger. Coda pushed upward on the stick, more gently than before, and made a series of small course adjustments, bringing the icon into the center of his vision. It grew steadily in size, and the numbers counted down until he was nearly upon it.

The checkpoint was an octagon, and as soon as Coda's fighter sped through it, his navigational information shifted, the yellow indicator pointing to the right side of his vision. Pitching the fighter perpendicular to the battle plane, Coda pulled back on the stick and brought his fighter around in a tight curve. Within moments, he'd sped through another checkpoint.

He flew through two more without incident then brought up the fifth and final one on his battle map. But there was something odd about it. While the other four had been stationary, the last appeared to be moving. The yellow indicator rotated around the perimeter of his HUD, and every time he got it in his sights, it slipped away as if it were an enemy fighter evading his pursuit.

Accepting the challenge, Coda kept on it, countering its movements. He began to gain on it. A few more seconds, and he was flying through its center. Coda hooted, taking his hands off the stick to celebrate. But as he did, the cockpit shook violently and was accompanied by a loud screech.

"What the hell was that?"

Before anyone could answer, his fighter was thrown off course with a sharp jolt, and blue fire shot past the cockpit.

"What is that?"

"You're under attack, Coda. Evasive maneuvers!"

Deep down Coda knew it was only a simulation, but the combination of the movement, the photo-real images, and Commander Coleman's not-messing-around tone made Coda's adrenaline spike. His drone flight training kicked into gear, and he stopped thinking.

He flipped the nose of the fighter around so that he was flying backward but still facing the enemy spacecraft. He couldn't see it with his naked eye, but the targeting system bracketed the ship as it had with the checkpoints before it.

More blue fire erupted from the enemy ship, covering the distance between them in a blink. A last-second course correction was all that saved Coda from becoming simulated slag. Centering the target in his view again, he pulled the trigger.

Nothing happened.

"You have to activate your weapons," Commander Coleman said.

Coda fumbled with the joystick, his thumb searching for the safety switch that would activate his weapons. Flicking it into place, he pulled the trigger again. The cockpit vibrated with a muffled rumble as simulated projectiles barreled out of the Nighthawk's nose-mounted cannon.

Two seconds went by. Then three. Nothing happened. He'd missed. But the enemy vessel *had* altered course, veering off at a ninety-degree angle.

It's fleeing.

Since the computer was regulating his speed, Coda

flipped his fighter back around, settling on a course that would bring him directly behind the enemy vessel. One eye on the yellow indicator highlighting the enemy craft, Coda kept the other on the distance between them. It wasn't getting any smaller. He wasn't gaining on it. He nearly squeezed the trigger again but flicked the weapons switch instead, toggling his missiles.

Successfully engaged, the targeting system changed. A circle appeared, trailing the enemy fighter. Keeping the enemy in his sights, Coda allowed the targeting system to lock on. Then, when the circle completely surrounded the enemy fighter, it stopped flashing, going solid with the dull sound of missile lock.

Coda squeezed the trigger, and a missile blasted forward. He quickly lost sight of it, but a new bracket appeared on his HUD, tracking it as it streaked toward the enemy fighter. A heartbeat later, and with a flash of light, the enemy ship was destroyed.

"Splash one!" Coda shouted, keeping his hands on the joystick and his eyes on his surroundings. No other fighters came, and a few brief moments later, the simulation dissolved.

"Good!" Commander Coleman said, bringing the ladder up to the edge of the simulator. "Very good. If that had been a real Baranyk fighter, you would have been shot to shit fifteen different ways to Sunday, but you weren't a complete disaster out there, and for today's purposes, that was good enough."

"Thank you, sir." Coda climbed out of the cockpit onto the ladder.

Commander Coleman laid a firm hand on his shoulder as his feet touched the deck. Having been spun every which way imaginable over the last several minutes, he was thankful for the added stability.

"So how was it?"

"Amazing, sir." Coda grinned. "Absolutely amazing."

14

Mess Hall, SAS Jamestown
   Alpha Centauri System, Proxima B, High Orbit

UNO DIDN'T COME TO LUNCH THAT DAY. CODA NOTED HIS absence, assuming it had to do with his throwing up in the Simulation Room earlier that morning. Uno was probably embarrassed, mopping the deck, or both, so Coda decided to give his friend some space. But when he didn't show up for dinner either, Coda knew the issue was more serious.

After shoveling in the last of his protein paste, Coda left Noodle and Squawks behind and sought out his friend. There weren't many places a pilot could be—Commander Coleman hadn't granted them access to the larger ship—so when Coda didn't find Uno in his bunk, the gym, or the bathroom, there was only one other place he knew to look.

The Simulation Room was dark when the doors slid open, and Coda almost left right then, but something drew him inside. It could have been his desire to find his friend or the allure of gazing upon the simulator again; he couldn't be sure.

The lights flickered on as Coda stepped inside, the room's motion sensors detecting his movement. Uno sat at the base of the simulator, his arms hugging the knees. He made no motion to see who had walked into the room, just continued to sit there, staring upward at the machine.

"We missed you at dinner," Coda said, stopping to the side and slightly behind Uno.

"Wasn't hungry." Uno still didn't so much as look in Coda's direction.

"Yeah? Still not feeling good?"

Uno took a deep breath but didn't say anything more. He obviously didn't want to talk about what had happened.

"You know what's crazy?" Coda said, deciding to take a different tack. "I grew up designing my own X-23s. Well, not the X-23. I'd call them the X-24 or X-25 or whatever, but I'd design them and print them out on our 3-D printer. They were just toys, of course, but I'd stage mock battles in my room, even run simulations, pitting them against the X-23 to see which was more powerful. The X-23 always won, of course. There was no way a twelve-year-old would design a better starfighter than the military's top minds. But it was fun."

Coda's words echoed off the walls, dissipating into silence. Uno made a face but didn't appear any closer to talking. Coda walked up to the simulator, took hold of one of the arms as Commander Coleman had, and gave it a push. The mechanism went into motion, the various arms and cockpit spinning with it.

"It's crazy," Coda continued, "because after they were decommissioned, I never thought I'd fly one. Hell, I never thought I'd *see* one again, but here we are." Coda turned back to Uno and took an exaggerated breath. "Here we are... And holy shit, do the things scare the crap out of me."

Uno's eyes found his, surprise plainly visible on his face. "No shit?"

"No shit."

"I thought I was the only one."

"No," Coda laughed. "Definitely not. I bet half the people who failed FAM Phase did it on purpose."

"I wish I'd thought about that," Uno said.

"I'm glad you didn't," Coda said. "Viking Squadron was a pretty tight group, and I didn't know if I'd ever find that again. But then I met you guys, and you're all right. I mean *you're* kind of a know-it-all, and I've never heard anyone complain about working out as much as Noodle. And Squawks... well, Squawks just never stops talking. But you've all been there for me. Without you, I wouldn't still be here at all."

"Not sure I did you any favors," Uno said, his lips curling into the tiniest of smiles.

"I'm not sure you did either," Coda said, matching his smile. "But whatever crap we go through, we go through it together, all right?"

Uno nodded, his gaze taking on a distant quality.

"So, are you going to tell me what happened?" Coda asked.

"There's not much to say. I got nervous, and I threw up."

"We both know there's more to it than that."

"Maybe." Uno shrugged.

"Care to elaborate?"

"I'm not like you and Squawks. I don't want the attention. I like to figure things out on my own. Not in front of a group."

Everything suddenly clicked. Coda had misunderstood.

Uno wasn't afraid of the simulator. He was afraid of learning in front of everyone, or more specifically, afraid of *failing* in front of everyone. His call sign suddenly took on a different meaning. Uno might have developed a reputation for shooting down fighters in a single shot, but what if he was a bit of a loner too? It made too much sense to be a coincidence.

"That might have worked back at the academy, Uno, but that's not going to fly here. There's too much attention on our entire group. Too much pressure."

"I know."

"That doesn't mean you can't log extra time, though," Coda said. "Try to figure things out on your own after hours. God knows I'm planning on it."

"You are?"

"Of course," Coda said. "I barely squeaked by FAM Phase, remember? I've got some ground to make up. We can do it together."

"You'd do that?"

"Of course. As far as I'm concerned, I owe you one, and like I said, I was already planning on it anyway."

"You're a good guy, Coda."

"Thank you, but don't tell anyone, all right?"

Uno laughed. It was a tentative thing, but it was a start. "All right."

"Here's what I propose. Morning workout is at oh six hundred, so we meet here every day at oh five hundred and get in an extra hour. If we're feeling up to it, we can log more time after hours too."

"Sounds good."

"Good," Coda said. "Let's get started then."

"Now? What happened to tomorrow?"

"You were the only pilot who didn't log simulator time

today. I'd be willing to bet the commander has you go first again tomorrow. Let's get you comfortable with it."

Uno looked as though he might be sick again, and shot a nervous glance at the simulator. "Do you even know how to use that thing?"

"I'm sure we can figure it out." Coda slapped Uno on the back. "Come on, let's get to work."

Uno took a deep breath and climbed to his feet, then together, they made for the simulator. Coda suspected it would be the first of many long nights.

15

Barracks, SAS Jamestown
  Alpha Centauri System, Proxima B, High Orbit

"WAKE UP! WAKE UP!" COMMANDER COLEMAN SHOUTED AS
he entered the barracks. "Rise and shine!"

It took Coda two precious seconds to register what was
going on. His first thought was that he had overslept their
morning workout, but as quickly as the thought came, he
dismissed it. Across the room, Uno and Squawks were just
as confused as he was. If he had overslept, then they had
too, and that was unlikely.

"Get your asses up!" Commander Coleman strode down
the center of the barracks, already dressed in the blue of the
Sol Fleet. "You can get your beauty sleep on your own
time!"

Coda kicked off his blanket and scrambled out of bed,
snapping to attention. The metal decking was cold against
the bottoms of his feet, and like most of the other pilots in
the room, he was dressed in nothing but his underwear.

"What's going on, sir?" Squawks asked. "Workout's not for another hour."

"That was yesterday's schedule," Commander Coleman said. "Today's is different. You have two minutes to get dressed and meet me in the gym. Move!"

Without another word, Commander Coleman left the room. Coda hastily pulled a navy-colored tank top and pair of gray sweatpants from the drawers below his bunk and threw them on. As soon as he had on his shoes and socks, he was hustling out the door.

Uno caught up to him before he'd made it more than few steps. "What do you think's going on? You think this is part of the training? Sleep deprivation and all that?"

"I have no idea," Coda said. "But I'm sure we're about to find out."

Commander Coleman was waiting for them in the back of the gym, his arms folded across his chest. Another officer stood at his shoulder. With graying hair and a disapproving scowl creasing his tan face, he was at least as old as Commander Coleman and every bit as intimidating.

Coda snapped to attention in front of them, waiting for the rest of the squadron to arrive. They made it seconds later, every one of them beating the commander's time. As the last stragglers fell into formation, Coda realized that the squadron had been split in half. The pilots in the gym had come from two barracks. Unfortunately, the other barracks was Moscow's. He apparently wasn't getting away from his academy rival any time soon.

"Someone tell me what time it is," Commander Coleman said.

"Oh four thirty, sir," someone said from behind Coda.

"That it is," the commander said. "As you've no doubt figured out, our training resources are limited, but in their great resourcefulness, the fleet has mustered up and installed a second simulator. But we still have more pilots than we do equipment, so this group is being rewarded with the morning shift. For the next two weeks, I want your asses in here by oh four thirty, working up a lather. Is that understood?"

"Yes, sir!"

"Good," the commander said. "Let me also introduce you to Commander Chavez, who will be aiding your instruction moving forward. For those that don't already know, the commander and I have flown many missions together, and I consider him one of the finest pilots to have ever flown in the fleet. More than that, before transferring to my squadron, he was my NFO aboard the *Pittsburgh*, making him one of the foremost experts of the X-23's systems and flight capabilities. I'm honored to have him as part of our squadron."

"The honor is all mine, sir," Commander Chavez said.

Commander Coleman nodded and returned his gaze to the squadron. "We'll see you in the Simulation Room at oh six hundred. Get to it."

They got to it, and for once, Noodle wasn't the person who complained the loudest.

"This is horseshit," Squawks wailed. "It's too early for—"

"Stow it," Coda shouted between sets. "No one wants to hear it."

Squawks grumbled some more but largely kept it to himself. By the time their workout was over, Coda felt more awake than he'd ever expected to, and after he'd showered and thrown on a set of clean clothes, he made for the Simulation Room.

True to Commander Coleman's word, a second simulator had been installed on the other end of the room.

Having been there late into the evening the night before, Coda had no idea how they had found the time to install it, but there it was, buttons glowing and waiting.

The commander quickly separated them into two groups based on their barracks then muttered the ten scariest words in the English language. "We're going to do things a little bit different today."

The commander had programmed four different training scenarios that escalated in difficulty, each one in the sequence adding a new variable. The pilots, broken into even smaller groups, took turns running through the simulation while the rest looked on. The largest variation between the day's training and the one previous was that after the subgroup's simulated run, they sat down with Commander Coleman or Commander Chavez to review their hop.

Coda was pleased to learn that while the commander could be a hard ass with the larger squadron, he was calm and patient with their smaller number. He went from being their CO to their instructor, and they listened to him all the more closely for it.

"Your approach vector is too shallow here," Commander Coleman would say, pausing the simulation replay. "Tell me how you could have done it differently."

And they would tell him—then put their words to action in their next run, redoing the scenario until the commander was pleased.

For three hours, they took turns running through the simulations, learning from their fellow squad mates and their combined mistakes. By the end of the first session, the vibe had shifted from exhausted frustration to positive excitement, and that carried over through breakfast and into their late-morning practice.

"Where is the rest of the squadron?" Uno asked during one of their evaluation periods. The Simulation Room was still filled with only forty or so members, all from the same two barracks.

"Class," Commander Coleman said simply.

"Class?" Uno asked skeptically. Minus the CAI—which in Coda's estimation barely counted—they hadn't had any class. "For what?"

"You'll find out soon enough," Commander Coleman said. "Now tell me why you flipped nose to tail here instead of altering course with a more gradual barrel roll."

The commander clearly wasn't going to explain further, and Uno didn't press the issue. He gave his explanation to the commander's question instead.

"It's faster, yes," the commander said, "and might have been a good maneuver if you'd had a Baranyk fighter on your ass, but at those speeds, the g-forces are enough to cause black out. Remember, these simulations are designed to help you learn to fly an X-23 correctly. Follow the flight rules until you know where you can bend them."

"Yes, sir."

"But...?" Commander Coleman said, obviously hearing the unspoken question on Uno's lips.

"But the X-23 is equipped with inertial dampeners, isn't it, sir?"

"It is," the commander said slowly. "Otherwise, you'd be ripped apart by even the most basic maneuver. But there are limits to every gravitic drive, even the most advanced, which I can assure you, do *not* come standard with the X-23."

"Which is why you're juicing us up with steroids and experimental growth hormones, right, sir?"

Coda and Squawks, who were in the evaluation group with Uno, shared a nervous look. That information hadn't made it beyond their circle or been spoken about since their first dinner on the *Jamestown*.

"Now where would you get a crazy idea like that?" Commander Coleman asked, the tone of his voice suggesting he was genuinely dismayed. There was something in his eyes, though, a hardness that hinted at his true feelings. Uno's question had made the commander uneasy.

Uno met Commander Coleman's gaze, not backing down but not exactly challenging him, either. "I don't know, sir," he said, obviously deciding not to push the issue. "You're right, though. It's a crazy thought."

Commander Coleman nodded, returning to Uno's evaluation.

At the tail end of their session, the commander posted their evaluations on the display board. Because most of the exercises had been timed, it showed their time of completion, along with accuracy, precision, and other success metrics. Coda's favorite was a calculated measure the commander called their "death probability," which the commander explained as the likelihood that their flight paths, vectors, and speed would either kill them or get them killed by enemy fire. It all culminated in a final score that was measured out of one hundred. The highest score barely cracked fifty.

Before Coda could find his name on the list, Commander Coleman called their attention to a red line separating a small number of pilots at the top of the list from the bulk at the bottom.

"This," Commander Coleman said, "is your failure line. Your training is about to get very real, ladies and gentlemen. I'm not interested in good pilots. I'm not even interested in great pilots. I need the best. The best of the best. And that means any pilots still south of this line at the end of the month will be excused from the program. Work hard, ladies and gentlemen. I'll see you tomorrow at oh four thirty."

Coda strolled out of the Simulation Room to a mix of hushed voices. The commander had changed the rules, upped the pressure. The real competition was about to get started, and Coda had no intention of giving up. He was having too much fun.

16

Corridor, SAS Jamestown
   Alpha Centauri System, Proxima B, High Orbit

AFTER THEIR MORNING SESSION IN THE SIMULATOR, AN officer escorted the pilots to a part of the ship they had never seen. Unlike their private section of the ship, the corridors here were occupied with the usual shipboard activity. Coda caught more than one confused look, though in true military fashion, nobody voiced their questions. Those conversations would happen over drinks or quietly over dinner, between shipmates, not out in the open.

"Take a good look, ladies," Squawks said loudly as he jogged past a group of female officers. "Heroes of the fleet, coming through. Heroes of the—"

"Can it, Squawks!" Uno shouted.

"I just want—"

"I said, 'Can it!'"

"Geez!" Squawks threw him an irritated look. "What crawled up your ass?"

"We have our orders. Follow them."

"It's not like they won't know soon enough, anyway," Squawks said.

"There's a huge difference between 'will know' and 'already knows,' so can it."

"What's the big—"

"Squawks!" several pilots shouted at once.

"Your mouth is talking," Coda said. "See to it."

Squawks snapped his mouth shut and defiantly blew a kiss in the officers' direction but remained quiet until they arrived at their destination. The classroom was like every other classroom Coda had ever been in, though like throughout the rest of the ship, the tables and chairs were bolted to the floor. And like the ready room, instead of the three-dimensional displays, the room was equipped with an aging digital touch board that took up the entire front wall.

"Take your seats," the escorting officer said. "Your instructor will be along shortly."

Coda found a seat with Uno, Noodle, and Squawks four rows from the front. Once they sat down, another group of pilots entered, Moscow at their lead. Seeing Coda, he smiled then nodded to his group. They found seats in front of Coda, but instead of sitting down, Moscow took a seat on the table, tossing a foot on the chair so that he was facing Coda.

"Funny thing, O'Neil," Moscow said in an amused voice. "I didn't see your name above the failure line. I guess you're just as much of a shit pilot as your father was."

The room fell into a hushed silence.

Coda opened his mouth to speak, but Squawks beat him to it.

"And your death probability was twenty-four percent.

How about you do us all a favor and raise that up a bit, huh?"

Laughter filled the room.

"He keeps talking, and it will," Uno said. "Even if I have to shoot him myself."

"What was that?" Moscow said, his cool voice at odds with his coloring face. "Oh, hold up." Moscow suddenly clutched his stomach and mock vomited in Uno's face. "The only thing you can hit is your own boots."

Coda was on his feet before he knew it, lunging at Moscow.

Squawks was on him immediately, grabbing ahold of him and pulling him back. "Simmer down, Coda. Simmer down. He's all talk."

If Moscow was all talk, Uno wasn't. He was on top of the table and diving at Moscow in an instant. The other man's eyes widened as the human projectile crashed into him, sending them both toppling off the table. They hit the deck with a loud thud and had just enough time to get in a few wild punches before the other pilots separated them.

Squawks let Coda go, and together, they pushed through the throng, making for Uno, then got between him and Moscow, who continued to shout obscenities at one another.

"Officer on deck!"

Years of military training took over, and Coda snapped to attention. Their instructor waited in the doorway, a tablet in her hands, watching the melee with a single raised eyebrow. She couldn't have been much over thirty and was short with closely cropped black hair that was only slightly darker than her skin.

"Someone tell me what the hell's going on in my class-room," she said in a thickly accented voice.

"Just getting in a quick workout, sir," Squawks said. "We're ready to learn."

"Good. Find your seats then."

Coda navigated Uno back to his spot then took a seat. "You didn't have to do that."

"Wasn't doing it for you," Uno muttered under his breath.

"My name is Lieutenant Commander Naidoo, though you may call me Dr. Naidoo. And I am no more a teacher than you are an astrophysicist, but we will make do. I am here because among all of you, I am the only one who has ever seen a Baranyk in person—a mistake we're about to fix together." Dr. Naidoo turned to the door and nodded. "Bring it in."

A pair of men wearing white lab coats wheeled in a gurney, its contents hidden under a thin sheet. They stopped it in front of Dr. Naidoo then turned and left. She thanked the men then, in a single quick motion, ripped the sheet away.

Half the class was on their feet in an instant. Many backed away, while others sat in frozen silence, hands over mouths. Lying on the gurney was a supine mass, flat black in color, with four legs, two arms, large lifeless black eyes, and a pair of thin antennae rising from a triangular head.

"I am not here to give you a shot or check your prostate. I am not that kind of doctor. I am a xenobiologist, and aboard this ship, that means I am the foremost expert of Baranyk biology. An area, if I'm not mistaken, your training has largely ignored. Now, please, return to your seats so we can begin."

Only half of the pilots returned to their seats, though the other half, primarily those nearest the prone Baranyk, refused to move.

"Oh, please," Dr. Naidoo said sarcastically, slapping the Baranyk on its oval-shaped abdomen. "It's not going to bite."

With the doctor making fun of the frightened pilots, the rest slowly made their way back, though if Coda wasn't mistaken, many of the front seats that had been occupied before were now vacant.

"Good," Dr. Naidoo said. "Now will someone tell me what you know about the Baranyk so we can begin?"

Uno raised his hand.

"Yes," Dr. Naidoo said, calling on him.

"The Baranyk—or the 'Astral Montodea,' as they're known officially—most closely resemble the praying mantis of Earth, though, of course, it's much larger and more deadly than anything back at home. Standing above two meters, it has four hind legs, with two forelegs that are bent and equipped with spikes used to snare prey and pin it in place. Their long neck is flexible enough that it can spin almost three hundred sixty degrees, similar to that of an owl. But unlike their cousins at home, the Baranyks' eyes are larger and can see in much clearer detail, though we're unsure if they see as we do or in some sort of infrared.

"Beyond that, they are thought to be tunnel dwellers since in our first encounter with them, they had primarily lived underground, going undetected for months. Since other Baranyk colonies were found underground, the evidence seems to support that theory. Unfortunately, since the fleet's ability to probe belowground remains greatly limited, the Baranyk remain nearly impossible to detect, and that remains one of our biggest challenges with the war."

"Good," Dr. Naidoo said.

"Show off," Squawks muttered.

"But spoken as if read out of a book," Dr. Naidoo said. "Tell me what you *know*, not what you've read."

"I... um..." Uno shifted in his seat. "I guess I don't understand the question, ma'am."

"Tell me its strengths. Its weaknesses. Tell me what they want or *why* we are at war with them."

Uno chewed on his lip, his face making a pained expression, as if not knowing the answer hurt.

"Anyone?"

Nobody took the bait.

"It's okay," Dr. Naidoo said. "We train you to fight, not to think. It doesn't matter *why* we're at war with them if those we are at war with threaten everything we know and love, does it?"

Several pilots voiced their agreement.

"But back to you," Dr. Naidoo continued. "You were trained to fly a drone, to fight distantly, not hand to hand. If you were a squad of marines, you would have no doubt received something similar to what I'm going to teach you, but you didn't. You didn't need to. But if you are to be pilots, you will have a very real chance of meeting one of these things in person, and I'm going to make sure you're ready."

"Ma'am," Ginger said. He was one of the experienced drone pilots who had joined them from the front. "We're fighter pilots. We'll be blowing the Baranyk out of space. Why would we ever run into one in person?"

"A fair question," Dr. Naidoo said. "Have you been trained on ejection procedures yet?"

"No."

"Well, let's just say if you're successful, you may be moored on an alien moon or planet. And if you are shot down, you can bet it'll be Baranyk-infested territory. If you want to survive until a rescue team can be assembled, you'll need to know how the Baranyk think, how they hunt, and where they're vulnerable."

"Understood, ma'am."

"Make no mistake," she continued. "This is not weapons training. It's far more important than that. So download the course curriculum onto your tablets, and we will begin."

An uncomfortable knot settled into Coda's stomach.

Learn to fly, Commander Coleman had said. *Save the world. Reclaim your honor.*

No one had ever said anything about battling the Baranyk in person. One-on-one. Maybe Uno had been right all those nights ago. Maybe he should have read the fine print.

17

Barracks, SAS Jamestown
   Alpha Centauri System, Proxima B, High Orbit

CODA RETURNED TO HIS BUNK, MENTALLY AND PHYSICALLY exhausted. The two hours of class with Dr. Naidoo had been followed by four more with a different instructor. That alone would have been enough, but the advanced mathematics and physics lessons had been followed by an evening work-out, dinner, and evening debriefing. By the time he staggered into the barracks, he felt as though he'd been run through the wringer, so his heart dropped when his tablet vibrated and he read its message.

My quarters. 2100. And it was signed by Commander Coleman.

The commander wanted to see him. Why? Even after performing well in the latest simulator scenarios, Coda was still below the failure line, but then again, so was everyone else in their quartet, and nobody else seemed to have received the message.

The incident in the classroom then?

That didn't make sense, either. It had been little more than a shoving match, and between Moscow and Uno more than anyone else. Why would Coda be summoned and not one of them?

Commander Coleman's quarters were near the rest of the barracks in their semiprivate section of the ship. Coda stopped outside the door. He looked for a communicator, something similar to what they'd had at the academy, but didn't find one and resorted to knocking.

The door slid open, exposing a small room with a bunk set into the bulkhead. A writing table, bookshelf, and two chairs spaced around a circular table filled the room. Commander Coleman sat in one of the chairs.

"Sir," Coda said, stepping into the room and snapping to attention.

"Have a seat."

"Thank you, sir." Coda made for the second chair and sat down.

"Dr. Naidoo said she walked into an issue in her classroom today."

It is about the scuffle then. Strange.

"It was nothing, sir. A few pilots were jarring, and it got a little out of hand. Nothing to be worried about."

"Nothing to worry about." The commander chewed on the words. "Dr. Naidoo said Lieutenant Krylov was at the center of it."

"I suppose, sir."

"There seems to have been a number of incidents between you two."

"Yes, sir."

Commander Coleman took a deep breath, rose from his seat, then made for the small bookshelf where a bottle of brown liquor waited. He poured two fingers' worth into a snifter, swirled its contents, and returned to his seat. After taking a sip, he exhaled through his teeth.

"You see," Commander Coleman said at last, "I've got a problem. My squadron is divided, and you and Moscow are at the heart of it. That's not going to work. The pilots of this squadron need to have complete and absolute trust in their wingmen. And I'm not talking about belief, Coda—they need to *know* that they can count on those they fly with. Do you think they can do that now?"

"No, sir."

"I agree. Unfortunately, it seems you and Moscow are more than just academy adversaries."

"Sir?"

"Do you know what the SAS *Benjamin Franklin* is, Coda?"

Coda's blood went cold. "The *Benjamin Franklin*, sir? Yes. I... It's..."

"The ship your father was stationed on when he turned on his wingmen." Commander Colemen took a sip, his eyes narrowing as they watched Coda over the rim of the glass. "When people speak of your father, they often talk about how many pilots died by his hand. What they usually leave out is how many people aboard the *Benjamin Franklin* perished as well."

"Sir." It was all Coda could do to get the word out of his throat. "What does this have to do with me and Moscow?"

Commander Coleman placed his glass on the table. "I did a little digging, Coda. And it appears that Lieutenant Kyrlov's mother was aboard the *Benjamin Franklin* during the attack."

"And she..." It was somewhere between a question and a statement.

Commander Coleman nodded. "She did. It's all right

there if you want to read it." The commander nodded to his tablet that rested on the table between them.

Coda followed the gesture, seeing a woman with a pale complexion and dark hair, before looking away. Even at a glance, he could tell she was Moscow's mother. He could see the pride burning in her eyes, the same pride that pushed Moscow to his limits and never allowed him to accept defeat. The same pride that Coda had thought was at the heart of their issues.

"I... I had no idea, sir. He never said anything about it. About her." Coda fought back the roiling mix of emotions raging inside him. Everything seemed so complicated all of a sudden. So confusing. "I just thought we were rivals."

Commander Coleman grunted. Like Coda, he seemed to be lacking the words and instead swirled his drink. "Then you see I have a serious issue."

"Yes, sir." Coda swallowed a lump in his throat. "Are you... are you sending me home, sir?"

Commander Coleman took another sip then winced from the bite. "No. But if I'd known the severity of the situation, I never would have taken both of you. Unfortunately, the urgency of our predicament didn't allow me enough time to properly vet the background of every candidate, so I focused on other attributes. But here you are, and I can't send either of you packing without a legitimate excuse. That would only divide the squadron even further. Nor do I *want* to send either of you home, to be honest. Despite your issues, you're both developing into a pair of fine young pilots."

"Thank you, sir," Coda said, breathing a little easier.

"But we need to find a way to fix this."

"Of course, sir."

"So here's what we're going to do. We're going to solve this the old-fashioned way—with a competition."

"Sir?"

"You heard me," Commander Coleman said. "I've heard him grumble about you ever since your squadron beat his back at the academy. So, we're going to give him his wish. You two are going to go toe to toe in the simulator."

"No offense, sir," Coda said skeptically, "but do you really think that'll work? That it'll fix our issues?"

Commander Coleman barked a laugh. "Of course not. But I hope it can be a start. And of course, if things don't get better, your one-on-one performance might give me grounds to get rid of one of you." He added the last bit as if it was an afterthought, but Coda knew better. There was likely more truth to that statement than he was letting on.

"Sir, if I may? Why tell me this?"

"A man deserves to know why someone hates him, Coda. More than that... well, I'll let you figure that out for yourself."

Walking back to his bunk, Coda replayed the conversation in his mind. If the commander's goal was to help him understand the true cause of his issues with Moscow, then he had done that, but Coda felt like he was missing something. The commander wanted him to understand something. Something important. But try as he might, Coda couldn't figure out what it was.

18

Simulator, SAS Jamestown
  Alpha Centauri System, Proxima B, High Orbit

CODA EXPECTED HIS COMPETITION WITH MOSCOW TO COME
the next day, but when they entered the Simulation Room,
Commander Coleman made no mention of it and instead
walked them through their normal routine. The showdown
didn't come during their late-morning session after breakfast, the following day, or the day after, either, and by the
end of the week, Coda had begun to wonder if he'd just
imagined his entire conversation with Commander
Coleman.

Knowing he was working on the commander's timeline,
he allowed himself to fall into his new routine: gym in the
morning, simulator, evaluations, breakfast, more simulator
and evaluations, class, lunch, more class, afternoon workouts, dinner, debriefing with Commander Coleman and the
entire squadron, all followed by his private after-hours practice with Uno.

By the end of the second week in the simulator, their fourth overall in the twenty-six-week program, Coda, Noodle, and Squawks were above the failure line. Despite being below the cutoff, Uno had made marked progress, and Coda believed he would make it above the line in time. That morning, Commander Coleman addressed the pilots as he always did, but his tone held something new.

"Congratulations on completing your first two weeks with the simulator. Every single one of you has put in a considerable amount of work, and you're all the better for it. If we look at the updated standings"—Commander Coleman punched something into his terminal, and the standings appeared on the Simulation Room's wall display —"you'll see that more than half of the pilots in the squadron are above the failure line. That's outstanding. That also means we're ready to move on to our second phase with the simulator: Combat Phase."

A ripple of excitement washed over the gathered pilots. Combat phase. The reason they were all here: not to study Baranyk biology or learn to rebuild a Shaw Drive with spit and gumption, but to feel the rush of flying on their edge of their seats, blasting down Baranyk fighters. As exciting as basic flight was, nothing got a young pilot hard faster than weapons training.

"Over the next two weeks," Commander Coleman continued, "you will face every other pilot in this squadron in a one-on-one competition. The objective is simple: shoot them down before they do you. Any questions?"

There weren't any.

"Good," Commander Coleman said. "Before we begin, there's one last thing I want to bring to your attention. With this new phase, we also enter a new evaluation period. Please see the board with the *updated* standings."

The red failure line that separated the safe pilots from the rest moved up. With one click of a button, Commander Coleman had just changed the fates of more than a dozen pilots.

"I don't understand, sir," one of the pilots in the front row said. "I thought you said anyone with an overall score of seventy would advance."

"You're absolutely correct, Fireball," Commander Coleman said. "There's been enough progress throughout this group that Command and I felt it was time to raise the bar. As I mentioned before, we don't need good pilots. We need the best of the best. That's why of the eighty-seven remaining pilots, only the top fifty will be moving on. Your battles will mean something, so make them count. Coda, Moscow, you're up first. The rest of you get with Lieutenant Commander Chavez and get your assignments. Let's get started."

Coda separated himself from the throng, making for the simulator. Moscow appeared at his shoulder, smirking.

"You ready to be embarrassed, O'Neil?" he asked quietly.

Coda had to chew on the inside of his cheeks to keep from snapping something back. *He lost his mother because of your father. Keep that in mind.* Always *keep that in mind.* "Good luck," he said instead.

Moscow looked at Coda skeptically and muttered something under his breath before they diverted and climbed up the ladders into their separate simulators.

Settling into the cockpit, Coda strapped in and adjusted the straps so that he was snug against the seat. When he was satisfied he wouldn't be thrown out of the simulator once it started rotating, he pulled on his VR helmet.

The simulation was already running, and Coda found himself looking down the barrel of the launch tube. A track nearly one hundred meters in length ran down its center and was attached to a pulley system that would hurl the starfighters out of the side of the battle cruiser like an arrow shot from a bow.

Coda went through his preflight routine, activating the various guidance, tactical, and weapons systems. When all glowed green, he settled into the gel seat and waited for instruction—except it never came. One moment, he was waiting patiently, visualizing his victory, and the next, he was hurtling down the launch tube, his Simulator attempting to replicate the force generated by accelerating to over three hundred kilometers per hour.

The small black dot at the end of the launch tube quickly grew larger until he was hurled into the black of space. The simulated environment nearly took his breath away. He was surrounded by the aftermath of what looked like a full-scale battle. Derelict ships and debris floated in high orbit around a blue-and-green planet, forming something of a ring around it. Streaks crossed the upper atmosphere where pieces of debris burned up, pulled down by the planet's gravity.

Coda punched his fighter to a more suitable combat speed.

"*Speed is life,*" Commander Coleman had taught them, and the old posters and quotes spread throughout their ready room had only reiterated the motto.

He oriented his battle map so that the planet was down. In this simulation, his orientation was a simple exercise, but in the black of space without reference points like the glowing ball below, it was much more difficult to maintain orientation and thus understand where one was located in the greater context of battle.

To solve that challenge, the early brass had devised a

strategy allowing pilots to orient their fleet based on an artificial plane extending from their capital ship to the enemy's capital ship. Everything above the plane on the z-axis, called "positive-Z," became up, and everything below, or "negative-Z," was down.

The simple exercise allowed battle commanders to keep the battle organized and execute complex strategies that made sense to every ship and fighter, regardless of their personal orientation. Of course, Coda was a fighter pilot, and his orientation might change twelve times in a three-second time span, so the exercise was necessity rather than preference. In the heat of battle, starfighters didn't have time to worry about minor details like up and down.

He set a course that kept him on the upper outskirts of the wreckage. His navigational thrusters spat out puffs of compressed air, allowing him to weave his fighter through the drifting debris as his targeting computer scanned the battlespace for Moscow's signature. In most instances, the computer was quick, easily distinguishing friend from foe, but having to catalog each piece of battle wreckage was slowing it down.

Keeping his eyes alert, Coda spotted the enemy capital ship cresting the curve of the planet at the same moment his targeting system beeped. A red box appeared around the vessel on his screen, marking it as an incoming enemy. Turning sharply and increasing thrust, Coda quickly left the debris field behind, settling into an approach vector. By the time Coda was halfway there, Moscow appeared, his location distinguished only by a red box bracketing his fighter.

Moscow must have seen him too, because in a heartbeat, the two fighters were racing toward each other on an intercept course. These one-on-one scenarios hadn't changed much since the early days of flight, and they almost always began with both fighters racing toward each other, opening fire. Then if both missed, they streaked past one another to loop back around for another pass. That was when things got interesting and when superior flying skills came into play.

As his and Moscow's fighters entered weapons range, Coda opened fire. His seat rumbled as his cannon hurled digital projectiles. Moscow did the same.

Tracer rounds cut through the black of space like shooting stars as Moscow and Coda used their navigational thrusters to juke and jank, avoiding the incoming fire. Then in less than a blink of an eye, they streaked past each other.

Coda watched on his battle map as Moscow flipped and burned, pulling a dangerous high-g maneuver to get on Coda's six. Coda had several options but decided to boost thrust, increasing the distance between them.

He made for Moscow's capital ship. Its dark exterior was accented with the yellow of the Sol Fleet and quickly grew larger. Identical to Coda's own capital ship, it was heavily armed with hundreds of port and starboard cannons, missile turrets, and secondary batteries but didn't open fire as he approached. This was a dogfight, not a race to destroy each other's capital ships.

Coda sped past the top of the vessel then turned in a downward arc that brought him around its underbelly, speeding toward Moscow's incoming ship. Coda opened fire, but Moscow immediately veered to port, bringing his fighter parallel to the capital ship.

Coda fired his forward thrusters, shedding speed, and spun to follow. But just as Moscow came back into view, he immediately disappeared, darting under the larger ship. Coda tried to follow, but he'd shed too much speed. By the time he made it under the ship, Moscow's fighter was nowhere to be seen. Corkscrewing his fighter back around the top of the capital ship, Coda searched for the missing fighter.

Tracer fire streaked past his cockpit. *Where did that come from?*

Wrenching his neck to see behind him, Coda searched for Moscow, but the multipoint harness restricted his movement, making it difficult to get a visual. More tracer fire flashed, and this time Coda's fighter shook violently as Moscow's shot found home.

"Shit!"

Coda was hosed. He maximized thrust and took evasive maneuvers, speeding toward the battle debris.

His fighter shook again. An alarm claxon blared. He wasn't going to make it.

I'm not a coward, and I won't run like one.

With Moscow closing on his six, Coda pulled the stick back, ascending above the battle plane, then flipped nose to tail so that he was flying backward, his guns facing his rival's expected trajectory. Tracer fire lit the black as he pulled the trigger, and the slugs ripped through Moscow's rearmost wing in a shower of sparks.

Coda hooted, expecting Moscow's fighter to explode, but excitement quickly turned to disappointment when he realized the damage was only superficial. Like the larger main wings, the offset rear wings were designed for atmospheric flight and weren't required for spaceflight.

Wounded but not yet destroyed, Moscow juked the remaining incoming fire before bringing his fighter into an attack vector. More alarm claxons sounded. They were different, more urgent.

He's locking on, Coda realized. *He's going to fire his missiles.*

A bright-yellow target appeared on Coda's HUD. It

streaked toward Coda's fighter, closing the distance between them faster than he would have imagined possible. Coda opened fire, targeting the incoming missile, only to have a second one appear.

You're hosed. You're hosed. You're hosed.

There was a brilliant flash, then all went black. By the time Coda blinked his vision back, he found himself spinning, a dozen emergency lights flashing. All of his maneuvering thrusters were offline.

It took him a moment to realize what had happened. He'd shot the missile, but it had been too close. Its shrapnel must have peppered his fighter. But that was the least of his worries. The second missile was almost upon him.

I lost. I lost to Moscow. Thank god it was only a simulation.

The second, blinding flash was accompanied by a terrible pain that burned through Coda's entire body. He cried out, his body paralyzed. He couldn't move. Couldn't breathe. Could barely think.

By the time the pain dissipated, Coda found himself in complete darkness, his body cold with sweat. With a shaky hand, he pulled his off his VR helmet and found himself back in the simulator.

Moscow was already standing, pumping his fist into the air and screaming his victory. Coda's friends looked on in disappointment, though Coda barely saw them. Deep down, he knew he was in shock, his body struggling to quantify the pain he'd experienced. Wearily removing his restraints, Coda climbed onto the nearby ladder and climbed down to the deck.

"Tremendous flying," Commander Coleman said, stepping forward. "Congratulations on your victory, Lieutenant Krylov."

"Thank you, sir."

"Sir," Coda said. "There at the end, when the simulation ended, there was... I... It *hurt*."

Moscow sneered, obviously not understanding what had happened in the opposite cockpit. Commander Coleman's reaction surprised Coda the most, though. He laughed.

"Of course it hurt," Commander Coleman said. "You were shot down."

"But, sir... It's only a simulation."

"It's a training exercise, Lieutenant. What you felt is a mild deterrent—one meant to prevent my pilots from getting comfortable with being shot down."

"I don't know about 'mild,'" Coda said sarcastically. He hadn't meant to say it aloud, but there was nothing he could do about that now, except mutter a quick "sir" and brace against the commander's wrath.

"The little jolt you felt is nothing compared to the pain of being shot down," Commander Coleman said. "That, I can guarantee you."

"Yes, sir. Of course."

"Good flying, both of you," the commander said. "Now take a seat at the debriefing monitor and wait for me to return."

"Yes, sir," they said in unison and started for the private alcove at the back of the room.

"I told you," Moscow said quietly. "You're nothing. You never were. And now everyone knows it."

Coda took a deep breath, trying like hell to ignore the insult. Commander Coleman had said the squadron was divided. That it needed to be unified. And that the battle was the first step in accomplishing that goal. As much as he wanted to punch Moscow's teeth in or challenge him to a rematch, Coda knew it would only counter whatever the commander was working on. So instead, he forced his best smile and said, "It was a good battle, Moscow. Congratu-lations."

Moscow sniffed, no doubt expecting the compliment to be followed up with a jab, but when it didn't come, his sneer faltered. He looked genuinely perplexed.

"I mean it, Andrei. Good flying."

Moscow grunted something Coda couldn't decipher and put some distance between them. Coda sighed. Playing nice with Moscow wasn't going to be easy—especially if the other pilot had no intention of meeting him in the middle. Still, considering that their last encounter had ended in a shoving match, he couldn't help but feel like this was an improvement. *At this pace, we'll be friends in no time.*

But even as he thought it, he knew it would never happen. They would never be friends, but maybe they could tolerate being in the same room, fly in the same squadron. That was something Coda wanted. Wasn't it?

19

Simulator, SAS Jamestown
  Alpha Centauri System, Proxima B, High Orbit

BATTLES. IT WAS BATTLES ALL DAY, EVERY DAY AS THE PILOTS worked through the remaining roster, taking each other one-on-one in custom simulations built by the commander himself. Battle became life, an all-encompassing game that they lived, breathed, and dreamed. There was no class or studies. Only the gym and the game. Only winning and losing. And losing meant going home, so when they weren't in the simulator, they were watching the battle unfold on the display board.

Coda spent his time studying the other pilots, taking detailed notes about their strengths and weaknesses. He'd then eavesdrop on the commander's evaluation to see how his own reviews stacked up. Oftentimes, he picked up on things that Commander Coleman highlighted, but the commander always had more to add, and Coda, even when he wasn't flying, continued to learn.

By the third day, a hierarchy was already beginning to take shape, and Coda was surprised to find that experience didn't necessarily translate into success within the simulator. He and Moscow continued to be outliers in that regard, both placing within the top fifteen pilots, well above the failure line.

Their friends weren't quite so fortunate. Noodle and Squawks rode the line, above it some days and below it others, while Uno was consistently below it. Moscow's friends were doing even worse.

That night at dinner, after a particularly embarrassing rout, Uno was even more agitated than usual. "I'm sick of it," he said. "It's too complicated. There's too much to keep track of."

He wasn't the first pilot to voice the complaint or the first to be overwhelmed by the sheer number of commands the pilots were responsible for. Unlike transports and bombers, the Nighthawk was a single-pilot starfighter. They didn't have the luxury of a navigator. It was just the pilot and the computer, and regardless of how much slack the computer picked up, there was still far more the pilots had to pay attention to than their previous drone training had prepared them for.

"The stick has over sixty combinations alone," Uno said, resorting to raw numbers and statistics as he always did when he was trying to make a point. "Did you know that? *Sixty!* Just tonight, I was trying to designate a target and turned off the cockpit lights. No joke. Yesterday, I thumbed the wrong weapon and dropped a bomb instead of firing my guns."

They all laughed. Noodle, caught in the unenviable position of having taken a drink of milk a moment before, spit it out all over his food.

"Probably make it taste better," Squawks said, and Noodle almost lost it again.

"I'm serious," Uno said. "I don't know if I can do this."

"You just need to calm down," Coda said.

"I can't," Uno said. "The commander calls it 'finger fire.' Says it's been around for hundreds of years. And he says it's only going to get worse when we start flying for real and there's radio chatter. 'Helmet fire,' he called it. I don't think I'm cut out for this."

"You just need more time in the simulator," Coda said.

Uno barked a laugh. "And when am I going to get that? The commander has it running all day, and we're already putting in extra time as it is."

"Wait," Noodle said. "You've been flying without us?"

"What do you think we've been doing every night?"

"It's the only personal time we get," Squawks said. "For all I know, you've been dating a pretty little lady."

"The only date we've had has been with the simulator," Uno said. "Little good it's done me."

"We'll be there again tonight," Coda said, ignoring Uno's bitter tone. "Come if you want. It might help your scores."

COMMANDER COLEMAN STEPPED OUT OF THE SIMULATOR Room just as Coda and the rest were approaching. Noodle and Squawks had taken Coda up on his offer to join them for after-hours practice, and they all froze as the commander spotted them.

"Good evening, Commander," Coda said.

"Coda," he said. "Gentlemen. You're not looking to sabotage my simulators, are you?"

"Just logging in some extra time, sir," Coda said.

"Personal time was built into your schedules to keep you sharp."

"We understand, sir. Thing is"—Coda nodded toward the door—"that's all we think about. All we dream about. And the way we see it, the better we fly, the better we'll sleep, and the sharper we'll be."

Commander Coleman nodded appreciably. "I completely understand, Lieutenant. Be easy on my equipment."

"Will do, sir."

The commander turned down the corridor as Coda and the rest entered the Simulation Room. Having been the pilots' home for the last few weeks, it smelled strongly of sweat and agitation.

"Squawks, Uno, get ready to go. I'll get you queued up."

"Who put him in charge?" Squawks asked sarcastically as he and Noodle made for their cockpits.

"You did by joining my extra sessions," Coda said then cycled through the various preprogrammed simulations in the control panel on the wall. After selecting one to his liking, he turned to join his squad mates. As he did, the door opened again, and Moscow strode in. He was joined by three of his friends, and all four of them froze, each eyeing the other. Apparently, Coda and his friends weren't the only ones planning to log extra time in the simulator.

Moscow appraised the scene and grimaced. "Come on," he said to the others, turning to go. "We'll come back later."

"No," Coda said as Moscow's friends turned to join him. "Wait."

Moscow stopped in the doorway.

"You're going to fly some extra simulations, right? So are we. Nothing says we can't do it together."

Moscow's eyes slid past Coda, finding the other three pilots behind him. "You want us to fly with you?"

Coda shrugged. "Why not?"

Moscow's friends looked at each other warily. *Why not?* They had a thousand reasons why not. But their common need outweighed them all.

Finally, Moscow shrugged. "Why not?" he repeated then strode into the room.

"Squawks," Coda said. "Take this one off." Then a little more quietly, he said to Moscow, "Uno's flying this one. Let's try to keep things even, yeah?"

"Sure," Moscow said. "Bear, you're up."

Bear, a female pilot with jet-black hair, had earned her call sign because she had a reputation for going "Momma Bear" when defending her friends. Though she and Uno were both below the failure line, Bear was in the bottom third overall, much lower than Uno.

Coda made for Uno's simulator, while Moscow and his group went for the other.

Squawks fell into step at Coda's shoulder. "What are you doing?" His voice was quiet, but there was an edge to it.

Coda felt Moscow's eyes on him. "We don't own the simulator, Squawks." Then just loud enough for Squawks, he added, "Besides, who would you rather shoot down? Uno or one of them?"

Squawks grinned. "Good point."

Coda slapped him on the shoulder. "Just play nice, okay?"

"Only down here," Squawks said. "I'm gonna kick some ass in the simulator."

"There you go." Coda climbed up the ladder. "How you feeling?"

Uno clicked the last latch of the harness into place then set the VR helmet on his lap. "Good."

Coda could hear the nervousness in Uno's voice but didn't mention it. It would only make him more self-conscious, and the last thing Uno needed was to think about himself instead of his opponent.

"All right," Coda said. "Listen, Bear is slow, and she's overly reliant on missiles. If you get in close and take her with your guns, she won't have a chance."

"Okay."

Coda wasn't sure how it was possible, but Uno somehow sounded even *more* nervous than before. "Hey." He let the word hang there until Uno met his eyes. "It's just us. No statistics. No board. No full squadron, okay?"

"Okay."

"Good," Coda said. "Have fun."

Coda stepped down the ladder then moved it out of the way. When both pilots gave him the thumbs-up, he toggled the start initiative on the wall panel, and the simulation began.

It was a relatively brief encounter, with both pilots flying tentatively, like a pair of amateur boxers unwilling to commit to the fight. Despite Coda's advice, Uno kept his distance, making sweeping movements at full thrust. The strategy played directly into Bear's strength, and Uno met his end when he failed to deploy his chaff in time, allowing Bear's long-range missile to take him clean in the fuselage.

"Sorry," Uno said to Coda as he and Squawks swapped positions.

"No need to apologize."

"I didn't listen to you."

"Maybe you'll fix that next time, huh?" Coda smiled to let Uno know he was joking, but he would've been lying if he'd said there wasn't an element of truth in his words. "Listen, Uno. You're flying stiff because you're thinking too much. Just let it go, and before you know it, the stick will be an extension of your body."

"Is that how it is for you?"

"Me?" Coda asked. "God, no. I'm flying by the seat of my pants too. It's just something my dad used to say…" Coda winced, wishing he could take back the words. "Anyway, just relax. Stop thinking. Let your training kick in."

Squawks's battle was smoother. Unlike Uno, Squawks had all the traits of a talented fighter pilot. Unfortunately, he flew like he talked: fast, confident, and reckless. He took unnecessary risks that worked as often as they got him into trouble. Commander Coleman would have to train that out of him before he ever saw action, though Coda struggled to see how that could be done. Telling Squawks to fly slower and not take as many risks would be akin to telling him to be quiet. It was an assault on who he was.

Maybe not train it out *of him then. Maybe the commander can teach him to channel it.*

By the time their hour of personal time was nearing an end, everyone had flown except for Moscow and Coda.

"Rematch?" Moscow asked, smiling wryly.

Coda couldn't tell if Moscow was trying to be an ass, or if his own feelings were still raw from the defeat. He decided Moscow was trying to have fun with it, nothing personal. "Not tonight."

"Still sore?"

Okay, maybe he is trying to be an ass. "Something like that."

"You guys here every night?"

"Yeah," Coda said. "I take it you're planning on making it a regular thing?"

"That was the plan," Moscow said. "The group needs the practice."

"So does mine," Coda said. "No reason they can't do it together, right?"

"I guess not."

Just like that, he found himself in a shaky truce with Moscow. Every night during their hour of personal time, Coda and his three friends logged extra time in the simulator, and every night, Moscow's group joined them. They didn't always battle opposing teams. Sometimes, Uno took on Squawks or Noodle flew against Coda, but as the nights wore on, they began to offer each other advice.

"When he's on your ass like that," Moscow said to Noodle one night after Bear had gotten in close and killed him with guns, "you can deploy your chaff. At those speeds, it'll tear her apart. Don't be afraid to think outside the box."

By the end of the week, the extra practice was already beginning to pay off. Moscow had cracked into the top five, with Coda right behind him. Noodle had worked his way into the top twenty, and every member of their alliance had broken into the top sixty. After that, it didn't take long for people to realize they were spending more time in the simulator than the others. Some of the pilots asked to join their after-hours practice sessions, while others complained to the commander.

Commander Coleman simply said that personal time was personal time and that he wasn't going to discipline pilots for working harder than everyone else. After that, the simulator became a buzz of activity, and it became next to impossible to log an extra session.

So Coda spent the time studying the other pilots in excruciating detail, augmenting the notes he'd already begun taking. Subconsciously, Coda knew that when it came to fighting the Baranyk, it wouldn't matter how well he could fly if he couldn't understand and outthink his opponent.

For the remainder of the week, he put the strategy into action, leveraging what he knew about the other pilots' deficiencies to destroy them in battle. When it was all said and done, he, like the rest of his group, had made his mark on the commander's standings. Unfortunately, it wasn't the commander's opinion that he should have been worried about.

20

Commander Chadwick Coleman's Quarters, SAS Jamestown
Alpha Centauri System, Proxima B, High Orbit

COMMANDER CHADWICK COLEMAN SIGHED AS LIEUTENANT
Hernandez left his quarters. The meeting hadn't been altogether unexpected. Pilots, after all, left programs for
personal reasons all the time, but what *had* surprised him
was who the meeting had been with. Lieutenant Hernandez
wasn't a bad pilot, and his scores were good enough to graduate to the next phase of his training, but if he didn't think
he had what it took, then Coleman wasn't going to argue
with him.

Unbuttoning his uniform, Coleman crossed the small
room to his bookshelf, where he poured himself a drink.
After a small sip that warmed his body from the inside, he
returned to the chair and pulled up the flight roster on his
tablet. He found Lieutenant Hernandez's name in the top
fifty and, with a second frustrated sigh, crossed it out.

The pilots had done well, all things considered, in large

part because their drone training had translated better than he had expected. Even then, it still wasn't an equal replacement for basic flight. In his day, any X-23 pilot would have first flown other spacecraft before being selected for the Nighthawk strike fighter program—Commander Coleman himself had built his early reputation on flying long-range reconnaissance vessels, so he'd possessed at least some experience with fast-moving, highly maneuverable spacecraft.

Still, transitioning from the larger, slower ships of the fleet to the X-23 was akin to jumping from a bicycle to a motorcycle. They were similar only in concept. But that concept created a foundation upon which everything else was built. The pilots of Coleman's squadron didn't have that foundation, or if they did, it was incomplete, the concrete not yet solidified into something that could be built atop of. That was why they'd logged so many hours in the simulator. During his day, a pilot only had to complete eight hours of simulated flight before moving to the real thing. Most of his pilots had already logged over fifty.

They're ready… or at least as ready as they'll ever be.

The only question left was with Lieutenant Hernandez's sudden departure, would he slide the person from the fifty-first position into the top fifty?

No, Coleman decided. *That would be an insult to those who've earned it.*

It was done then. What had been one hundred was now forty-nine. Only half of the original recruits had made it to the midpoint in their training. He took another sip and set his tablet aside, then sinking deeper into his seat, he rested his head back and closed his eyes.

The tablet buzzed. Coleman was alert in a heartbeat,

noticing the red border that now filled the edges of his terminal, noting the priority message.

With the development of the Shaw Drive, humanity had unlocked the keys to faster-than-light travel, but faster-than-light communication was still little more than a science fiction concept. That meant the ships of the fleet were often both battle vessels and mail carriers, carrying important information to other ships in the area like a bucket brigade. For high-priority messages, though, command leveraged courier drones whose sole mission was to jump to a single location via a jumpgate and deliver its message. Even with the receiving vessels reusing the courier drones for subsequent communications, the system was beyond expensive and only available to those with a captain's rank or higher. Whoever had sent him the message had gone to a lot of trouble for him to get it as quickly as possible.

Commander Coleman played the message. The man on the screen was in his early sixties, his skin smooth and showing little sign of his age. His hair, however, was pure white, matching his admiral's uniform, and styled meticulously. But Admiral Orlovsky's lively blue eyes were bloodshot and rimmed by dark circles, as if he hadn't slept in days.

"Commander," the recording of Admiral Orlovsky said, "enclosed, you'll find footage of a recent Baranyk encounter. The target was the mining colony of Numina 3, and as you'll see, the enemy once again employed the use of their Disrupter. Despite recent fleet R&D upgrades, our forces were still rendered inoperable. The colony was lost, as were the *Boston* and *Charleston*."

The admiral paused, taking a deep breath. The hardness of his eyes melted away, and the façade of command disappeared as the admiral turned into the man Coleman had known for his entire military career.

"They're going for our supply lines, Chadwick. Destroying not only our drones, but our ability to manufacture more. The courier carrying this message is equipped with a new Shaw Drive prototype. I need your report, including roster updates, capabilities, and battle readiness. And, Chadwick, I hope your work is going better than it is out here, because we're going to need your pilots. We're going to need you. I look forward to your report. Good luck, Commander."

The image of the admiral disappeared as the screen faded to black. Coleman sat there for several moments before toggling the vid attached to the message. By the time it ended, Coleman was ready for a second drink. It was bad form for a commander to get sloppy drunk, so he did the next best thing: he slid the fifty-first pilot into the fiftieth position.

The rest of the squadron might not know it yet, but they were going to need every pilot they could get.

21

Ready Room, SAS Jamestown
Alpha Centauri System, Proxima B, High Orbit

"Where's Uno?" Coda asked, surveying the half-empty ready room.

The remaining pilots of Commander Coleman's squadron mingled, sharing smiles, attempting to ignore the vacancies left behind by their departed friends. That was the fighter pilot way: to move on and act as if the cut, the loss, or the death had never happened. Dwelling on it meant confronting failure. Confronting death. One's own mortality. To a pilot, that meant losing their edge. And the moment a pilot lost their edge, they became slag.

"Have you seen Uno?" Coda asked, turning to Squawks, who, like Noodle, sat next to him.

"He's probably taking a dump," Squawks said.

Noodle snorted, but Coda didn't feel like laughing. "I haven't seen him all morning."

"Maybe it's a stubborn one."

"A what? No, never mind, I don't want to know." Coda shook his head, trying to get the mental image to disappear. "He should be here."

"Settle down," Squawks said. "He will be."

"Yeah..." But for some reason, Squawks's words didn't make Coda feel better. Objectively, Coda knew he shouldn't be worried. Like every other member of their group, Uno had finished above the failure line and would advance to flight status, but Coda still couldn't shake the uneasy feeling in his gut. Something wasn't right.

"Attention on deck!"

The pilots snapped to attention as Commander Coleman stepped into the ready room.

"Take your seats," he said, taking his usual position behind the podium.

Once the pilots had found their seats, the room fell deathly quiet—something that was even more pronounced by the number of empty seats. When the pilots had first arrived, they'd been excited, nearly bursting at the seams, but that energy had suddenly dissipated, leaving a gloom as if the squadron had lost a major battle and taken fifty-percent casualties.

"Congratulations," Commander Coleman said, giving his obligatory speech. "The men and women in this room have advanced to basic flight. The chief is still readying your fighters, so despite my better judgment, I'm giving you the day off. Enjoy it, because it'll be the last one you get before the end of your training."

The room erupted into cheers, pilots clapping and laughing, slapping each other on the back.

A day off. Coda couldn't remember what that was like. Twenty-four hours to himself. He didn't know what he would do. *Sleep*. Yes, that sounded nice. *Sleep*. His eyes felt heavy just thinking about it.

"Flight schedules have been downloaded to your tablets," Commander Coleman said once the ruckus had died down. "Check then double and triple check your flight times and craft number. Failure to arrive on time and at the correct spacecraft will result in an automatic SOD."

A SOD—or a "sign of difficulty"—was the pilots' version of a strike, and as in the great American pastime of baseball, after three strikes, the pilot was out of the program.

"This is the real thing, ladies and gentlemen. I expect you to be ready. I'll see you tomorrow."

Coda turned to his friends as the commander strode out of the room. "Come on."

"Where?" Squawks asked.

"Just follow me."

Coda pushed his way through the pilots, making for the ready room door, then chased the commander down the corridor. "Sir!" Coda shouted. "Sir!"

Commander Coleman stopped and turned to face him. "What is it, Coda?"

"It's Uno, sir," Coda said. "We haven't seen him and were wondering if you knew where he was."

"Lieutenant Hernandez?"

"Yes, sir."

"Coda," Commander Coleman said, "Lieutenant Hernandez is set to depart with the rest of the washouts at oh nine hundred."

"Washouts?" Coda said. "Sir, there must be a mistake. Uno was above the line."

"Yes, he was," Commander Coleman said. "Which is why it was so unexpected when he came to my quarters last night and withdrew from the program."

"He quit?" Coda couldn't believe what he was hearing. "I thought you said we couldn't quit."

Commander Coleman's face grew hard. He apparently didn't like having his words thrown in his face any more than anyone else did. "I won't have a pilot in my squadron who endangers everyone else he flies with. The lieutenant didn't believe he had what it takes, and I didn't disagree with him. Anything more than that, and you'll have to ask him."

"He's still here?"

"As I already said, Coda, he departs at oh nine hundred. You can find him in the hangar bay."

———

THEY FOUND UNO SITTING AGAINST THE WALL, HIS ARMS draped over his knees, watching as specialists worked under the watchful eye of the chief, frantically trying to get the remaining Nighthawks ready for flight. When he saw Coda and the rest approaching, his mouth fell open, and his face grew several shades redder than it had been before.

"Hey," Coda said, crossing his arms and stopping in front of him.

"What are you guys doing here?" Uno asked.

"What are we... Uno, what are *you* doing here? The commander said you quit."

Uno turned away.

"Uno—"

Snapping his head around, Uno jumped to his feet. "What do you want me to say? I told you I couldn't do this, but you wouldn't listen. 'You just need more time,'" Uno said, giving Coda an exaggerated impersonation of himself.

Coda felt his blood rise and forced himself to take a

deep breath. "Uno, you were above the line. You want to say you couldn't do it? You're full of it. You did it. You passed."

"Anyone can pass a test, Coda."

"What's that supposed to mean?" Coda asked defensively. Was that a shot at Coda nearly failing FAM Phase?

"It just means I can pass whatever test the commander puts in front of me, but that doesn't change anything. I *know* I can't do this. I *know* I don't have what it takes."

"We don't believe that," Noodle said.

"It doesn't matter what you believe," Uno said. "Do you know what I've been doing in my bunk the last few nights?"

"I'm not sure I want to know..." Squawks said.

"I've been watching the flight vids," Uno said, ignoring Squawks's failed attempt at a joke. "Mine. Yours. All of them. And you know what I saw? I saw someone who was slow. Someone who was mechanical. Someone who *thought* too much. Not like you guys. Not like everyone else."

"Uno—"

"No, Coda. I already made my decision."

Coda clamped his mouth shut. There was no arguing that. Uno had quit on his own, and even if Coda somehow convinced him it had been the wrong thing to do, there was little chance the commander would take him back. A fighter pilot with self-confidence issues wasn't exactly a prized commodity.

"You should have said something," Coda said. "We're supposed to be friends."

"I know." Uno blew out a long breath. The anger and frustration in his voice disappeared, and for the first time since they'd confronted him, he seemed truly disappointed. "But you guys know me. I like to fail on my own."

"Deep down, you're just as selfish as I am," Squawks said with a smile.

"I guess so," Uno said, smiling back.

Coda didn't know how Squawks did it. He'd basically just insulted the man, but instead of getting mad, Uno had thought it was funny. If Coda had done something like that, Uno probably would have decked him.

"Where are they sending you?" Coda asked.

"The *Philadelphia*."

"They're sending you to the *front*?" Noodle asked.

"Yeah," Uno said. "I was surprised too. They have me flying a drone again."

The front. The one place Coda had dreamt about since joining the academy. At any other point in time, he would have been jealous, annoyed that a washout was being stationed in the one place he wanted to be while he was left behind. But strangely, he didn't feel any of those things, and if someone had given him the opportunity to swap places, he wasn't sure he would have taken it.

"Anyway, it looks like I've got to go." Uno pointed to where a group of former pilots were boarding a transport ship. "Seriously, though, guys. I'm sorry. Thanks for coming. Thanks for everything."

Coda clapped hands with Uno and pulled him into a quick hug. "Good luck."

"You too, Coda."

Noodle was next, repeating the embrace. "Take care, man."

"Save some Baranyk for us," Squawks said, punching him in the arm.

"No promises," Uno said, then with a final, half-hearted smile, he nodded and turned to go.

Watching Uno walk away, Coda couldn't help feeling as if the squadron had just had its first real casualty. He also knew it wouldn't be the last.

22

Ready Room, SAS Jamestown
   Alpha Centauri System, Proxima B, High Orbit

CODA ENTERED THE READY ROOM TWO HOURS BEFORE HIS scheduled flight. Commander Coleman was already there, sitting in a chair in the front row of the auditorium seating. His eyes were alive in a way Coda hadn't seen since joining the squadron. When the commander stood and strode toward Coda, his step was light, almost giddy.

"Good morning, sir."

"Good morning, Coda. You ready?"

"Can't wait, sir."

"Good." Commander Coleman stepped past Coda and, grabbing a black stylus from the tray, stopped in front of the large digital display board that took up the entire front wall. "You reviewed your flight packet?"

"Yes, sir."

Commander Coleman handed the stylus to Coda. "Write it out for me then."

"Sir?"

"I said write it out for me. Who's flying? What are their call signs? What are our takeoff and landing times? What ship numbers? Communications frequencies? Diversion information? I want all of it, and I'm going to want to know all of it before every flight."

"Yes, sir."

Coda started writing. *Who's flying? Lieutenant O'Neil and Commander Coleman. Call signs? Coda and Spitfire. Taking off at 0700 from hangar bay 7B in Nighthawks One and Two. Landing at 0800 at the same location.* He listed communications frequencies, both primary and emergency, as well as alternative flight paths in the event of engine trouble, carrier malfunction, and invasion. The whole process took nearly twenty minutes. When he was done, he handed the stylus back to Commander Coleman and stepped back to let him review it.

"Well done."

"Thank you, sir."

"Can you tell me why I had you do this?"

"Because you wanted to be sure I knew it, sir."

"Because it helps avoid accidents. This is your first flight, so your ship is unarmed, but I've flown in training exercises where the pilot accidentally climbed into the wrong fighter and fired real rounds instead of the simulated rounds we'll be working with today. His mistake nearly cost his CAG his life. Don't forget that, Coda. Mistakes cost lives."

"Understood, sir."

"Good, because you'll do this before every flight. I'll take two minutes to review it, but other than that, you'll be on your own to fill it out properly. Get anything wrong, and you're grounded for the day."

"Yes, sir."

"Follow me."

The commander led Coda through the ready room into the adjoining locker room, where they stopped in front of a locker with Coda's call sign. Hanging inside was one of the best presents he'd ever received.

"Do you know how to put that on?"

"I think so, sir."

"Do it."

Coda began shedding clothing until he was dressed in nothing more than his underwear. The black flight suit, known as a G-suit, fit snugly around every part of his body. During flight, it would squeeze his legs and abdomen, preventing the flow of blood from his brain to help avoid grayout, the loss of vision or awareness, or even blackout, the loss of consciousness altogether. Because it was so snug, the commander had to zip it up in the back for him. Coda repaid the favor.

Once dressed, they moved down the short corridor into the hangar. They passed a number of ship personnel, garnering confused looks and double takes. While their presence was becoming known throughout the ship, there was a difference between knowing and seeing, and seeing two pilots striding purposefully down the corridors of their ship, especially the legendary Commander Coleman himself, was akin to seeing a living legend.

Commander Coleman led Coda through the hangar, avoiding technicians and machinery with an efficiency gained through years of practice. Their fighters were set apart from the rest of the hangar, hitched to a pair of fork-lifts that would assist loading them into the launch tubes. A middle-aged man with thinning dark hair and a round face covered in grease was overseeing the last of their preparations.

"Chief," Commander Coleman said.

The chief looked up. "Sir," he said, giving the commander a quick salute. "We're just wrapping up now, sir."

"Very good. We'll take it from here."

"Of course, sir." The chief stepped away from the fighters and ordered his specialists to do the same. Rather than disappearing entirely, though, they only gave the commander some space.

"What are you doing, sir?" Coda asked, watching as Commander Coleman ran a hand down his fighter's fuselage.

"Visual inspection."

"Isn't that what the chief was doing?"

"Mm-hmm."

"Then why are you doing it again, sir?"

"Because it's *my* ass in the cockpit."

That was good enough for Coda. He circled his own fighter, trying to mimic his commander's steady gaze. The only problem was, he didn't know what to look for. The commander seemed to sense his confusion, and without taking his attention away from his own fighter, he told Coda what to look for.

"Loose parts, dents, cracks, anything that can cause friction or come apart in a high-g maneuver."

Coda started his review again, taking in the finer details of the fighter, running a careful hand down its fuselage, offset wings, and rear thrusters. It was the first time he'd seen one of the fighters since the first day of FAM Phase, and after flying countless simulations since that day, he found it even more impressive.

"Looks good, Chief," Commander Coleman said. "Good work."

"Thank you, sir."

"Coda?"

"Looks good to me, sir."

"All right. We've got four minutes 'til launch. Load up."

One of the specialists rolled over a ladder, which Coda used to climb into his cockpit. Settling down inside, he immediately secured his harness then slid on his helmet. The specialist helped him lock it into place, and a moment later, cold oxygen blew into the flight suit, giving the entire thing a miniature pressurized environment. The cockpit would be pressurized too, of course, but in the event of an emergency, the suit would give him roughly another thirty minutes to get to safety.

Manned spaceflight was built around contingency after contingency after contingency, and while many called it redundant, Coda, who was seconds away from shooting into the cold, lifeless void of space, was beginning to understand that redundancy might save his life.

With everything in place, he closed the cockpit, maneuvered the emergency lever to lock it into place, and powered on his guidance, engine, and communication systems.

"Hawk Two, this is Hawk One. Do you copy?" Commander Coleman's voice sounded slightly tinny through the speakers of Coda's helmet.

"Copy, Hawk One. Loud and clear."

"Copy that, Coda. Begin final systems check and prepare for launch."

"Yes, sir."

Coda ran through the final check, verifying that each of his systems was online and functioning properly. Once confirmed, he radioed back to the commander. "Final systems check complete, sir. I'm good to go."

"Same here, Coda. Strap in and have fun."

"Yes, sir."

The forklift moved him into the launch tube, locking the bottom of his fighter to a pulley that was attached to a track at the bottom of the deck. When it was time to launch, the pulley would rocket forward, dragging his fighter along with it, and hurl it into space.

"*Jamestown* Tower, Hawks One and Two are green and ready for takeoff."

"Roger, Hawk One," Lieutenant Commander Chavez said over the radio. "Hawks One and Two are cleared for launch from launch tubes three and five, firing at one-second intervals in ten seconds."

The prelaunch sensation reminded Coda of being a kid and riding a roller coaster. His legs felt light, and he thought he had to pee. And this time, he didn't have the reassuring smile from his father to let him know everything was going to be all right. Worst of all, just as it had been when he was a child, once he was strapped in and the ride started moving, there was no shutting it down. He was truly at the mercy of whatever came next.

"Five seconds."

I really do have to take a piss.

"Three."

There was a muffled banging noise followed by hissing air. Was something wrong?

"Two."

Two? Why's he still counting down? Where's the emergency abort?

"One."

Another bang. Another hiss. Both louder than before. Then like a bolt fired from the world's largest ballista, Coda rocketed forward. Thrown back in his seat, he watched as the distant black dot at the end of the tunnel grew alarmingly fast. He had just enough time to blink before he was spit out into the night.

I'm flying, Coda thought as the *Jamestown* grew smaller behind him. *I'm actually doing this!*

And then the panic hit him.

23

Cockpit, Nighthawk
  Alpha Centauri System, Proxima B

CODA'S HEART WAS IN HIS THROAT. ADRENALINE COURSED through his veins, making his hands tremble, his movements sharp. The *Jamestown* was little more than a shadow against the orange glow of Proxima B, but its subtle shifting out his starboard window, coupled with the null gravity, was more than enough to send his body into a panic.

Up became down and down became sideways as he fought to find some semblance of gravity. In that terrible moment, he realized that regardless of how realistic the simulator was, nothing could ever truly replicate the experience of spaceflight.

"Breathe," said a calming voice on his radio. Who? Who was talking to him? "Breathe, Coda." Commander Coleman's X-23 appeared at Coda's wing, close enough that Coda could see the other man seated inside the cockpit. "Just follow the blues of my thrusters. Acknowledge?"

"Acknowledged," Coda said, forcing the words through the lump in his throat.

Commander Coleman's fighter moved ahead of Coda's effortlessly. Coda took a deep breath then pushed the throttle forward with his left hand, increasing speed, and formed up behind Commander Coleman's left wing in the dash-two position, using the blue of his Shaw Drive thrusters as much as the navigational path that had popped up on his HUD. They followed the path for several minutes, leaving the various orbits of fleet ships and satellites behind.

"All right, Coda. Just like we practiced in the simulator. Stay with me."

Commander Coleman's fighter rocketed forward, quickly leaving Coda behind. With the aid of his computer, Coda initiated his main thrusters and matched speed. One second, he was moving at a comfortable five kilometers per second; the next, he was moving at more than twice that. Thrown back in his seat, with what felt like the weight of the world on his chest, he finally understood what five G's truly felt like, and along with the sensation came something else: true, unbridled joy.

Letting out a long yell, Coda fell in behind Commander Coleman, but because the commander had launched forward before him, the blue of his thrusters appeared as little more than a pair of blue stars shining in the distance. Coda brought up his targeting computer, identified Commander Coleman's ship, and locked on. No sooner had he done so than the commander strafed right, turning forty-five degrees.

Coda followed, and the G's increased. If he hadn't been harnessed in so tightly, he would have been thrown against the left side of his cockpit. As it was, his body cried out against the restraints, and he could *feel* the blood inside his body forced from his extremities. The flight suit tightened, compensating for the movement, keeping the blood where it belonged and preventing him from blacking out.

Before he'd fully adjusted to the sensation, the commander turned again, bringing his fighter around ninety degrees to the left. Coda followed again, and again, the harness and flight suit adjusted for the increased g-forces. Coda still felt his vision grow fuzzy.

This is going to take a lot of getting used to.

Zigging and zagging, they flew, Coda always matching Commander Coleman's maneuvers. For an hour, Coda followed him, doing barrel rolls, corkscrews, aileron rolls, and split-S maneuvers—everything he'd already mastered in the simulator—and by the end of the hour, the over-whelming panic he'd felt when he'd shot out of the *Jamestown* had been replaced by a growing confidence.

"All right, Coda. That's enough for one day. Lead us home."

"Copy that, sir."

With the *Jamestown* behind them, and Coda once again in the dash-two position behind Commander Coleman's starboard wing, the correct maneuver would have been to make a wide one-hundred-eighty-degree turn, but his confidence was growing by the second, and Coda wasn't inter-ested in correct. He wanted some fun.

Coda fired his nose thrusters, flipping the front of his ship backward. It was a maneuver he'd done in the simu-lator a thousand times, but in the short time since the begin-ning of the exercise, he had forgotten how little the two had in common. He was thrown up, down, and backward, then all three all over again. By the time he stabilized the fighter, he was still facing the wrong direction.

Breathing heavily, Coda reoriented himself, finding the

two other ships, and braced himself against the comman-der's impending rebuke. However, what he heard was even more unnerving.

Commander Coleman was *laughing*. He appeared in front of Coda, their fighters nose to nose, Commander Coleman flying *backward* so that he was looking directly into Coda's cockpit.

"That didn't look comfortable," Commander Coleman said.

"I feel like my brain was put on spin cycle."

"I bet. Are you hurt?"

"Only my ego, sir."

"What did you learn?"

"That I'm an idiot?"

"I won't argue with you there," Commander Coleman said. "That wasn't very good headwork. But tell me *why* you're an idiot."

"Because I can't do things out here the same way I did them in the simulator."

"Very good, Coda. I won't argue with your stupidity, but part of this was my fault. In my day, a pilot would fly eight simulations before flying their first real flight. You've flown more than eighty. We never had the opportunity to get comfortable in the simulator. You did. And you're going to have to unlearn a lot of it."

"Understood, sir."

"It's going to be a process, and we're going to spend some time getting comfortable. After that, the real work will begin."

"Sounds good, sir."

"All right. Let's try that again, shall we? Home's that way." Commander Coleman pointed behind Coda, laughed again, then used his forward-facing thrusters to create some distance between them, giving Coda space to turn around and plot a course back to the *Jamestown*.

As they drew closer, Coda radioed in. "*Jamestown* Tower, this is Hawk Two requesting clearance to land."

"Roger that, Coda. You are cleared for landing in hangar bay 7C."

"Copy, *Jamestown* Tower. Thank you."

Coda set a course that would bring them into the fighter recovery bay then toggled up the landing procedure on his HUD. Selecting the automated sequence, he let go of his stick. Instead of following the designated path, though, the fighter drifted off course.

Cycling through his systems again, Coda made sure his autopilot was activated. After confirming it was, he reattempted to connect with the *Jamestown*'s auto-docking procedure. It failed a second time.

"Is there an issue, Lieutenant?" Commander Coleman asked.

"My auto-docking isn't engaging."

"That's because we're not using the auto-docking procedure."

"Sir?"

"The enemy has a way to disrupt our connection with our drones. Who's to say they couldn't do the same with an automated landing? We'll be hands-on the whole way in."

Hands-on. The words filled Coda with dread. He'd practiced landing in the simulator, of course, but he'd already learned that the simulator wasn't the same. Now he was supposed to land on a ship that was traveling at eight thousand meters per second while coming in on an adjacent flight path.

"Is that going to be a problem, Coda?" Commander Coleman asked.

Coda had no idea what to say. *Yes, sir, I'm petrified?* He would never live that down, especially since he knew his radio communications were being broadcast in the ready room for anyone who wanted to listen. He didn't expect a big draw; he wasn't the first pilot who'd flown, but he had been the first out of his friends. That meant Noodle and Squawks were likely listening in.

"No, sir. Not a problem at all. Plotting my landing now."

Coda readjusted his flight path, aligning it with Hangar Bay 7C, then swung around so that he was flying parallel to it. Once his fighter and the *Jamestown* were traveling at matching speeds, the only thing he had to do was ease the fighter in, like an old car switching lanes on the highway— at eight thousand meters per second.

"Clear one, Coda," the tower officer said. "Call the ball."

"I've got the ball," Coda said.

"Just like the simulator," Commander Coleman said. "Trust your training, and you'll be fine."

It went against every instinct in Coda's body, but trust his training, he did. The digital display on his HUD traced a line moving from left to right. His job was to keep a small circle inside a second, larger one. The farther out he was, the more leniency he had, but as he drew closer to the *Jamestown*, even the smallest movement had amplified effects.

Using the line on the HUD as his guide, Coda used his portside thrusters to ease his fighter starboard closer to the *Jamestown*. It was close enough now that he could make out the individual cannons lining its surface out of his peripheral vision. Coda kept his eyes locked on the ball, sweating as it veered up and down, side to side, fighting him as if the fighter itself were an energetic puppy that didn't want to go back into its kennel.

His gaze never veering from his HUD, Coda felt the lights of the *Jamestown* more than he saw them. Having been in the black for an hour, he found them bright and oppressive. But he was inside the ship now, and squinting against the bright lights of the hangar, Coda brought the fighter gently onto the deck.

After several deep breaths, Coda looked to see if the commander had landed yet. He spotted him only a few meters away, already pulling off his flight helmet. He saw Coda looking and gave him a thumbs-up.

I did it, Coda thought, returning the gesture. *I don't know how, but I did it.*

By the time they'd been towed back into the main hangar, Coda had removed his flight helmet and popped the cockpit hatch.

Commander Coleman met him at the bottom of the ladder. "Well done."

"Thank you, sir."

"How are you feeling?"

"A little wet in the breeches, but other than that..."

Commander Coleman laughed. "The first landing is enough to make any pilot's butthole pucker. We'll continue to work on them, and before you know it, you'll be able to land without leaving a mess inside your flight suit." He turned to survey the hangar. "Chief!"

"Yes, sir," the chief said, appearing behind Commander Coleman. "Here you are, sir." He handed something to the commander, who in turn held it out to Coda.

"This is yours," the commander said.

Coda took the small flight badge and studied it. Roughly six centimeters by four, it depicted a stylized pair of Nighthawks flying against the backdrop of the sun. Under the image were the words The Forgotten.

"We'll have it sewn onto your flight suit," the commander said. "You earned it."

"Thank you, sir," Coda said, never looking up. "What are the Forgotten?"

"We are, Coda. The war moved on without fighter pilots. The world left us behind. But where they have forgotten us, so has our enemy, and that will be their downfall. We are the Forgotten Squadron."

Coda rubbed a reverent finger across the flight badge. Usually, only full pilots were given badges.

The Commander seemed to read his mind. "It doesn't mean you've made the squadron yet, Lieutenant. But there aren't a thousand people left in the world who have flown a Nighthawk, so as far as I'm concerned, you're one of us."

It was too much. During the days of manned starfighters, each squadron had its own badge, and Coda could remember early memories of donning his father's flight jacket, looking at himself in the mirror, and dreaming of one day growing up to be just like him. That had been before the incident, but his father's downfall had only increased his desire to earn a badge of his own.

"It's... It's amazing, sir," Coda said, meeting the commander's eye. "Thank you. I'll wear it proudly."

24

CODA SET DOWN HIS TRAY. AS HE SLID INTO THE METAL CHAIR, Noodle sucked in a sharp breath and held it. His eyes twinkled with amusement, darting in Coda's direction. When Noodle didn't release the breath, Coda finally took the bait.

"What's he doing?"

"Breathe, Noodle!" Squawks said in an exaggerated impersonation of Commander Coleman. "Come on, Noodle! Just breathe! Breathe, goddamn it!"

Noodle burst into laughter, and Squawks joined him. A couple people sitting nearby looked at them, obviously wondering what the hell was so funny.

"You guys are assholes," Coda said, which only made them laugh even harder. "Why am I even friends with you?"

"Oh, please," Squawks said, wiping tears from his eyes. "This is *exactly* why. Someone has to keep you from believing your own bullshit."

"You, maybe," Coda said. "But not him. Noodle is more of the cool, quiet type."

"It's true." Noodle nodded.

"Yeah, you're a real rock star," Squawks said sarcastically.

"I take it you guys were listening?" Coda asked.

It hadn't been more than ninety minutes since his flight —just enough time to shower, change, and go through a short preliminary debriefing with Commander Coleman. The full evaluation would come later that night, once more of the pilots had flown.

"Every glorious second of it," Squawks said. "Breathe, Coda! Breathe!"

Squawks and Noodle erupted into laughter again.

"I'm glad I didn't say what I really was feeling then," Coda said, unsure if either of the two assholes even heard him.

"Don't let them razz you too bad, Coda."

Coda looked up to see an older pilot wearing the standard gray flight suit of Commander Coleman's squadron. With thinning salt-and-pepper hair and a face sporting lines of age, he was easily one of the oldest in the squadron. Coda didn't know him well; he bunked in one of the other barracks and was on a different schedule than Coda's.

"There ain't many pilots who wouldn't cry for momma while making a landing in high orbit."

Noodle and Squawks looked at the newcomer and exchanged a look that said, "Who the hell is this guy?" But between the newcomer coming to Coda's defense and his thick southern drawl, Coda immediately liked him.

"It's Tex, right?" Coda asked.

"Yeah."

"I take it you had your first flight?"

"Naw, not yet," Tex said. "Not in the Nighthawk, anyway."

"What do you mean?"

"I've flown other ships. Made some hands-on landings. They ain't fun."

"No, they're not," Coda agreed.

"You mind if I sit?"

"Sure."

"Thanks." Tex slid into the seat Uno normally occupied, a detail that didn't go unnoticed by Noodle and Squawks. Tex must have felt their uneasiness, because he offered them a kind nod.

"So," Coda said, interrupting the growing silence, "you've flown spacecraft before?"

Tex stabbed his food paste and shoveled in a bite. "I'm a puddle jumper," he said, talking around the mouthful.

"A what?" Squawks asked.

Tex swallowed. "A puddle jumper. A bus driver."

Squawks's confused face made it clear he had no idea what the man was talking about, but he shrugged, apparently not interested enough to figure it out.

"You flew transports?" Noodle asked.

Tex pointed at him with his fork, nodding. "Marines, mostly."

"On the front?"

"Where else?"

A quiet appreciation filled the table.

"Then why'd you leave?" Suddenly interested again, Squawks asked the question that was on all of their minds. They all dreamed of getting to the front and making their mark on the war, even if each had his own reason. To leave that behind was like walking away from a winning lottery ticket.

"Same reason I joined the fleet the first time," Tex said. "Wanted to fly a Nighthawk. My folks thought I was crazy. Told 'em I didn't want to wake up at sixty-three and regret not following my dream. 'You won't have to worry about waking up at sixty-three,' they told me. 'You won't make it to thirty-six flying one of them things.' Well, the way I see it, I've already made it to thirty-six, so I don't have to worry about that no more."

Coda grinned. "My mom said something similar when I joined up."

"Mine too," Noodle said. "They wanted me to go to school. Get one of those advanced robotic manufacturing jobs Captain Hughes was always talking about. I couldn't do it, though. The drones were just too damn cool."

"They never did it for me," Tex said. "I was actually in the strike fighter program before they shut it down. Had a chance to be one of the first drone pilots. But like you said, I just couldn't do it. I wanted to *fly*. So when the opportunity came again, I couldn't pass it up."

"But the front..." Squawks said.

"Ain't as glorious as they make it out to be," Tex said. "'Specially for a marine transport pilot. I'd be on the same shit planet, eating the same shit food, sleeping in the same shit housing, staring at the stars, wondering where my life had gone wrong. You don't know how good you got it here."

"I think you've been roughing it for too long," Squawks said, stirring his meat paste with a disgusted look.

Coda laughed with the rest of them. Still, he couldn't help but feel that Tex was right. The food wasn't *that* bad—

and whatever Commander Coleman was packing into it was working. They were only about halfway through their training, and he was already working out with twice as much weight and had more than tripled the distance he ran on the treadmill while dropping his per-kilometer time by a third. He'd thought he was in great shape before, but any remaining baby fat had disappeared. Even Noodle, the skinniest person in their squadron, had noticeably filled out.

But it was more than that. Coda had no way to confirm it, but he felt as though his reaction and processing times had improved too. Not to mention his recovery periods. Every day, he was growing faster, stronger, and smarter. To top it all off, they were being trained by the great Commander Coleman himself.

Yeah, Tex is definitely right. The members of the Forgotten don't have it bad at all.

That night after their evening debriefing, Commander Coleman told them that because the squadron had shrunk by half, they no longer needed four barracks, and ordered them to reassemble in Barracks One and Two.

Coda groaned. Even though it had only been a day and a half since the other pilots had left, he'd started growing accustomed to the extra space and relative privacy.

At least I'm in Barracks Two and don't have to move.

Tex was one of the first pilots to make his way into their barracks. He pointed to the open bunk once occupied by Uno. "You mind?"

Something told Coda that the older man hadn't connected with any of the other pilots in the squadron, likely because of his age and unique background, but he was still reluctant to give up Uno's place in their quartet so easily. To Coda's surprise, though, Squawks answered first.

"It's all yours," he said. "But only if you promise to tell us some stories from the front."

Tex gave him a small laugh and nodded. "Deal. But I ain't gonna promise they'll be interesting."

25

Ready Room, SAS Jamestown
  Alpha Centauri System, Proxima B, High Orbit

TEX WAS THE FIRST OF THEIR NEWLY FORMED QUARTET TO FLY after Coda, and the older pilot was what Squawks called "a real hoot to listen to." Every increase in speed and high-g maneuver was accompanied by a hoot, yee-haw, or woo-hoo, and it got so bad that the commander had to tell him to cut the chatter. But that night during their group evaluation, Commander Coleman hadn't been able to keep from smiling with the rest of them.

"Tex was obviously meant to be in the cockpit," Commander Coleman said. "And his excitement is infectious. But if you're going to hoot and holler, Tex, do so off the radio, and make sure you don't miss a critical order."

"Yes, sir," Tex said.

"But I'm glad you're having fun."

Noodle went up after him, and the slender pilot earned

high praise from the commander, even if Noodle secretly believed he didn't deserve it.

"I couldn't decide if I wanted to throw up or wet myself," he had said after the flight.

"When?" Squawks asked.

"During all of it," Noodle said. "You don't know what it's like. It's nothing like the simulator; that's for sure."

Squawks just laughed and called him a wuss, but Coda could see that under the bravado, their friend was growing increasingly uneasy. When it was Squawks's turn to go up, Noodle and Coda gathered together in the ready room to listen in. They weren't the only ones, either. Moscow and his gang were hanging out in the back of the auditorium, keeping to themselves.

Since the uneasy truce had been made in the simulator, Coda hadn't had much interaction with Moscow or his gang, and it was a welcomed change since it provided him with fewer distractions.

"All right, Squawks," Commander Coleman's voice said over the ready room speakers, "well done today. Let's bring it in."

"Roger that, sir," Squawks said, his pride barely masked behind military decorum. By all indications, his flight had gone well. Like Coda and Noodle, he'd been able to perform the basic flight maneuvers they'd mastered in the simulator, but as Coda had already found out, when it came to performing a hands-on landing aboard a moving vessel in high orbit, there was a canyon of difference between the simulator and the real thing.

The seconds ticking by, Coda listened to the commander's instruction, piecing together the landing sequence in his mind's eye. Squawks would be parallel to the *Jamestown* by now, ready to begin his landing procedure.

"Squawks, you're a kilometer out. Call the ball."

"Roger that. I have the ball."

Coda slid to the edge of his seat, growing increasingly nervous. This was the most difficult part of the landing sequence, and Squawks was already muttering curses under his breath.

"You're too shallow, Squawks," Commander Coleman said. "Just like in the simulator. Keep the two together, and you'll be fine."

"Copy that, sir," Squawks said, though Coda thought he could hear panic in his voice.

"You're still too shallow, Squawks," Commander Coleman said a few seconds later. "Abort and prepare to circle back for another pass."

"Negative, sir," Squawks said. "I've got this."

"Lieutenant—"

"Almost there, sir."

"Pull up, Lieutenant. Pull up. Squawks, pull up. Pull up! Pull up! Pull up!" Commander Coleman's shouts were followed by an eerie silence.

Silent seconds ticked by, the quiet punctuated only by Commander Coleman's heavy breathing. Coda didn't move, didn't think, fearing the worst.

Had Squawks successfully landed or had he crashed into the side of the *Jamestown*? Would they have felt the impact? Heard the explosion? Or would it be the equivalent of hitting a bug on the freeway, a nuisance that would have to be washed off when it was convenient?

Then he heard it. The faint voice of his friend.

"Oh my god, oh my god, oh my god."

"Oh my god is right." Noodle ran a hand across his closely shaven scalp. "What just happened?"

"Your friend is rubbing off on him," Moscow said,

striding down the auditorium stairs. "It's the O'Neil curse."

His emotions already flying high, Coda seethed. His feud with Moscow might have taken on a different tenor lately, but that didn't undo the months of comments, digs, and verbal jabs. Before Coda could reply, Moscow and his gang continued down the stairs, leaving the ready room behind.

"I'm seriously going to kick that guy's ass someday," Noodle said.

"Don't worry about it," Coda said, his words at odds with his emotions. He wanted nothing more than to let Noodle kick Moscow's teeth in—hell, he wanted to do it himself—but he was tired of his temper turning him into a failure.

"You're just going to let him get away with it?"

"We're supposed to be part of the same squadron, Noodle. Fighting him won't do any good. It'll just make it worse."

Noodle stared at him as if he had just turned into a Baranyk. "What happened to you?"

"Nothing."

"He and his gang get to you? Push you into an empty room and have their way with you?"

Coda's anger was quickly moving from Moscow to Noodle. If he wasn't careful, he'd take it out on his friend. "Drop it."

"The commander talk to you? Tell you to bury the hatchet?"

Coda let out a sharp breath, less because Noodle was right, and more because he was being such a persistent little asshole.

"He did, didn't he?" Noodle said. "What did he say?"

"It doesn't matter."

"The hell it doesn't. Look, Coda, you tell me to sic him, and I'll bite his leg like a Jack Russell terrier. If you tell me to stand down, I'll do that too. Just tell me why."

Coda imagined Noodle with his teeth around Moscow's calf and had to hold back a smile. "Then as my friend, listen to me when I say don't worry about him. Moscow's an ass, but..."

"But what? Coda, I don't know what the hell happened, but you spent every day fighting with that guy for months, and now you're defending him? What changed? What do you know that I don't?"

Coda drew in a deep breath. "Let's just say I understand where he's coming from."

"Coda—"

"It's not my story to tell. Okay? Just drop it."

Noodle snapped his mouth shut and looked away, irritated. That was fine as far as Coda was concerned. Noodle could be mad. He could even think that Coda was defending Moscow. Anything was better than having the squadron know that Coda's father was responsible for Moscow's mother's death. That would drive a wedge between him and everyone else in the squadron so deep that there would be no recovering from it. And at that point, the commander wouldn't have to choose between Moscow and Coda. The squadron would choose for him.

THE NEARLY BOTCHED LANDING EARNED SQUAWKS THE FIRST SOD in the squadron. If he got two more, he would be expelled entirely. For nearly a day and a half, he steamed, running landing simulation after landing simulation, obsessing over the mistake. Tex had tried to help him through it by sharing stories about his own experiences and offering small tips and tricks that he'd learned over the years, but Squawks made it abundantly clear that he wanted none of it.

His mood only improved when other pilots had similar issues. Fortunately for him, the mistakes weren't uncommon. Of the fifty remaining pilots, nearly one third had to abort their approach and try again, and of them, nearly half failed to accomplish a clean landing on the second attempt. Squawks hadn't flown the cleanest, but he wasn't the worst, either, and for the time being, that seemed to be enough for him.

As the weeks wore on, Coda settled into his new routine. Because the squadron had only two instructors, he was lucky to go up every other day, so when he wasn't in class or at the gym, he spent most of his time in the simulator. But after he'd tasted the real thing, simulated flying couldn't scratch the itch. Flying had become a drug and he needed his fix.

When he had gone up the second time, the commander spent the first part of the training session putting him through the same basic flight maneuvers and critiquing him on the finer details, but they spent the majority of their time doing touch-and-go landings aboard the *Jamestown*. Coda flew approach after approach, getting ten for the price of one. It was terrifying work, but by the end of the fourth week Coda could approach without pissing himself.

Once each of the pilots had gone up twice, they began group instruction, flying courses and beginning formations. Then, when the commander was confident they wouldn't accidentally crash into each other, began dogfighting.

Their only reprieve was that their flights were no longer scored and tiered. They had progressed to a review phase, and as Commander Coleman and Lieutenant Commander Chavez had done during one-on-one post-Simulation debriefings, they instructed the pilots instead of graded them. But like all breaks, Coda knew it wouldn't last.

26

Commander Coleman's Quarters, SAS Jamestown
Alpha Centauri System, Proxima B, High Orbit

CODA TOOK A DEEP BREATH, STRAIGHTENED HIS UNIFORM, AND knocked on Commander Coleman's door.

"Come in," Commander Coleman said as the door slid open. Coda stepped in and snapped to attention. "At ease. And have a seat." The commander gestured at the unoccupied armchair opposite the one the commander had obviously been sitting in.

Coda sat. Commander Coleman had turned his back to Coda and fumbled with something on his bookcase. His eyes drifting from the commander to the small room, Coda made a mental note that it was the second time he had been summoned to the commander's personal quarters, and for the first time, he realized the older man didn't have a personal office.

The realization surprised him. Commander Coleman was a true, real-life war hero on a secret mission to construct a squadron that might very well save humanity, and he couldn't even get a personal office? Secrecy, it appeared, didn't afford luxuries.

When the commander turned around, he was holding two glasses, one filled with a brown liquid, the other with water. He handed the one filled with water to Coda and sat down in the chair across from him.

"Thank you, sir," Coda said, oddly thankful he wasn't holding the glass with the alcohol. It wasn't that he wasn't of age—he was, even if the United States federal government hadn't long since lowered the drinking age for all enlisted personnel to eighteen years old. Drinking hadn't been accepted at the academy, and despite stories of fighter jocks being heavy-drinking womanizers, Coda's experience in the Forgotten had been very different—though he supposed that was likely due to their equally different training circumstances.

"You're doing well," Commander Coleman said, leveling his gaze on him. "You completed FAM Phase by the skin of your teeth, but you were near the top of your class in the simulator, and you've made the transition to real flight look surprisingly easy."

Coda let the smile wash over his face but played it modest. "I don't know about easy, sir."

"Oh?" Commander Coleman took a sip. "Then tell me how you're feeling."

"I feel good, sir. Confident."

"That's good. A timid pilot is a danger to themselves and everyone they fly with."

Coda felt a stab of guilt as his mind wandered to Uno. A lack of confidence had been his friend's undoing. It had rendered him slow and tentative—"mechanical," as Uno had put it. Perhaps the commander was right.

"You don't have to worry about that with me, sir. I feel... at home out there."

Commander Coleman took another sip, his eyes never leaving Coda. "Is that why you're here?"

Coda cocked his head to the side, caught off guard by the question. What was the Commander really asking? "I'm here to become the best fighter pilot in the squadron and protect the fleet, sir."

"No." Commander Coleman shook his head. "Not *here*. I mean here, fighting in this war."

Coda stalled, taking a sip of his water. He hadn't openly expressed his feelings on too many occasions, though they probably wouldn't come as any great surprise, either. After all, Buster had guessed his true motivations, and he hadn't exactly the fastest ship in the hangar. Would it help his cause if the commander knew the truth?

Commander Coleman had flown with his father and had spoken highly of him. Maybe in this instance, separating himself from his father would be counterproductive.

"You obviously know my father's story," Coda said, deciding to take the chance.

Commander Coleman nodded. "It couldn't have been easy growing up under that shadow."

"It wasn't," Coda agreed. "Though it wasn't as bad at home as it was at the academy. Either way, when I'm done, the O'Neil name won't be something to be cursed. It'll be celebrated. Revered."

"You want to be a hero."

"No." Coda shook his head. "I don't *want* to be a hero. I want to restore honor to my family name. Being a hero is just the quickest way to do it."

"That's a very noble goal."

Coda shrugged. Something about the way Commander

Coleman had spoken the words made Coda uncertain if the other man truly meant them or if the commander was somehow poking fun at him.

"You know I flew with him."

"That's what you said, sir."

"The man I knew and the man the world *thinks* it knows are very different."

Coda shifted uneasily. Having someone suggest that the person he'd despised his entire life was actually a good person was discomforting. More than discomforting. It went against every mental image he'd crafted of his father and threatened to destroy the entire world he'd built atop it.

"Unfortunately," Coda said, "the man I knew was closer to what everyone else sees."

That wasn't entirely true. Coda had many fond memories of his father: playing catch in the backyard, going to the zoo, sitting in the cockpit of his father's Nighthawk. But the pain caused by his father's betrayal greatly outweighed whatever positive feelings he felt for the man.

Commander Coleman leaned back in his seat, pursing his lips. Coda was growing increasingly confused by how well the commander had known his father and just how close they had been. Coda wasn't interested in getting to the bottom of it at the moment. He wasn't there to talk about this father. He decided to change the subject before the commander had a chance to muster up his response.

"Why are *you* here, sir? What's a decorated war hero doing on an ancient ship flying patrol over a worthless mining colony?"

"I'm here to assemble the best fighter squadron known to man and protect the fleet."

It was obviously a play on Coda's politically correct response, and hearing it from the commander helped him realize just how ridiculous it really sounded. Because the commander had said it without even the hint of a smile, Coda took his true meaning. Commander Coleman wasn't going to tell him a damn thing.

"The truth is, Lieutenant," Commander Coleman continued, "even though this squadron has surpassed even my wildest expectations, it's still woefully behind the schedule the fleet needs us on. As much as I would like to continue with basic flight maneuvers and formations for another month, we simply don't have the time. We need to move forward."

Commander Coleman set down his drink then slid his tablet across the table and gestured for Coda to take a look at it.

"What's this, sir?"

"Your flight."

A "flight" was a smaller subset of fighters from the same squadron, numbering anywhere from four to six. What a squadron was to a wing, a flight was to a squadron.

"This is where the training gets fun, Lieutenant. For the next three months, we're playing war games, and for this mission, I want you to lead other pilots. Assuming you want to, of course."

Coda looked up from the names on the tablet. "Yes, sir. Of course." His eyes went back to the terminal. "But this list... Surely you don't mean..."

"Don't mean what?"

Coda's eyes fell back to the tablet. At the top of the list was Moscow's name. Commander Coleman not only expected them to work together in the same flight, but he expected Moscow to follow Coda's orders. It was almost laughable. But how could he say so?

"Is there a problem, Lieutenant?"

"No," Coda said. "It's just that... well... I think we'd be more successful if I had Noodle and Squawks under my command."

"Which is exactly why I didn't put them there. The squadron needs to fight as a single unit, and that means you must be comfortable flying with *everyone* inside it. More than that, you need to know, in intimate detail, the strengths and weaknesses of everyone around you. That's not possible if you only surround yourself with your friends."

Coda bit his tongue. The Commander was right, of course. Why else had Coda been taking notes on every pilot in the squadron?

"You'll get a chance to fly with your friends," Commander Coleman continued. "There are no set rosters here, not yet. Not until the squadron gets closer to its final number. For now, the pilots that make up each flight will change with every mission. And the person giving orders will change with every mission as well. For now, at least."

"What kind of missions, sir?"

"They'll be simple at first," Commander Coleman said. "Flight versus flight. Basic combat. But after a while, they'll get increasingly complex. Multiple objectives. Stacked odds. Scenarios you can expect on the front."

"When will they start?"

Commander Coleman grinned. "Your pilots are already waiting for you, Lieutenant. Launch is at nineteen hundred."

27

Simulator, SAS Jamestown
   Alpha Centauri System, Proxima B, High Orbit

THE FIVE PILOTS THAT MADE UP CODA'S FLIGHT WERE ALREADY
waiting for him in the Simulation Room when he arrived. If
they were surprised to see him, they didn't show it, so Coda
assumed they'd received their orders separately and had
known to expect him as their leader.

Moscow was there, of course, watching Coda with an
expression that he couldn't place. Joining him were Tex and
Bear, Reno and NoNo. The only thing he knew of the latter
two was that they had performed well in the simulator,
finishing in the top thirty overall, and had both been reassigned from drone squadrons on the front.

*At least Commander Coleman isn't giving me a completely
green flight.*

"Good morning," Coda said. "Our hop is in two hours.
The details are unclear, but our objective is simple: destroy
all enemy fighters. Your flight information has already been

downloaded to your personal tablets. Read it. Memorize it. Preflight is in one hour. Any questions?"

There weren't any.

"All right. Let's get warmed up."

Coda loaded Reno and NoNo into the simulator first, keying in a scenario that had them flying as a fighter pair against an enemy force outnumbering them three to one. Coupled with the notes he'd taken from their previous simulations, he intended to study their flight patterns and better understand who he was flying with.

Both pilots were deft—even if NoNo had a bit of a habit of shouting, "No! No! No!" when things got hairy—and made short order of the enemy fighters, falling effortlessly into working as a pair. That had likely become second nature to them while on the front, where the drone squadrons flew in complex, highly coordinated formations. To them, staying on the wing of their wingmen was as natural as breathing.

Coda ran Moscow and Bear through the simulator next, with the former flying lead. They weren't nearly so smooth, lacking the training and experience that Reno and NoNo had benefited from, but they weren't completely clueless, either. Having spent dozens of extra hours in the simulator flying with each other, they knew each other's styles well, even if their instincts were often at odds with one another.

He didn't have time to run through the simulation with Tex, so rather than have the other man fly his wing, Coda opted for another strategy. If the others were his scalpels, cutting into the enemy with precise, synchronized attacks, then Tex would be his bat, ready to crush any unfortunate fighters flying into his strike zone.

An hour before flight, they began their preflight routine. Commander Coleman sat in the ready room but made no

effort to instruct, direct, or review their preflight information. Coda stepped into the role, ensuring that each of his
pilots had memorized their flight information and that
there wouldn't be any accidents. After they'd confirmed
their information, they stepped into the locker room and
suited up. By 1850, they were climbing into their cockpits,
ready to be loaded into the launch tubes. Once loaded,
Coda radioed his pilots and had them perform systems
checks.

"All right, *Jamestown* Tower," Coda said after everyone
had confirmed they were green across the board. "We are go
for launch.

"Copy that, Coda," the tower said. "You are go for launch
at quarter-second intervals. Prepare for launch in five, four,
three..."

Coda didn't listen to the rest. He settled into his seat,
waiting for the sudden but welcomed g-forces to slam into
his body like a stack of bricks. Maybe it was because of his
time in the gym. Maybe it was the growth hormones that
strengthened his body from the inside out. Or maybe it was
just his state of mind. But no matter the reason, when the
forces came, they wrapped him like a warm blanket,
comforting him.

He'd been anxious before. Now he was calm. At peace.
The commander was right. Flying was in his blood. He was
born for this.

28

Cockpit, Nighthawk
  Alpha Centauri System, Proxima B

SIX X-23 NIGHTHAWKS SHOT OUT OF THE BOW OF THE *Jamestown*, entering space at quarter-second intervals. It took one-point-five seconds from the time the first fighter entered space to the last.

"All right," Coda said, plotting a course that moved them away from the *Jamestown* toward the coordinates outlined in the mission briefing. "Form up, and keep your eyes peeled. They're out here somewhere."

Silence stretched out before them, interrupted only by the slight rumble of their Shaw Drive thrusters and the soft sounds of breathing through Coda's helmet speakers. The sea of stars and image of the ever-shrinking orange globe behind them might have been relaxing if they hadn't been flying into battle.

"Contact!" NoNo bellowed as a group of red dots

appeared on Coda's HUD. "I've got six bogeys, negative-Z twelve degrees. Thirty thousand kilometers and closing."

Coda adjusted the battle map in his HUD, switching the battle plane from the original plane to the new one between his fighters and the enemy bogeys. Once completed, he sent it to the rest of his flight, using his power as flight leader to automatically switch theirs, ensuring they all continued to operate under the same information.

"Copy, NoNo. Let's go get 'em." Coda brought his fighter into an intercept course with the incoming enemy, the rest of his flight falling into formation behind him. "Fighter pairs. Just like we practiced. Tex, you and I will play centerfield."

Several affirmatives came through the coms at once, and Coda dug himself deeper into the gel seat. He had three seconds before the enemy vessels were in firing range, but since they were on a direct heading, their combined speed prevented missile lock. It was all guns.

"Let's see if we can break them up," Coda said. "Fox-four!"

Coda thumbed the firing switch to guns and pulled the trigger. The cockpit came alive, rumbling as the nose-mounted M-66 cannon hurled thirty-millimeter rounds at the incoming enemy to the tune of four thousand rounds per minute. They were simulated rounds, of course, all tracked and cataloged by their onboard computers, but the effect felt very, very real.

The X-23 held only three hundred rounds, so he kept his trigger finger light, shooting in controlled bursts that lasted only a fraction of a second. The firing bursts had their desired effect, and two seconds from contact, the enemy formation broke apart. Two fighter pairs broke off in opposite directions, veering to the three- and nine-o'clock positions relative to Coda's incoming squadron. The last pair held course, splitting Coda's formation down the center.

"Break!" Coda bellowed, and as one, his formation broke apart.

Reno and NoNo who had taken the dash-3 and -4 positions directly behind Coda's portside wing, brougt their fighters around and went after the bogey that had veered off to their left. Moscow and Bear mirrored their movement, going after the fighter to their right, while Coda and Tex dove above and below the battle plane, taking opposite routes but both making for the third pair that had split their formation.

The g-forces were incredible, slamming Coda into his gel seat hard enough that black spots crept into his vision. Coda's G-suit tightened in response, constricting around his extremities, preventing his blood from rushing out of his brain. Without the suit, he would have lost consciousness; instead, he felt as though he were being squeezed in an old trash compactor. It was uncomfortable, but he was alert.

Completing the turn, Coda found that the enemy fighter pair had broken apart, making for opposite ends of the battle. Coda keyed on the nearest one. The pilot brought the fighter around level with the battle plane. The angle left Coda's flank open, and if he had been any slower, the enemy fighter would have managed missile lock. Instead, Coda brought his fighter around, setting himself up on another head-on course.

As he and the other fighter sped toward each other, Coda opened fire, forcing the enemy fighter to dive below the battle plane to avoid the incoming slugs. Coda threw the stick forward then barrel-rolled, bringing his fighter directly behind the other. The steady, single note of missile lock sounded in Coda's ears.

"Hawk One, Fox Two," Coda said, squeezing the trigger. A yellow blip appeared on his HUD, shooting toward the enemy fighter. Half a second later, the fighter's cockpit lights went dark, and the fighter disappeared from the battle map. "Splash one!"

The enemy fighter vanquished, Coda reassessed the battle map just as another enemy fighter disappeared from the battle map.

"Splash two!" Moscow shouted.

He and Bear harried the lone fighter left of their original battle pair while Reno and NoNo were involved in a series of complex flight maneuvers with the second pair struggling to gain the advantage.

"Keep it tight!" Reno yelled. "Don't get acute!"

Acute meant Reno's wingman was too wide to be in firing position. A quick glance at his HUD showed that Reno was manipulating the enemy's flight course in a tactic as old as aerial combat. Time-tested and time-approved, it was still the foundational tactic of space combat.

"You're too acute, NoNo! You're too acute! Goddamn it! Break off and come back around."

"We've got a tail, Bear!" Moscow shouted. "You see it?"

"Uh…" Coda could almost hear Bear processing the information on her battle map. Precious moments ticked by as she searched for the enemy vessel. "Oh, no! It's coming around on our tail. Moscow, it's on our asses."

"Break formation," Moscow said. "See if you can draw it off. I'll stay on this one. Tex, I think it's time you brought your bat."

"Copy that, Moscow," Tex said. "I've got your back."

Coda grinned. His loose strategy had so far proved effective. Now it was up to the individual pilots themselves to ensure their victory.

Bear's fighter altered course, attempting to draw the incoming enemy vessel away, but to everyone's surprise, he stayed on Moscow.

"Tex!" Moscow shouted. "Tex, I need—"

"On it," Tex said. "Three seconds."

"I don't have three seconds." Moscow darted left and right in a series of evasive maneuvers, delaying the inevitable, all while trying to keep the other enemy fighter in his sights. "He's almost got missile lock! Tex, where the hell are you?"

Before Tex could respond, the red marker on Coda's HUD suddenly disappeared.

"Splash three!" Tex shouted. "You're clear, Moscow. I repeat, you're clear."

"Nice shooting, Tex," Moscow said, relief palpable in his voice. "Bear, you still out there?"

"Still here, Moscow."

"Good. I'm sending updated vector information now. We can't let Coda and Tex have all the fun. There's only three left."

"Copy that."

Coda let the words wash over him, keeping his eyes on the larger battle, never listening to any one thing. There was too much going on, too much to keep track of. He had to trust that his brain was able to keep it organized and prioritize what needed to be prioritized. That was easier said than done, though.

Coda screamed as two fighters cut upward through the battle plane, only meters from the nose of his Nighthawk. The thrusters of the other craft cooked the glass of his cockpit, skyrocketing the temperature inside to a near boil. Coda glanced back at the battle map to make sure he wasn't about to become an improbable casualty of a space collision—and saw how truly messy the battle was.

The battle was like a knot that had been tied over itself again and again, the fighters pulling the ends of the string tighter and tighter. In the infiniteness of space, the battle became a single point of violence less than twenty kilometers in the diameter—something impossibly small at their speeds.

Still recovering from the near collision, Coda didn't notice the enemy fighter opening fire. By nothing more than an impossible stroke of luck, the digital projectiles missed, and the enemy fighter zipped past him, but not before Coda caught a single important detail.

Where the wings of both flights were accented with the gold of the Sol Fleet, this one was accented with red. Unlike the rest of the pilots in the squadron, this pilot had earned his colors—he'd shot down enemy fighters. He'd fought real battles. Had drawn real blood. The enemy fighter was piloted by none other than Commander Coleman himself.

29

Cockpit, Nighthawk
   Alpha Centauri System, Proxima B

CODA WATCHED AS COMMANDER COLEMAN BROUGHT HIS fighter around, angling for another pass. Such were the ways of fighter combat, both pilots attempting to outmaneuver the other, often making several runs until one of them made a mistake. Unfortunately, Coda knew that if either of them was going to make a mistake, it would be him. If he stood any shot at defeating the commander, he needed help.

"Tex," Coda said, "where are you at?"

"Occupied."

"I'm going to need a hand over here."

"Bite off more than you could chew?"

"You could say that."

"Fifteen seconds."

"Negative," Coda said. "This one's too important. Break

off and meet me..." Coda keyed in on a point on his HUD and sent the coordinates to Tex. "There."

Tex sighed. "Breaking off. Rendezvous in six seconds."

Coda cursed silently. Even six seconds was too long. He and Commander Coleman would be coming around for another pass by then, and already, the commander's more precise flight paths were giving him the advantage. He would have Coda dead in his sights before Tex could come to his aid. Worse, if Coda broke off his attack and tried to run the commander would have a clear path to his six.

This is why you don't fly solo. Then again, the commander was flying solo too, and that gave him a chance. *In theory.*

Coda and Commander Coleman's fighters raced toward each other. Coda squeezed the trigger again, loosing another triple burst. But unlike the nugget pilot, Commander Coleman didn't flinch. The commander mirrored Coda's strategy, letting off a burst of his own. Both pilots missed, their fighters zipping past each other faster than their eyes could register.

Coda started his turn almost immediately. Eyeing his HUD, he saw the commander doing the same.

"Tex?"

"Coming. Hang on."

"Trying..." Coda's voice was strained by the excessive G's of the turn. "He's closing... Tex... the commander..."

"Say again, Coda," Tex said. "The commander? You want me to fire at the commander?"

"Yes!"

"This is going to be fun."

Coda leveled off and turned, adjusting course to come around into another pass, but the commander had already completed his maneuver and was coming in on Coda's flank. He would have missile lock any moment.

Coda's Hornet training took over. He threw the joystick to the side, rolling his fighter in a series of tight corkscrews, then with his wings perpendicular to the battle plane, he pulled back, performing a tight high-g turn.

The yellow indicator of a missile appeared on Coda's HUD.

Shoved hard against the gel seat, he prepared to drop his chaff. At worst, the debris would cloud Commander Coleman's missile sensors, hindering its ability to target Coda. At best, the missile would explode against one of the sand particles.

But he never had a chance. Even his G-suit couldn't keep him from blacking out during the high-g maneuver. The last thing he saw was the yellow indicator racing toward him.

He had no idea how long he was out. It could have been a second, an hour, or anything in between. When he returned to consciousness, his head pounded as blood returned to the places it should have been. But with every throbbing pulse, Coda's awareness grew.

He still had controls. By some miracle, his fighter was still operable.

And someone was screaming. No... they were yelling. Moscow. It was Moscow. Why would Moscow be yelling?

Coda blinked, trying to focus. The yellow blip of the missile was gone, as was Tex's fighter, but so was the red marker of the commander. Trying to shake away the remaining cobwebs, Coda worked to make sense of the situation. Something was wrong. Coda had been dead in Commander Coleman's sights.

Unless...

Moscow's shouts suddenly made more sense. Lieutenant Andrei "Moscow" Krylov, Coda's former rival at the Terran

Fleet Academy, had just eliminated Commander Coleman and saved Coda's ass in the process.

Coda wanted to be sick.

30

Hangar Deck, SAS Jamestown
  Alpha Centauri System, Proxima B, High Orbit

A CROWD OF PEOPLE WAS WAITING IN THE HANGAR AS CODA and the rest of the flight arrived. They clapped and cheered as the victorious pilots cracked their cockpits and removed their helmets. The pilots pumped their fists and yelled excitedly in return, celebrating their first win as a unit.

When Moscow took off his helmet, the crowd erupted, and the few people who weren't already around his fighter flocked to it. There was no doubt who the crowd thought the hero of the battle was, and Moscow basked in it. He stood on top of his seat, hollering back at his screaming admirers like a rock star trying to make his audience earn an encore.

Coda removed his own helmet and gloves without fanfare. Except for the specialist who rolled over a ladder so that he could climb out of his starfighter, nobody even seemed to realize he was there. He struggled to swallow the bitter lump in his throat. The recognition Moscow was receiving was the same recognition he'd dreamed about since joining the academy.

Tex was the first to come to him, finding him as Coda began his postflight visual inspection. "I'm sorry, Coda."

"For what?" Coda asked.

"You needed me, and I wasn't there."

Coda sighed and brushed off his hands. "To be honest, I don't even know what happened. I blacked out from the turn. The last thing I saw was the commander's missile headed my way."

"I took care of that then got the commander's attention before he could turn you into slag. That was a mistake, let me tell you. He's good, Coda, real good. Took care of me in no time. But that's when Moscow snuck up on him and took *him* out."

"Moscow left his wingman?"

"Reckon so."

Coda shot another look in Moscow's direction. He was stepping down the ladder, grinning and high-fiving his admirers. Leaving your wingman was a cardinal sin. Space was too large, too empty, the battles too chaotic for one person. The first pilots had long since learned that when facing that alone, they often ended up like... well, like Coda. An afterthought in battle—or worse. That he'd broken the first rule of flight cheapened Moscow's victory even more.

"You took out the commander's missile?" Coda asked.

Tex grinned, puffing out his chest. "Sure did."

"I'll have to check out the vid," Coda said. "That must have been a hell of a shot."

"Like shooting a can in the backyard."

Coda and Tex found Noodle and Squawks as they headed for the locker room. Even they were commiserating, regarding Coda and Tex as if Coda had lost, as if he'd failed.

Coda wanted to scream. He might not have shot down the commander, but damn it, his flight had won! Beginning his breathing exercise, Coda slowly wrestled his emotions back under control. Then Moscow's voice cut through the din.

"You're welcome, O'Neil!"

Coda froze. Hearing Moscow call him out, hearing him address him by his last name took him straight back to their fight at the academy.

Turning, Coda locked eyes with Moscow. He couldn't be sure from the distance, but Moscow's sneer seemed to falter.

"For what?" Coda shouted back.

Moscow looked at the crowd gathered around him as if deciding whether pushing Coda was worth it. He must have decided it was, because when his gaze returned to Coda, so did his smirk. "For saving your ass."

Coda barked a sarcastic laugh then wiped the bottom of his nose with his thumb, starting toward him.

"Don't," Squawks said, attempting to grab him.

Coda ripped his arm from Squawks's grip.

Moscow started toward Coda, ready for his rematch, his admirers falling into step behind him. Moscow had at least twenty to Coda's four, but Coda didn't care. He had to wipe that patronizing sneer off Moscow's face.

Before he got his chance, the commander appeared between them. Still dressed in his flight suit, he stood like a rock ready to withstand the force of two incoming tidal waves. Coda and Moscow froze at the same time, their attention shifting from each other to the commander, who stood unfazed between them.

"Congratulations," Commander Coleman said, though his tone was anything but congratulatory. "It's not often a pilot takes down their instructor in their first battle. Let alone when that instructor is me. Well done, Moscow."

The jubilant atmosphere that had filled the hangar before returned, and Moscow was once again at the center of it. The crowd behind him shouted their praise, slapping him on the shoulders and back in congratulations. Moscow took it in, smiling, though his eyes never left Coda.

Commander Coleman turned his gaze from Moscow to Coda. "You flew well. Whether by skill or sheer dumb luck, you flew *together*. And that's how you're supposed to do it. Together. For each other." He appraised Moscow and Coda again, then apparently content with his ability to de-escalate the situation, he nodded. "Get out of those flight suits and shower up. Your debriefing starts in ten."

With that, the commander strode past Coda without a word, exiting the hangar. Moscow and Coda watched each other for several long seconds before Moscow inclined his head and turned back to his fighter, putting an end to the situation.

Coda started back toward the locker room.

"Well, that was close," Squawks said behind him.

Coda showered up, dressed, and grabbed a seat in the front row of the ready room. The rest of the flight's pilots joined him, and to his surprise, so did the rest of the squadron. The commander's evaluations were going to be a public as public could get.

Any remaining excitement from the flight quickly dissipated when the commander began his evaluation. He was ruthless, cutting into their strategy from every angle. Coda's initial plan had been sound, except Coda and Tex never should have been flying alone.

"Had you been paired up like the other fighters, you would have had me long before the second pass," Commander Coleman said, addressing Coda directly. "You have wingmen—use them. It's no mistake Reno and NoNo killed three fighters to your one. They flew together, and the other pilots didn't stand a chance."

Then he graded their speed, approach vectors, accuracy, flight maneuvers, and reaction times—and declared them all subpar. He grounded every pilot in their flight until they completed the updated exercises and scenarios he'd plugged into the simulator.

"And you will stay grounded," Commander Coleman continued, "until you've completed them to my satisfaction. Before the rest of you get too excited, I recommend you look at them too, because I expect you to learn from your fellow pilots. They were graded harshly today, but I assure you, the pilots who fly next will be graded even harder. And then harder after that. It's a moving goalpost, ladies and gentlemen, but I still expect you to get there."

That night at dinner, Coda watched as Moscow was surrounded by yet another group of admiring pilots. He was retelling the flight from his perspective, using his hands in place of fighters.

"You're going to drive yourself nuts comparing yourself to him," Noodle said.

"I'm not comparing myself to him," Coda said.

"Of course you're not," Squawks said. "I mean, why else would you stare at him your entire dinner?"

"I haven't been..." Coda's face grew hot. How long *had* he been watching him? "Whatever. I'm just trying to figure out why everyone is so infatuated with him all of a sudden. It's not like he shot down the most fighters."

"No," Noodle said. "He only shot down the best one."

"But it was still my strategy that made it happen."

"So?"

"So why is everyone all over him?"

"You mean why isn't everyone all over *you*?" Tex said. "What do you want, Coda? To win? Or to win glory?"

Coda stewed on the question long after dinner and lights out. He lay on his bunk, his curtain closed, wide-awake. The question had been more insightful than Coda would have expected from Tex, whose slow speech and deep-Southern drawl did little to suggest he offered much in the way of intelligence. But after knowing Coda for little more than a few days, Tex had understood the feeling that plagued Coda every day.

When the commander had asked him why he'd joined the Forgotten, the answer had been so clear. But for some reason, life didn't seem as simple as it had before. Things weren't as cut and dry. Even his feud with Moscow was confusing. Were things getting better or staying the same? He couldn't tell. And more than that, did he *want* them to get better?

Questions, questions, questions. So many questions. What do I want? To win or to win glory? And most perplexing of all, if he couldn't have both, which would he choose?

31

Mess Hall, SAS Jamestown
  Alpha Centauri System, Proxima B, High Orbit

"You're doing it again," Noodle said. Then to everyone else at the table, "He's doing it again."

"Yes, he is," Squawks said, his voice somewhere between amused and annoyed. "Hey! Dumbass!"

Something wet and slimy hit the side of Coda's face. He glanced down, saw a glob of food paste on the stainless-steel table, then looked up at Squawks, who was still holding his food-stained spoon, smiling wryly.

"What?" Coda snapped, grabbing his napkin and wiping the meat paste off his face.

"You're staring at him again." Squawks nodded toward Moscow, who sat on the other side of the mess hall. "It's getting creepy."

"I wasn't staring."

"You were staring," Noodle said.

"You looked like you were about to ask him to dance," Tex said.

"Got the hots for Moscow now?" Squawks joked. "Didn't think he was your type, but I guess he is kind of a celebrity now."

"Shut up," Coda said.

"Seriously, Coda," Squawks said. "You're obsessed. You need a hobby."

Coda snorted. "A hobby?"

"I'm not kidding, man. You may be a badass in the cockpit, but you're kind of a stick in the mud outside it."

"A stick in the mud?"

"Are you just going to repeat everything I say?" Squawks asked. "Yes, a stick in the mud. Boring. Dull. Someone who needs a life. And staring at Moscow like you're going to ask him to prom isn't helping."

Coda could feel his face growing red. He stirred his food absently. Squawks wasn't wrong, but Coda liked to think of himself as determined, not boring. He had a goal, and he wasn't going to stop striving for it until he achieved it. He didn't have time for anything else. It was as simple as that.

"And when am I going to find time for a hobby?" Coda asked defensively. "It's not like you guys have anything going on outside of our training, either."

"Are you serious?" Squawks asked, suddenly irritated. He turned to Noodle and Tex, who wore equally vexed expressions. "Is he being serious right now? God, Coda, you can damn near recognize someone by their flight patterns, but when it comes to everything else, you really are clueless, aren't you?"

"What are you talking about?"

"What do you think we do during our free time?"

"I don't know..." Now that Coda thought about it, since

Uno's departure, their extra practices in the simulator had all but ended, and most nights during their free time, his friends *did* disappear. He'd never thought to ask where. He'd barely even noticed they were gone.

"Unreal, man. Tex has his own garden in hydroponics, growing carrots and potatoes and crap. And Noodle, you telling me you haven't seen him scribbling in his notebook? He's writing a book, man. By hand. Swords and dragons and all that nerdy stuff. *I'm* working on something more *communal*. Everyone has their own thing. Everyone but you. And it kind of sucks that you didn't know that."

Coda looked at the three of them as if seeing them for the first time. Squawks was right. He barely knew anything about them. He might call them friends, but they were anything but. They were his wingmen, his squad mates, and that was it. He'd known he'd built a wall around himself— he'd done that years ago—but he hadn't realized he hadn't entered anyone else's, either.

"I'm sorry," Coda said. "You're right. I am... Are you really writing a book, Noodle?"

His slender friend nodded, his face turning crimson.

"Mind if I read it sometime? I apparently need a hobby."

"No," Noodle said softly.

"No?" Coda raised an eyebrow. He hadn't expected to be rejected.

"Not until it's finished."

"All right. How long will that be?"

Noodle shrugged as if to say he had no idea. Since he clearly had no desire to talk about it, Coda turned to Tex. "And you, growing food. I thought you said this stuff wasn't so bad."

"It's not," Tex said. "But there's nothing better than fresh veggies."

Squawks snorted. "*Everything* is better than fresh veggies. Well, almost everything," he added, sticking his spoon back into the meat paste.

"I had no idea," Coda said. "I haven't been a good friend, and I'm—"

"Stop," Squawks said. "You don't need to baby us. Just get out of your own head sometime."

"All right."

For the remainder of lunch, Coda tried to play a larger role in the banter, but try as he might, his eyes kept drifting back to Moscow. He'd decided the night before to suck it up and bury the hatchet. And he meant to tell Moscow as much. So when Coda's friends finished and stood to return their trays into the washing dispenser, Coda made for Moscow.

Squawks groaned behind him. "He really is going to ask him to dance."

Ignoring the comment, Coda continued toward Moscow. He was sitting at another table with his friends, and they were laughing, in the middle of a story about how poorly the morning flight had gone. If the commander had heightened expectations following his pep talk the day before, then he must have been very disappointed with the morning's session.

Their laughter died away as they spotted Coda approaching. Bear nodded to him, her previous disdain having been damped down in their hours spent training together in the simulator. Moscow, however, smiled when he noticed Coda, and it wasn't an inviting thing.

"Can I talk to you?" Coda asked.

"Come to congratulate me on our victory yesterday?" Moscow asked. "Or maybe thank me for saving your bacon?"

Coda ground his teeth. *Why can't he make this easy?* "Something like that."

Moscow shrugged and rose from the table. Coda quickly led him out of the mess hall into an adjoining corridor.

"Look," Moscow said before Coda could start. "I'm just busting your balls, okay? Nothing personal. If you didn't take offense to everything, people might tone it down."

"That's good," Coda said, "because that's exactly what I wanted to talk to you about. This thing, this rivalry—it needs to stop. Because like it or not, we're two of the best pilots in this squadron, but even that won't guarantee our spot in the squadron. *If* we make it, then we have to trust each other, and we can't do that if we're constantly looking over our shoulders."

"Why wouldn't we both make it?"

"Huh?"

"If we're two of the best pilots, why wouldn't we both make it? Why would one of us get reassigned?"

"That's not the point," Coda said, trying to steer the conversation back to center. "I'm just saying—"

"It's not the point, but it's important. Why wouldn't we both make it?"

"Because there's a chasm in the middle of our squadron a mile wide, Moscow. We were about to go at it in the hangar and it wouldn't have just been us. It would have been your group and mine. It would have been a brawl."

"You sound like the commander."

"Well, he's right." Coda regretted the words the moment they left his mouth. Moscow was already suspicious, and the way Coda had phrased his reply left little doubt that he'd had help coming to the conclusions.

"You talked to him?" Moscow voice went quiet. "What did you talk about?"

"Nothing," Coda said. "He just told me to fix this."

Moscow eyed him as if deciding whether or not to believe him. Was he always this on guard? This suspicious?

Moscow shook his head. "And here I thought you were doing something honorable. Instead, you're just following orders."

"I was!" Coda said, exasperated. "I am. Damn it, Moscow, what's wrong with you? I'm trying to make life easier for both of us."

"Just stay away from me, O'Neil, and we'll be fine." Moscow started back toward the mess.

Coda grabbed his arm, stopping him. "It doesn't work that way, and you know it. Yes, I talked to the commander, and if we can't get this stuff worked out, one of us is going home."

"Then you better step up your game, Coda, because it ain't going to be me."

Moscow tried to pull away again, but Coda wasn't letting go. "Look, man, I know why you hate me, and I get it—"

"You don't know anything."

Coda had stepped on a land mine, and he knew it. He let out a long breath. "No, Moscow, I don't know everything, but I know enough. And for what it's worth, I'd hate me too. Hell, I already do."

Moscow's eyes blazed in anger. "Who told you?"

"Nobody," Coda lied. "And nobody else knows. Just me."

"You're lying."

"I'm serious. I was doing research on my father when I came across her name on a file. I'm s—"

"Don't!" Moscow shoved a finger in Coda's face. "Don't."

"Andrei..."

Moscow's hand became a fist, and for a second, Coda thought Moscow was going to hit him. Moscow regained control at the last moment, though, his fist falling to his side. "Stay away from me, O'Neil. If anyone finds out about this, I swear on my mother's grave, I *will* kill you."

"Fine," Coda said.

"I mean it, Coda."

Coda shrugged. "So do I."

They stared at each other for several moments. When Moscow finally turned to go, Coda let out a long breath. *Maybe he's right. Maybe I just need to leave him alone.*

But even as he thought the words, Coda knew keeping his distance wouldn't be enough. He would never feel comfortable flying in a squadron where he knew someone hated him. Where someone wanted him dead. No, the commander was right. There was only enough room in the squadron for one of them. The only thing Coda could do was make sure that person was him.

SAS Jamestown
  Alpha Centauri System, Proxima B, High Orbit

AVOIDING MOSCOW PROVED TO BE SIMPLER THAN CODA anticipated. With flights occurring every day, the squadron's previous schedule was thrown out the air lock. Workouts and classes on Baranyk physiology and biology were still required, and they still logged dozens of hours a week in the simulator, but all of those things came in at a distant second to logging time in their starfighters.

When they did occupy the same space, mostly during dining hours and squadron briefings, Coda didn't so much as even acknowledge Moscow's presence. And Moscow did the same. If the commander noticed the sudden change in how they stepped around each other, he didn't say anything.

As the days turned into weeks, Coda spent more and more time in the cockpit, flying hop after hop, sometimes as flight leader, sometimes not, sometimes as the flight with offensive objectives, sometimes as the defending force. And he dedicated himself to his training like never before. When he wasn't in the cockpit, he was in the simulator, and when he wasn't in the simulator, he was studying the recent flight vids, analyzing and learning from his fellow pilots. Squawks had said he needed a hobby, but that was a luxury Coda couldn't afford. Not yet.

He won, he lost, and he was shot down, but every hour of every day, he grew more confident. As his notebook filled up, he began to understand his wingmen like never before. He leveraged the knowledge when he was flying with them and exploited it when he was flying against them. Their flight strategies became as recognizable to him as their voice, their laugh, or even their walk.

After their fourth week of Nighthawk battles, the commander unveiled his new leaderboard. Coda wasn't surprised to find his name near the top but had to grind his teeth when he saw he was still trailing Moscow.

The commander never said as much, but Coda assumed it was because the quality of kills were weighted in the ranking. Shooting down a pilot who was in the bottom quarter didn't count as much as shooting down someone in the top or, for that matter, shooting down the commander himself. Moscow's kill of Commander Coleman continued to pay dividends, but Coda was gaining on him, and he knew that before long, he would knock his rival out of the top spot.

But seeing Moscow's name atop the leaderboard proved to Coda one thing above all else—try as he might, there was no way he could avoid Moscow forever. Sooner or later, their paths would cross again. What he didn't know was just how soon that would be.

Or that it would coincide with the first catastrophic training accident.

Cockpit, Nighthawk
  Alpha Centauri System, Proxima B

CODA DIDN'T KNOW WHAT HE ENJOYED MORE: THE SILENCE OR
the stars. The brief moments between sliding on his VR
helmet and the following radio chatter had always been one
of his favorite moments back at the academy. It offered free-
dom, as if he were floating on a pristine lake nestled somewhere deep in the heart of Earth. There was no
responsibility, no rivalry, no fight to regain honor. There
was... nothing. And because Coda knew the silence would
never last, it was something to be cherished.

But those moments, like the simulator he'd experienced
them through, had been artificial. Here, though, the silence
was real, and it was unique. The absence of radio chatter
was new, different, and unnerving. Not like the stars. They
burned like distant embers, flashing and flickering blue,
white, and gold. They called to him, inviting him to join

them like beautiful sirens beckoning an old seafaring captain.

But both moments had one thing in common: they were always interrupted.

"Something feels different about this one," Squawks said. His voice was slightly muffled, cracking through the speakers of Coda's helmet.

"Forget your lucky underwear?" Noodle asked. It was the first time Coda had flown with the two of them together.

"No," Squawks said. "It isn't that. I've got them on, and I didn't wash them either."

"That's disgusting," Noodle said.

"Gotta keep the streak alive, you know?" Squawks added.

"What kind of streak are you talking about?" Tex asked.

"Okay, too far, too far," Noodle said. But he was laughing. Laughing was good. Laughing kept them loose. Because Squawks was right—something *did* feel different.

"Stay sharp," Coda said. "This one feels different because it's bigger."

He didn't necessarily believe his own words, but they seemed to sate the growing concern among his wingmen. Like all good lies, there was just enough truth sprinkled in to make it sound credible. Of course, it really was a bigger hop, the largest they'd flown yet, and unless Coda was mistaken, it was about to turn into a real mess.

He glanced at his HUD. Twelve fighters made up two flights of six. He was flight leader of Alpha Flight, Tex the flight leader of Bravo. Their recent hops had put them up against increasingly numerous enemies, often outnumbering them by fifty percent. If that trend continued, how many enemies could they expect today? Sixteen? Twenty?

The latter would mean more than thirty Nighthawks in the entire engagement. Not a small number by any stretch.

At the moment, though, the HUD was empty, showing only the green indicators of the two flights and the Proxima B's moon to their left. Like Earth's moon, its surface was rough and littered with craters, though instead of the light gray that Coda was accustomed to, Theseus was a mix of reds and oranges, almost like the surface of Mars.

Coda eyed it closely. According to their mission detail, an enemy mining colony existed on the back side of the moon, but intelligence was spotty, and they didn't know the size of its defensive force. The primary mission was to scout the moon and relay the information to Command, but if the mining station was vulnerable, they were to take it out. In Coda's mind, that left only one option.

"Bravo One, Alpha One," Coda said. "Tex, you copy?"

"Loud and clear, Coda."

"You ready to see what they got cooking?"

"Is a frog's ass watertight?"

"Say again, Tex?"

"Does Howdy Doody have wooden balls?"

"Uh…"

"Yes, you dumb Yankee!"

"All right," Coda said, still more than a little confused. "Then take your flight around the moon, full burn, and we'll meet you on the other side."

"Sounds good, boss."

The green indicators marking Tex's flight on Coda's HUD veered away, darting toward the moon.

"All right, Alpha Flight," Coda said, "new coordinates coming your way. Keep the formation tight and stay on me."

A series of affirmatives came in through the radio, and Coda punched it, settling in on a course that would have him rendezvous with Tex's flight on the back side of the moon. The flight path brought them close enough to the moon that he could make out individual rock formations. Their red peaks glinted in the sunlight, hinting at the valuable metals beneath the surface. Like Proxima B, Theseus was critical to the Centauri system's mining operation, and being the closest star system to Sol, the operation was one of the most important in the fleet.

"Entering communications blackout," Tex said. "See you on the other side, Coda."

Since they didn't have access to the satellite system orbiting the moon, the moon's natural body would restrict their window of communication, creating dead zones proportionate to where the two forces were in relation to each other. For the next two minutes, each flight would be entirely alone.

"Acknowledged," Coda said. "Good luck."

The next two minutes felt like an eternity. Coda didn't know what to expect, and his imagination ran amok. He imagined the entire squadron waiting for them, thirty-eight fighters ready to take on Coda's twelve, and helmed by the commander himself. It would never happen, at least not this early in their training. Besides, Coda knew that his imagination was always worse than whatever reality held in store.

Except when it wasn't.

"Coda!" Tex's voice erupted on Coda's radio. "Coda! Goddamn it, can you hear me? Requesting immediate assistance! I repeat, immediate assistance!"

"Coda copies." He struggled to keep his voice even. "Approaching from the east, two degrees positive-Z in… fifteen seconds. I repeat, Alpha Flight, rendezvous in fifteen seconds."

"Hurry, Coda," Tex's voice came again. "They're on us like a pent-up bull."

Coda toggled his flight's private frequency. "Be alert and prepare for contact. We're coming in hot."

The curve of the moon blocked their view of the battle, but after a few moments, it came into focus. From the distance, it looked like little more than a swarm of mosquitos flying above a pool of water, but as they sped closer, Coda was able to take in the full situation. His HUD showed almost thirty contacts, and it was changing every second as green dots disappeared and more reds materialized. It was a true rat's nest, and even with Coda's flight, their total forces would still be outnumbered nearly two to one. Fortunately, despite the previous panic in Tex's voice, his flight appeared to be holding up better than expected.

The enemy had obviously known they were coming, but in space, there was only so much they could do to prepare. The enemy could come from any position, from any angle, at any time, and that meant defending forces were limited in the defensive measures they could prepare. Space combat had become a mano a mano fistfight built around three foundational pillars: track, deploy, and attack.

Coda had scratched off the first two. It was time to move to the third.

34

Cockpit, Nighthawk
Alpha Centauri System, Theseus

"FIGHTER PAIRS," CODA SAID. "TARGET THE PURSUING fighters first. Let's get them off our friends' backs. Prepare to break in... three, two, one, break."

Coda's formation broke into three pairs. Squawks, who was in the dash-two position, was his wingman, and together, they zipped into the fray. Toggling his weapons switch, Coda ensured it was set to missiles and let his computer select a nearby enemy fighter harassing one of Bravo Flight's pilots. Then matching course, Coda performed a tight maneuver to get on its six.

"Bravo Four," Coda said. "Bravo Four, this is Alpha One. I've got your enemy in my sights. Prepare to break to positive-Z, six degrees in three. Acknowledge."

"Acknowledged, Coda," came the voice on the radio. "It sure is good to see you."

With the enemy fighter nearly in his sights, Coda didn't have time to chat. "Break!"

Bravo Four suddenly veered course, and as Coda expected, the enemy pilot took the bait. Moving to intercept, Coda waited for his targeting computer to get a lock. The X-23's anti-radar did its job, slipping missile lock like a banana peel in an old cartoon, but that would delay the inevitable for only so long.

After two more breaths, Coda had lock and fired his first missile. The yellow icon streaked toward the red indicator on this HUD, and a moment later, the enemy vessel disappeared from the battle map. In real life, the fighter went completely dark, save for its emergency markers as the ship's onboard computer steered it safely from the battle.

"Splash one!" Coda boomed into the radio.

"Thank you, Coda."

"No problem, Bravo Four. Let's get back in there."

Coda brought his fighter around in a wide arc, targeting the next fighter that had unwittingly opened up its flank to Coda's incoming vector. As quickly as Coda registered the opportunity, he got tone. Less than a second later, another missile was on its way.

"Splash two!"

Coda completed the arc and made for another pass through the knot of fighters. It was the equivalent of running through a swarm of yellow jackets. At breakneck speeds, fighters zipped in every direction. He and Squawks took out two more fighters before they erupted through the far edge.

Coda brought his fighter back around, preparing for another pass, then spotted an enemy fighter in pursuit. "Evasive maneuvers," Coda said.

Squawks split from Coda, pulling above the battle plane. The enemy stayed with Coda, moving into firing position.

"He's coming around on my six," Coda said. "Where are you, Squawks?"

"I've got you, Coda. Continue course."

Coda strafed left and right, weaving in and out of the edges of the dogfight, using its natural chaos to his advantage. Fighters were everywhere, blazing so fast that he barely had time to see them, let alone take evasive maneuvers to avoid a collision. He was nearly clipped more than once, and the encounters left him in a cold sweat. The commander had armed them with digital rounds and missiles, and he'd even put restrictions on speed and elevation as it pertained to the moon—there would be no canyon runs on this flight—but there was nothing the commander could do to prevent fighters from colliding with each other.

Despite his attempts to shake him, the enemy drew closer. "I can't hold him much longer, Squawks!"

"Two seconds."

An alarm claxon blared. Coda didn't have two seconds.

"Alpha Two!" Squawks shouted. "Fox Three. Bingo!"

The enemy indicator disappeared from Coda's HUD. "Good shooting, Squawks. I owe you one."

"Like shooting fish in a barrel, right, Tex?"

Tex's laughter echoed through the comm. "Easy as fallin' off a log."

"Whatever that means," Squawks said, reappearing on Coda's wing.

Coda focused his HUD, studying the mass of ships. "Squawks, break formation. It's not going to do us any good in there."

"The commander's going to have your ass," Squawks

said, reminding Coda of the commander's disdain for fighters going at it alone.

"Break formation but follow my lead. Make it appear as if I'm a lone wolf and see who takes the bait."

"Copy that."

Squawks's fighter veered off perpendicular to Coda's, darting into the mass of fighters with complete disregard for his own safety. Coda followed a moment later, entering from a different angle.

Fighters zigged and zagged in every direction, moving faster than Coda could track, but though he'd been overwhelmed in his first two passes, the world seemed to slow now. His actions were measured, never rushed. His heartbeat remained within its resting boundaries. Again, he allowed the computer to analyze the various flight trajectories. This time, he let it select his targets for him.

Targeting brackets appeared around another enemy fighter. It moved more slowly than the rest, its movements timid, as if the pilot was afraid of making a mistake.

Uno was right. He never would have made it out here. Coda followed his target through the mass of fighters, recognizing the other pilot by her flight style. *Bear, how many times has the commander told you that speed is life?*

Getting into firing range took less than three seconds, and even then, seeing no reason to waste his missiles, Coda switched to guns. As the fighter moved into his crosshairs, Coda let off a quick double burst.

Bear's cockpit went black as she vanished from Coda's HUD. Coda didn't take any time to celebrate before moving on to the next target. He thumbed the switch back to missiles, then took out two more fighters before spotting an incoming third.

Pulling back on the stick, Coda darted above the battle

plane, then rolled into a steep-pitch turn, and let the enemy craft fly beneath him. Then he pulled out of the turn directly behind the other fighter. The pilot never saw him coming.

"Splash twelve!" Coda boomed as its cockpit went dark. "Keep it going, boys. We've got them on the ropes now."

But Coda's celebration was interrupted as Squawks's voice cut through the rest of the radio chatter. "Coda, you've got company. Incoming bogeys. Ten o'clock, six degrees positive-Z."

Coda found the fighter pair on his HUD. "I see them."

"Move to intercept and hold course," Squawks said. "I'll provide cover."

"Acknowledged."

Coda pulled his fighter into a head-on course, daring the incoming fighters to engage. Tiny sparks shot from the front of the crafts as their cannons came alive. Coda fired his own bursts, but like the enemy fighters', his weren't effective. Squawks's cannons, however, were. He cut in from negative-z, taking out the enemy wingman from below.

"Sorry, Coda," he said as he zipped past the lead fighter. "Thought I could get both of them."

Coda had no time to respond. The incoming fighter was coming in too hot. Coda offset left, avoiding a collision as he and the other fighter passed each other in the black, then he pulled above the battle plane in a tight loop. Crossing over, Coda rolled out behind the other fighter, who was angling for another pass.

The other fighter saw his own mistake and increased speed to get away from Coda's pursuit. Only one pilot had the ability to recognize his own mistake so quickly: Moscow.

Grinning, Coda punched the throttle, going after the other fighter. He toggled his long-range targeting system, preparing to switch to the accompanying long-range missiles, but Moscow was too elusive. He ducked and dodged, flying dangerously close to other spacecraft, providing himself with cover, just as Coda had done before.

Coda kept pursuit, giving chase as if he were playing a childhood game of tag. And like those early games, it was only a matter of time before the pursuer gained the advantage. Little by little, Coda drew closer.

Moscow must have seen it too, because he suddenly veered off course, diving steeply below the battle plane in what looked like a reverse high yo-yo maneuver. At their increased speeds, Coda barely had time to replicate the maneuver...

And spot his mistake.

Moscow wasn't performing a high yo-yo—he was performing a high yo-yo *defense*. Where the first maneuver was designed to maintain speed, the high yo-yo defense was deceptive, allowing the defender to shed velocity and cause the pursuer to overshoot. Moscow was trying to force Coda in front of him, where he could turn the pursuer into the pursued. But it worked too well. Coda was coming in hot— way too hot.

Throwing the stick hard to the right, Coda tried to avoid colliding with Moscow's fighter. His nose missed, but a terrible shriek crossed the underbelly of his fighter. After a brief flash of light, Coda was spinning.

Up became down then down became forward as his fighter tumbled out of the fray. He had just enough time between spins to see Moscow's fighter spiraling out of the battle too, its starboard wing completely ripped away. A second flash illuminated the dark, this time brighter and tinged with orange.

An explosion.

Oh god! A third fighter had collided with the wreckage from Moscow's fighter.

"Mayday! Mayday!" the voice on the radio screamed. Coda couldn't tell who it was. "Multiple collisions. I repeat: multiple collisions. Send immediate recovery!"

Coda shut away the panicked voice. Multiple claxons in his cockpit told him he had more immediate problems of his own.

Quickly assessing the situation, he found the underbelly of his fighter had been breached, and the collision had knocked out several of his portside navigational thrusters. The cockpit was leaking oxygen and losing pressure, but his flight suit was designed to protect him in situations like that. Correcting the spin without full navigational thrusters would be much more difficult, though.

Worst of all, his HUD showed that he was well below the battle plane and streaking toward the moon. With no friction to slow him down, he was flying toward the moon at nearly the same speed that he had been flying in pursuit of Moscow. If he didn't correct it and fast, he would provide the moon with a brand-new crater. Fortunately, his onboard computer was still active, and the fighter's spin was correctable—even with his fighter's damaged thrusters.

Coda had the computer measure his spin and leveraged the autopilot to counter its rotation with several well-timed bursts. Almost immediately, he felt the spin subside, then quickly thereafter, it stopped altogether.

And that was when he saw it.

Like Coda, Moscow was streaking toward the moon's surface, but his fighter appeared to be entirely inoperable. Its cockpit and marker lights were completely dark, and there was no sign of its navigational thrusters. The X-23 was little more than battle debris caught up in the moon's gravitational pull.

"*Jamestown* Tower," Coda said. "Alpha One. What's the ETA on the recovery vessels?"

"Alpha One, *Jamestown* Tower. ETA in four minutes."

"Four minutes." Coda chewed on the words. Moscow didn't have four minutes. He didn't have anything even close to that. Unless Coda did something, it wouldn't be him that would be leaving a fresh crater on Theseus.

It would be Moscow.

35

Cockpit, Nighthawk
Alpha Centauri System, Theseus

CODA'S FIRST THOUGHT WAS TO LET MOSCOW FALL, LET HIS fighter crash into the surface of Proxima B's only moon. That would certainly solve many of his problems. No more rivalry. No more looking over his shoulder. No more trying to play nice with a man who wanted nothing of it. And Commander Coleman wouldn't have to choose between two of his best pilots—chance would do it for him.

But even as the thought came to him, Coda knew he couldn't let it happen. He wasn't wired that way. He hadn't grown up drowning in his father's misdeeds only to let something similar happen on his watch—regardless of how much he hated Moscow. Shoving the throttle forward, Coda directed his damaged fighter toward Moscow's.

Halfway there, he realized he had no idea what he would do once he got there. He didn't have any tow cables or anything to latch to Moscow's fighter that he could use to pull him to safety. What was he going to do?

I'll crash into him again if I have to. Throw him off course. Wait... That gave him an idea.

Coda adjusted his course. Rather than intercepting Moscow's spacecraft, he would arrive at a point *below* it. Only, no, that wouldn't be enough. He had to arrive well below Moscow's fighter in order to provide himself with enough time.

That means I'll only get one shot at this.

Well, if he was only going to get one shot at it, he had to give himself as much room for error as possible. Plotting a revised course, he settled into his seat, preparing himself for what would amount to little more than a suicide run.

What are you doing, Coda? Why are you risking your life for the only person you hate more than your... The only person more than your father?

That was it, wasn't it? He was willing to risk his life to save Moscow's because he had dedicated his entire military existence to undoing the damage his father had done. He couldn't undo the deaths, and he couldn't bring back Moscow's mother, but he could do everything he could to save her son.

"Charlie One, Charlie One, this is Alpha One. Do you copy?" Coda waited for a response, then when none came, tried again. "Moscow, it's Coda. Do you copy?"

Still nothing.

Following the flight path indicated on his HUD, Coda moved into position, bringing his Nighthawk into a low orbit around Theseus and directly into the middle of Moscow's incoming trajectory.

"Andrei, it's Coda. Are you there?"

Moscow never responded. His comms were likely dead. After all, Coda hadn't heard his mayday on the radio.

Unless he's injured... or worse.

Was Coda trying to save someone who couldn't be saved? Risking his life for someone who was already dead? There was no way to be sure, and he didn't have time to radio the tower and have them check the vitals measured by his flight suit. Moscow's fighter was coming in too hot.

Coda brought up Moscow's Nighthawk on his HUD, measuring its incoming velocity and rate of spin. Like an outfielder tracking down a pop fly, Coda calculated the multiple points where he could catch Moscow's vessel. Then, firing his forward thrusters, he propelled his fighter *backward*, deeper into the moon's gravitational pull. The maneuver meant that Moscow's fighter was still gaining on his but at a slower rate than before.

As Moscow's fighter came closer, Coda feathered his thrusters, gaining more reverse speed, thereby slowing the rate of Moscow's pursuit until they had nearly matched speed. Moscow's fighter was in visual range now. Its portside wing was missing, and the glass of his cockpit was cracked.

Still plummeting toward the moon, Moscow's fighter closed the remaining distance. With one eye on the catch point, Coda gave his rear thrusters a single short burst, slowing his rate of descent. Half a second later the two fighters collided in a second crash of metal and...

...Coda *caught* Moscow's damaged fighter.

"I've got you!"

The two fighters were lodged against each other, their wings and fuselages intertwined like two hooks looped together. The positioning brought their two cockpits side by side, and Coda could finally see Moscow. The other pilot was slumped against his seat, not moving. He was either dead or unconscious, but there was nothing Coda could do about that at the moment. Increasing power to his rear thrusters, Coda gently slowed their descent. His Nighthawk groaned under the combined strain. The fighters were designed to deal with intense g-forces. They wouldn't break apart, would they?

Coda couldn't do anything about that, either. He continued to increase his thruster power, and within seconds, they had settled into a dangerously shallow orbit, neither falling nor climbing.

"Come on," Coda said, encouraging the fighter. "You've got this. You can do it. Come on."

Little by little, he increased thruster power, never more than half a percent at a time. His fighter was intact, with only moderate damage, but Moscow's was barely hanging together.

The seconds ticked by, becoming minutes, and despite the occasional metal groan, they eventually escaped the moon's gravity well. Breathing a sigh of relief, Coda surveyed the battle space. The other fighters had disappeared, and a quick glance at his HUD showed that they had all returned to the *Jamestown*.

"*Jamestown* Tower, this is Alpha One. What's the ETA on that recovery ship?"

"There was a malfunction with the hangar bay doors, Alpha One. The recovery ship is still several minutes out."

Coda cursed. After literally catching him in space, Coda couldn't afford to sit around and wait.

"Copy that, *Jamestown* Tower. Alpha One requesting clearance for emergency landing."

"Coda," Commander Coleman's voice said over the radio. "What's your status?"

"I've got Moscow, sir. His ship is... *attached* to mine."

"Alpha One, repeat," Commander Coleman said.

"I said he's attached to me, sir. Our wings are criss-crossed, wedged together. It's not pretty, but I've got him."

"What's his condition?"

"Unknown, sir," Coda said. "His ship is intact, but..." Coda heard other voices in the background and realized the commander hadn't been talking to him.

"Increased heart rate... blood pressure dropping..." He could barely make out the words, but what he heard didn't sound encouraging.

"Coda," Commander Coleman said. "This is what you're going to do..."

Coda's mouth went dry as the commander gave him his emergency landing orders.

"Do you copy?"

"Copy, sir."

"All right. We'll see you aboard soon."

"Alpha One, *Jamestown* Tower. Proceed to Landing Bay 7C and prepare for emergency landing."

"Acknowledged. Proceeding to Landing Bay 7C. Coda, out."

Coda's ship was already moving—slowing down would likely mean their two fighters would separate again—so he angled the nose of his ship around to point toward the *Jamestown*. Or at least where the *Jamestown* would be. They'd practiced emergency landings in the simulator but never anything like what Coda was about to attempt.

His course plotted and speed set, Coda's only job was to make the small adjustments needed to keep his fighter on the designated path indicated on his HUD. This far out, that task was simple, but as he grew closer, it would become increasingly difficult. What he hadn't counted on, and what his computer struggled to compensate for, was the added mass of Moscow's fighter and the reduced navigability due to his damaged thrusters.

For the first time since the first week practicing landings, Coda almost succumbed to his fear. But what he had now that he hadn't had before was hours of training. Experience.

Banishing the emotions from his mind, he focused only on the task at hand. He adjusted, readjusted, and felt the ship moving under him, always anticipating what he would need to do next. When the *Jamestown* finally came into view, he was still green, his ship well within the range of error. But then he realized just how fast he was truly going.

Unable to slow down, Coda and Moscow were approaching the *Jamestown* at more than ten times the speed of a normal landing. Terror seized him as the *Jamestown* grew at an alarming rate.

This is going to hurt, Coda thought, squeezing his eyes shut.

The last thing he saw before shooting into the landing bay was the giant net that had been erected in its center. Then there was groaning, crashing, sparks, and above all, incredible, excruciating pain, followed by deep, impenetrable darkness.

36

Sick Bay, SAS Jamestown
Alpha Centauri System, Proxima B, High Orbit

CODA'S EYELIDS FELT AS IF THEY WERE WEIGHED DOWN WITH lead weights. It took nearly everything he had to open them, and when he finally succeeded, keeping them open was twice as difficult. The blinding white light wasn't doing him any favors, either.

He found himself in sick bay, surrounded by empty gurneys and a distracted medical staff. Unlike the rest of the *Jamestown*, the sick bay was pristine. No industrial walls accented with the signs of old battles. No dated equipment or furniture. The place was immaculate. Everything white or chrome, and it all seemed to be alive, glistening from the lights of the various monitors and equipment spread throughout the room.

A nurse appeared at his side. She laid a hand on his forehead and shushed him, telling him to take it easy, then brought a small cup of water up to his dry lips. The water was cool and soothing and felt like heaven as it tamed his scratchy throat.

"Thanks," Coda said once he'd drunk his fill. "How long have I been out?"

"Shhh," she said again. "Save your questions."

"For what?"

The telltale sound of a door hissing open caught her attention, and she looked up. "For him."

Coda followed her eyes, spotting a thickly built man with closely cropped black and white hair and ebony skin. Commander Coleman. Coda swallowed reflexively, but the commander's customary hard expression softened when he saw Coda was alert.

"Sir," Coda said, trying to sit up to give him a proper salute.

"No," Commander Coleman said, stopping beside Coda's bed. "No need for that."

Coda was thankful for the commander's sudden lack of military decorum. The movement had *hurt*.

"How are you feeling?" Commander Coleman asked as the nurse left to go back to whatever she'd been doing before Coda had woken up.

Coda laughed softly, and even that stirred more pain. "Funny. I was just thinking my body felt like a giant bruise."

"Something that's not far from the truth, I'm afraid. There's a reason we don't practice emergency landings. They're... *painful*."

Coda couldn't argue with him there. "How bad is it?"

The commander shrugged. "You had some significant bruising, a couple broken ribs, multiple lacerations, separated shoulder, whiplash, and a minor concussion. Nothing too serious."

Nothing too serious. Any one of the ailments the

commander had mentioned would have been enough to send anyone to the doctor. With all of them combined, there was no telling how long he was going to be grounded. Still, even as pained as he was, he didn't feel as bad as the commander's words suggested.

"How long have I been out?"

"Two days. You're healing quite nicely."

Two days. That wasn't enough time to heal but only the most minor of cuts. *What exactly are they pumping me full of?* The thought brought another to the front of his mind. "How's Moscow?"

"Moscow's fine. Better than you. He was discharged this morning."

Coda closed his eyes, nodding. The pain was worth it then.

"That was a brave thing you did," Commander Coleman said. "And for someone you dislike."

"He's part of my squadron," Coda said.

"*Your* squadron?"

Was that a smile at the edges of the commander's lips? "Don't make me laugh, sir."

"My apologies." There was something else in the commander's expression, something he left unsaid.

"He would have done the same thing for me, sir."

"Would he?" Commander Coleman raised an eyebrow. "Perhaps. I pray we never have to find out. In either case, you have my thanks. You prevented a terrible accident from claiming even more lives."

"Even more lives, sir?"

Commander Coleman's gentle demeanor vanished, replaced by the hard expression Coda was more accustomed to. "Sooner or later, death comes to all pilots, Coda."

"Who was it?"

"Don't worry about that right now," Commander Coleman said. "Right now, you need to—"

"Who was it, sir?"

Commander Coleman exhaled. He had to know that if Coda didn't get the information out of him now, he would get it from his next visitor. At least this way, he could control the message. "Whiskey."

"Whiskey..." Coda repeated, ashamed of the sudden wave of relief flooding through him. It hadn't been Squawks or Noodle. Hadn't been Tex. Coda closed his eyes, trying to reconcile the guilt.

Commander Coleman must have misunderstood the gesture, because he rested a hand on Coda's shoulder. "Do this long enough, Coda, and you will know more. Whether we're dealing it out or falling victim to it, death will always surround us. Get some rest." The commander patted him on the shoulder before making back toward the door.

"Sir?"

Commander Coleman stopped and turned.

"When will I fly again?"

"I don't know, Coda. All flights have been grounded until the investigation has been completed."

Coda felt his blood go cold. "Investigation, sir?"

"Yes. A review board is being assembled to investigate the death of Lieutenant Jones. It's standard procedure following a mishap of this nature."

"Who's being investigated, sir?" Coda asked, already knowing the answer.

"Coda—"

"No, sir, I need to know what to expect."

Commander Coleman sighed. "You and Lieutenant Krylov are under investigation for exhibiting a trend of unsafe behavior that culminated in the death of one of your squad mates. After a review of the facts by the officer board, you, Lieutenant Krylov, or both may be expelled from the squadron and never allowed in the cockpit of a Nighthawk again."

Coda watched as Commander Coleman turned to go. *This can't be happening! It's a nightmare... an absolute nightmare. No matter how hard I try, I'm no better than my father.*

Struggling to cope with the array of conflicting emotions, Coda replayed the training scenario again and again in his mind. When he could do that no more, he requested his personal tablet back then watched the training scenario itself, deconstructing the flight from every angle.

The simple fact of the matter was Coda had a blind spot the size of the Milky Way where Moscow was concerned. He'd abandoned the battle at large, focusing all of his effort and energy on shooting down the one fighter that would bring him the most personal gain. And it had cost him. Again.

"When you're in battle," Captain Hughes had said after Coda had beaten Moscow to a bloody pulp in the Terran Fleet Academy corridors, "your fellow wingmen need to have absolute trust in you. There's no room for grudges. There's no room for ego. And there sure as hell isn't room for pilots who aren't capable of learning from their mistakes."

Captain Hughes had been right. Not only was there no room for personal animosity, but Coda also couldn't learn from his mistakes.

The realization was like a blow to the gut. Coda thought he'd been doing well. God knew there'd been times when he'd wanted to slam Moscow's head into the deck, but he'd held back. He'd even *stopped* a fight between Moscow and

Uno in Dr. Naidoo's classroom. But it was all fool's gold. When push came to shove, Coda could always be counted on to follow Moscow into a foxhole. This time, neither he nor Moscow had died. Whiskey had.

There was no question who the review board would conclude was at fault. Bile crept into the back of Coda's throat. He could taste its sour burn. He was responsible.

"The hero is awake," Noodle said as he strode into sick bay with Squawks and Tex.

Coda looked at his friends. The words cut deep. "Don't feel like a hero."

"Please," Squawks said. "Everyone's talking about it. Even Moscow doesn't have anything bad to say for once."

"Yeah?" Coda asked. "And what are they saying about Whiskey?"

His friends' smiles and easygoing nature vanished, and it quickly became obvious that they had talked prior to coming in. Make sure Coda was in good spirits. Don't pull him into the muck with everyone else.

"Nobody's saying much," Squawks said. "You know how it is. Everyone acts like nothing happened."

"Well, it happened," Coda said, then he told them about the pending investigation.

"I was wondering why everyone was grounded," Noodle said.

"It's standard procedure," Tex said. "Maybe not grounding the entire squadron, but that's how these things go. The top brass needs to find something to cover their ass."

"You mean someone to blame," Coda said.

"It's really not a big deal," Tex said.

"Not a big deal?" Coda repeated. "Tex, Whiskey is *dead*."

"I wasn't talking about that," Tex said. "I was talking about the review itself. I've been through one too."

"You have?" Squawks said. "For what?"

"Failure to complete a training syllabus," Tex said as if reciting the description from an official memo. "But they can be called for almost any reason. Too many SODs, a failure to meet goals, actions discrediting space aviation, mishaps—whatever blows their hair back."

"Exhibiting a trend of unsafe behavior that culminated in the death of one of your squad mates?" Coda said. "That's what me and Moscow are under investigation for."

Tex whistled. "That's not good, Coda. That means they'll be elbows deep in your cookie jar. They'll dig into your whole life. Not just what's happened on the *Jamestown*, but everything. The academy. Your school. Your..."

"My what?"

"Your family, Coda," Noodle said.

"You think they'll rope his dad into this?" Squawks asked.

All eyes went back to Tex, but the older man looked like he was trying to find a place to hide. Unlike Squawks and Noodle, who had spoken with Coda about his father on a few occasions, the subject was still taboo to the older pilot.

"I..." Tex stammered. "I wouldn't be surprised."

"That's ridiculous," Noodle said. "He had nothing to do with it."

"It doesn't matter," Coda said softly. "It's never mattered. Whatever weakness flowed through him flows through me. That's how everyone's always acted. How everyone has ever looked at me."

"That's not true," Noodle said.

"Isn't it?"

"No," Squawks said. "Noodle is right. Forty-eight pilots and Commander Coleman himself just watched you risk your life to save Moscow's. Whatever they say, your squad mates know you're nothing like your father."

"We'll see," Coda said. It was the only thing he could think of. He didn't want to talk about it anymore, but he didn't have anything else to talk about. Except for the vids on his terminal and the random conversation with the medical staff, nothing else had happened. There was nothing to share with his friends.

"Keep your head up," Tex said. "You'll get a chance to speak your piece. Just know what you want to say before you go in there, and you should be all right."

"You don't think they're coming *here*, do you?" Noodle asked.

"Well," Tex said, "that's how mine were done."

"Yeah, but you were at a training facility with training staff. We're light-years away from the top brass."

"That's true," Tex said. "Huh. I don't know what they're going to do then."

The sudden uncertainty did little to improve Coda's mood. At least in a face-to-face conversation, he would have had a chance to make his argument. The board could see his remorse, and he could explain what had been going through his mind. He would have been able to attack the questions about his father head-on and quell any similarities that could be drawn between the two.

"I bet they do it through written questions," Noodle said. "They'll get their information, and it'll be cheaper than shuttling them out here."

"That makes sense," Tex said. He turned his attention back to Coda. "Know what you want to say, and say it. That's the best advice I can give. And be honest. They can smell bullshit like it's stuck to the bottom of your boot."

37

Private Room, SAS Jamestown
  Alpha Centauri System, Proxima B, High Orbit

NOODLE'S PREDICTION THAT THE REVIEW BOARD WOULD USE written questions and statements was only partially true. When the official questions came in, they did arrive in a written format but only to supplement the video messages they accompanied. The commander brought Coda, who was still recovering from his injuries, into a private room and moderated the interview, recording Coda's responses to the video's questions.

Tex's prediction was spot on, though. For two hours, Coda was grilled about his time at the academy, including every minor and major success and failure. Fortunately, his time there had been marked more with awards of excellence than demerits. They reviewed his scores and recommendations, even shared statements his former squad mates had made about him, always asking him to respond.

Admiral Orlovsky, whom Coda couldn't believe was

overseeing the review, asked specific questions about Coda's first interactions with Moscow: when and where they'd met, how, and in Coda's estimation, why their feud had escalated.

Coda attempted to keep his answers short and succinct, relaying the facts as he remembered them. When it came to the why, he purposely left out all knowledge of Moscow's mother's death. The information had helped Coda understand the true depths of Moscow's hatred and even helped him understand Moscow himself, but it wouldn't do anything to help his case with the board.

The questions about his time in Commander Coleman's squadron were even more tedious. They questioned the speed of the training and the mental and physical strain it put on all the pilots. They compared brain scans, heart rates, and other information taken during his physicals on the *Jamestown* with his previous records from the academy to show his deteriorating psychological state.

The longer the questions about the squadron's training wore on, the more Coda began to get the impression that he and Moscow weren't the only people under review. Commander Coleman didn't flinch or show any outward sign of emotion, but Coda could feel the anxiety emanating from him like heat from a fire. But why would the commander be under review? Accidents happened, and death was no stranger to the pilots. So why the extra scrutiny now?

Because not everyone in the fleet wants the commander to succeed, Coda realized. The idea was tantamount to treason. Commander Coleman's squadron was the ultimate fallback, a redundancy of a redundancy of a redundancy, only to be used if all other methods to counteract the Baranyk disrupter failed. Rooting for the squadron's failure was the equivalent of rooting for the destruction of the human race.

But it was never that simple. The military was the ultimate bureaucracy full of competing desires, agendas, and methodologies that all battled for the same limited budget. On some line of some memo in some stack of papers on some admiral's desk there was a cost breakdown of Commander Coleman's efforts. From the direct costs of transporting, housing, and feeding the pilots to the indirect costs of pulling them from other service, everything had a dollar sign. And even those paled in comparison to the money required to supply, retrofit, and repair a full squadron of aging X-23 Nighthawks.

Surely someone somewhere thought that money could be better spent elsewhere. More scientists researching the Baranyk weapon. More engineers trying to counteract its effects. More manufacturing equipment to rebuild the drones that had been destroyed during battle. It was no wonder the entire squadron had been grounded.

The realization that he wasn't just fighting for his own future but the future of everything they had been working toward woke something inside him. The anger strengthened his resolve, banishing the self-pity that had been plaguing him since he'd woken up in the infirmary. He knew what he was fighting for now, and he wasn't going to go down without giving it everything he had.

His first answers had been short and succinct, offering little additional insight. However, Coda let himself embellish his answers about the squadron. He talked about the growing camaraderie, their unprecedented skill and confidence, and how they would be ready when the fleet called on their aid. Keeping his flattery to a minimum, he praised the commander's instruction, using specific examples of how his one-on-one evaluations had improved their piloting skills and how his reputation meant his students listened to him all the more.

He fell into a groove, his words coming out smoothly and exactly as he intended them. When the conversation shifted abruptly to his father, Coda went blank. He stared at the camera recording the interview as if he had just been bludgeoned in the back of the head and forgotten his name.

"Coda?" Commander Coleman said from behind the device.

"I'm sorry," Coda said. "Could you repeat the question?"

"The captain asked what you know of your father."

"Right," Coda said. "Thank you, sir. My father..." He'd known the question was coming and had followed Tex's advice. He'd even written out his responses beforehand, but in that moment, his mind was as empty as space itself. "I know what most anyone knows, I suppose. The official information is classified, but the general understanding is that he turned on his wingmen, resulting in the loss of his squadron and the subsequent deaths of hundreds more aboard the *Benjamin Franklin*. He was executed for treason and wasn't given a proper military burial. But I doubt that's what you were asking.

"Unlike the rest of the other sixteen billion people that populate the Sol System, I also knew Lieutenant O'Neil as my father. He taught me how to play catch, how to ride a bike, a hoverboard. He..." Coda's vision went blurry. "He wasn't the man I saw on the vids or the man I read about on the web. To me, as much as they're the same person, they're different.

"Lieutenant O'Neil betrayed those he had sworn to protect, but Joseph O'Neil tucked me in at night and read me stories of great heroes. He taught me what it meant to be selfless, how to put others ahead of myself. That man, the man I knew, loved the fleet. He loved flying. I don't know why he did what he did, but I know in my heart that he would have had a damn fine explanation."

Coda blinked. The words had slipped out of his mouth as little more than a stream of consciousness. For those brief moments, he was alone with his memories, pen to paper, writing out a path to his deepest secrets—secrets that even he hadn't acknowledged in a long time.

Commander Coleman watched him for several silent seconds, for some reason, his face growing harder.

Did I do something wrong? Was I too honest?

Coda replayed his words in his head, trying to figure out how they had sounded to his audience. He cursed himself. There was no doubt about it, he had gone too far. The review board wouldn't care about his father teaching him how to throw a baseball, and they wouldn't like hearing Coda defend him.

Part of him wanted to backtrack and attempt to clarify what he had said. But what would he say? And how could he say it without sounding like he wasn't trying to backpedal? The commander moved on to the next question before Coda figured it out.

When the strange interview finally ended, Commander Coleman dismissed Coda, remaining behind to provide his own statements. As Coda left the small room and returned to his barracks, he couldn't tell if he'd helped his case or doomed the military careers of himself and everyone else in the squadron for good.

38

Hangar Deck, SAS Jamestown
  Alpha Centauri System, Proxima B, High Orbit

A DAY LATER, CODA ASSEMBLED WITH THE REST OF THE Forgotten in the hangar bay for Whiskey's funeral. A squadron of Nighthawks surrounded their group, providing them with an element of privacy from the rest of the ship's personnel.

The ceremony itself was conducted in crisp military fashion. Because Whiskey was from the United States, her casket was draped with the stars and stripes of the American flag. An old bugle recording played over the speakers as her casket was loaded into one of the X-23 launch bays. Something about the scene, combined with the aftermath of uncovering his deep-seated emotions during his interview, made it difficult not to compare the proceedings to his father's burial—or lack thereof.

For Lieutenant Joseph O'Neil, there had been no

lamenting music. No tears. No gathered friends to say their final farewells. Not even a casket. He'd just been spaced out an air lock, where the frigid black and lack of pressure ravaged his traitorous body and did the fleet's dirty work for them. The whole thing made him angry. Lieutenant O'Neil might have deserved that, but Coda and his mother hadn't. They had deserved a chance to say goodbye. A chance to find closure.

Commander Coleman said a few words—more talk about how death was too often a pilot's unwelcomed friend —then they gave Lieutenant Autumn "Whiskey" Jones her final salute and watched as her casket was launched from the tube into her final resting place.

Noodle blew out a breath as the proceedings concluded. "What now?"

It was a good question. The squadron was still grounded, and save for the gym and the simulator, there was little else to do.

"I've got just the thing," Squawks said, giving Tex a knowing look. "Follow me."

———

SQUAWKS'S IDEA, IT TURNED OUT, WAS TO GET WELL AND truly drunk. How, exactly, Coda didn't know at first, but Squawks led them to a secluded corner in a seldom-used parts locker where he and Tex, with the aid of a couple handy crewmen, had built a metal contraption that looked like little more than two buckets connected by a copper tube.

"What is that?" Coda asked, thoroughly confused.

"A still."

"A what?"

"I thought your old man was in the military?" Squawks said. "It's a still, Coda. You know, to make alcohol?"

"Oh," Coda said, finally understanding what he was looking at. "What kind?"

"The kind that'll get us messed up."

"And hopefully not make us go blind," Tex added.

"Blind?" Noodle asked, suddenly looking nervous.

"Yeah," Tex said. "Bad alcohol can make you go blind."

"Seriously?"

Tex erupted into laughter, his deep voice booming off the walls.

"Quiet, you dumb hick," Squawks said. "If we get caught with this, going blind will be the last thing we have to worry about." He grabbed the container that the metal hose emptied into and held it out to Coda, who reluctantly took it.

The container was nearly three-quarters full with a brown liquid. Coda sniffed the bottle's contents and instantly regretted it. Pulling his head away in disgust, he held the container as far away as possible. "It smells like engine solvent."

"That's how you know it's the good stuff," Squawks said, taking the cup back. He took a sniff of it himself and smiled. "Oh yeah, definitely the good stuff." He handed the cup to Tex. "You did most of the work. You do the honors."

Tex held the cup to his nose and took in a long, slow breath before taking a sip. He immediately started coughing. It was a deep, raspy sound, as if his lungs were full of smoke, but even before he was finished, he was smiling. "Not bad," he said between coughs then handed the cup to Noodle.

The slender pilot looked at the cup's contents as if it

were poison. "If this makes me go blind, I'm going to kick your ass."

"You'll have to find it first," Squawks said.

Noodle shrugged at Coda then took a sip. Like Tex, he immediately began coughing, his face turning red. But also like Tex, he smiled, his eyes glassy. "This is terrible." But that didn't stop him from taking another, bigger sip before passing the cup to Coda.

"I'm going to regret this, aren't I?" Coda asked.

"You know what the commander says," Squawks said. "If you aren't making mistakes, you aren't trying new things. Well, try that."

Coda sighed and brought the cup to his lips. The alcohol, whatever it was, may have smelled like engine solvent, but it tasted like pure rubbing alcohol, and it burned like liquid fire. In an instant, his entire midsection was warm, and his face felt flushed.

"There you go," Squawks said like a proud parent. He took the cup from Coda then gave each of the four pilots a smaller cup and filled them with the alcohol. "All right. Let's do this."

They settled into a small circle, sitting on various boxes and pieces of equipment as if sitting around a campfire.

Tex held his cup high. "To Whiskey."

"To Whiskey," they repeated then took a sip in salute.

Coda winced as the fluid burned its way down his throat. "It's weird," he said. "I've been so focused on making the squadron, I barely knew her."

"None of us one did," Noodle said.

"That's what I'm talking about," Coda said. "You guys were right when you said I was clueless. Outside of you three and Moscow, I barely know anyone. Hell, I barely know anything about you guys." He turned to Tex. "Like, I know you were in the Nighthawk program before it was discontinued, but that's it. I don't even know where you're from."

"His call sign is 'Tex,' dumbass," Squawks said sarcastically. "Where do you think he's from?"

"I'm from Georgia," Tex said, throwing an amused look in Squawks's direction. "But you dumb Yankees can't tell one southerner from another."

Everyone laughed.

"Other than that, there's not much to know."

"There's always more to know," Coda said. "You lived there your whole life?"

"Yeah," Tex said. "Family's owned a cotton farm for eight generations. My brother's running it now."

"Didn't want to go into the family business?" Noodle asked.

"No." Tex shook his head. "When you ain't ever been more than a hundred miles away from home your whole life, sometimes all you want to do is get as far away as possible. And you can't get no farther away than space, you know?"

Coda found himself nodding. He knew all too well what it meant to get away, but the one thing he wanted to run away from was the one thing he could never escape. "You been back since you left?"

"Naw," Tex said. "They wouldn't want me back, anyway. I didn't leave on the best terms."

"Me, neither," Noodle said. He stared into his cup as if it held the secrets of life. "Parents both went to Stanford. Dad's in Advanced Robotics. Oversees the plant that builds the processors for the Hornets. Mom's in Communications. They both expected me to follow in their footsteps, go to the family school and all that. But I grew up around the drones, saw the early models, and watched as they became what they are today. When it came down to it, I didn't want to build them. I wanted to *fly* one. So I joined the academy."

"How'd they take it?" Coda asked, knowing how his own mother had taken his decision to enlist.

"Dad blew a gasket, and Mom..." Noodle winced. "Well, I've never seen anyone cry so much." He took a deep pull. Coda couldn't tell if Noodle's glassy eyes were from the drink, the memory, or both. "I get it," Noodle continued. "I'm their only kid. Their whole life. And I just up and abandoned them."

"A man needs to find his own way," Tex said.

Noodle's eyes found Tex, and he nodded. The two couldn't have come from more different backgrounds, and yet in that moment, they were the same.

"So why join the Forgotten?" Coda asked. "If flying Hornets was your dream, then why are you here?"

Noodle grinned. "Because as cool as the Hornets were, the Nighthawks are even cooler. Besides, as Squawks likes to say, chicks dig pilots."

"Damn right," Squawks said.

Everyone laughed. Coda found that his smile lingered. He couldn't remember the last time he'd sat around with friends, with nothing to do except enjoy each other's company. It had probably been his last day at the academy, before his fight with Moscow, before his entire world had been upended. He'd forgotten how *good* it felt.

Coda's story was well known to everyone, his friends most of all, so it didn't come as any surprise when their eyes passed over him, falling on Squawks. What did surprise him was how much it stung. His friends might know about his father and how driven Coda was to fix his mistakes, but they knew little about the person he was. Before he'd been Coda, he'd been Callan O'Neil, with his own hopes and dreams, his own hobbies and loves. And some day after his service, he would become that man again. It hurt that his friends didn't want to know who that person was.

Squawks, it seemed, wasn't enthused, either. He stared back at Noodle and Tex as if irritated that he was expected to share next. "Are we here to talk or to drink?"

"Both," Noodle said. "Come on."

"It's not a happy story," Squawks said.

"Has anyone's been?" Noodle pressed.

"Well…" Squawks paused, winced, and shifted uncomfortably. "While all of you were disappointing your families, I was trying to find out who I was. I grew up in the system. Don't know who my mom or dad are. They could be drug dealers or Stanford grads—I don't know. Maybe I'll never know, but I can guess. You guys wanted to fly? You wanted to wipe the shit off your family name? That's great. I was just looking for some clothes, three squares, and a place I didn't need to move out of every six months."

A heavy silence fell over the group. Coda looked from Squawks to Noodle then to Tex. Nobody said anything.

"I don't know what to say, Squawks," Coda said, breaking the silence. "None of us knew."

"It's not something I usually talk about." Squawks looked toward Tex. "Every man needs to find his own way, right? Well, every man has his own secrets too."

"I wish I was entitled to my own secrets," Coda said. "I can't take a dump without it being compared to my father."

He'd meant it as a joke, but he didn't get more than a slight chuckle.

"This is going to sound sappy, or maybe this stuff's stronger than I thought it was," Noodle said, twirling the remaining alcohol in his cup. "But I think you found more than some clothes, three squares, and a roof, Squawks."

"Yeah?"

"Yeah. You found us, man."

"Lucky me," Squawks grinned. "A hick, a nerd, and a traitor's son. The three worst friends anyone could ask for."

"Says a guy who talks more in his sleep than most do awake," Noodle said. "We didn't do much better."

"Ha! No, you didn't." Squawks said. Then again, more introspect. "No, you didn't."

A gentle quiet permeated the group. In the wake of their squad mate's death, they had found a way to grow closer, to become better friends. Three of them had shared something deeply personal about themselves. Coda couldn't believe it, but he had the strong urge to participate. His mind drifted back to the first time they came together as a group, the first time they had shared something else about themselves.

Coda turned to Squawks. "You once asked me where my callsign came from." He kept his voice soft, not wanting to violate the peace. "The truth is, it's something I came up with."

"What's it mean?" Squawks asked.

"A coda is something that comes at the end of a play or a dance," Coda said. "Like the final moment when the actors come back on stage to be recognized for their performance. To me it's the end of the whole story with my family... to my father. And when I'm done it'll reshape the way the world looks at us."

Coda took a sip, too afraid to make eye contact with any of his friends. Said out loud, it sounded ridiculous. Somewhere between arrogant and self-righteous.

"The call sign's a constant reminder of why I'm here,

what I'm fighting for," Coda continued. "That's the idea anyway."

"You fly with the weight of the world on your shoulders," Squawks said.

"Yeah." It really felt like it sometimes.

"No wonder you're so slow," Squawks deadpanned. "You're overloading your thrusters every time you go out."

"I was going to say 'no wonder he's so short,'" Noodle added, "but he's taller than I am so that wouldn't have made sense."

"Or so frumpy all the time," Tex added.

The three of them roared with laughter. Coda couldn't believe it. He had shared something about himself that he hadn't shared with anyone, not even Buster, and they were *laughing* at him. Anger growing, he shot a look at Squawks... and saw something in his expression that calmed his frayed emotions.

"You're such an asshole," Coda said.

"That's what you like about me," Squawks said.

Coda shook his head, eyeing the three of them. "You really are the three worst friends anyone could ask for."

"Hell yeah." Noodle raised his cup, laughing. "To the three worst friends anyone could ask for."

Tex followed his lead. "To the three worst friends anyone could ask for."

Coda and Squawks shared a look, then did the same. "To the three worst friends anyone could ask for."

Taking a swig, Coda's eyes fell on the group, and he was struck with an overwhelming sense of camaraderie. It was even stronger than what he'd felt at the academy. He wanted to graduate with these men. Fly with them. Fight with them. More than anything in his entire life, he wanted to remain part of the Forgotten. But he also knew that the decision wasn't up to him. In that, he was completely and utterly powerless.

"Guys?"

"Yeah, Squawks?" Noodle said.

"Do I really talk that much in my sleep?"

Laughing, Coda banished thoughts of the squadron from his mind. For tonight at least, he was with friends.

39

Hangar Deck, SAS Jamestown
   Alpha Centauri System, Proxima B, High Orbit

COMMANDER CHADWICK COLEMAN TRACED A FINGER ALONG the wrecked fuselage of Coda's Nighthawk. Unlike Moscow's fighter, which had lost a wing, Coda's was mostly intact. The main damage was to the navigational thrusters along its nose and the puncture in the fuselage's belly. Had the X-23 still relied on combustible fuel instead of the electromagnetic propulsion created by the Shaw Drive, the accident would certainly have claimed another life. Unfortunately, one death had been enough to ground the entire squadron for over a week.

Coleman sighed, rounding the back of the fighter and starting back toward its nose. Their training was falling farther and farther behind schedule, something he couldn't afford. The timelines had already been tight. Beyond tight. They'd been downright impossible. And in all reality, it was remarkable how far his pilots had come. Still, for the first time since accepting the post, he felt that the squadron had no chance of success.

If I just had another eight weeks, we could have built something special. Something to be honored. Something to be feared.

But no, that wasn't the whole story. He'd been challenged with more than just compressed timelines. Coda and Moscow had been able to set aside their differences or if he hadn't uncovered the root cause of their rivalry before inviting both to join the squadron. He'd made so many mistakes. So many *unnecessary* mistakes.

What's done is done. There's nothing you can do about that now.

The real question keeping him up at night was whether or not he would get a chance to correct those mistakes. Whether his squadron would ever get a chance to fly. To fight. To prove to the world that their time—and Whiskey's sacrifice—had been worth it.

Coleman's tablet vibrated, and for a moment, he wondered if some sardonic god had heard him and granted his wish.

Pulling the device from his pocket, Coleman froze. The edges of the normally transparent tablet were outlined in red, marking the message as urgent. Even more concerning, the message was from Captain Baez, commander of the *Jamestown*, not someone at Sol Command. The emergency was local, maybe even aboard the ship. Had one of his pilots gotten into trouble?

Coleman opened the message to find a simple note requesting his immediate presence in Captain Baez's quarters. Coleman sent his reply, saying he was on his way, and started across the hangar. He was barely halfway across when his tablet vibrated again. Thinking it was the Captain's reply, Coleman pulled the tablet back out of his pocket.

His step faltered.

The message was from Admiral Orlovsky and was coded *Priority One*. Like the first, the second message was text-based, allowing Coleman to read it where he stood without fear of a security breach, and what he read sent shivers down his spine. Commander Coleman broke into a run. His wish had been heard and granted.

40

Barracks, SAS Jamestown
  Alpha Centauri System, Proxima B, High Orbit

CLAXONS BLARED.

Coda's eyes snapped open. Flashing red lights bathed the barracks in a bloody light, intensifying the alarm as fifty pilots woke to the same scene. He was out of his bunk in a flash. His bare feet touched the cold floor, the sensation bringing with it a level of alertness that banished any lingering fatigue.

Tex rolled out of the upper bunk, colliding with Coda. The larger man was denser than Coda had expected, the collision rattling his teeth.

"Sorry," Tex muttered, his drawl more pronounced in his sleepiness.

"You're fine." Dressed in only his underwear, Coda pulled out a pair of standard issue flight pants and began pulling them on. "What do you think is going on?"

Before Tex could answer, the door to the barracks

opened, and Commander Coleman, already dressed in a full flight suit, stopped in the doorway. "I need you in the ready room in two minutes. This is not a drill."

Commander Coleman disappeared, no doubt going to the second barracks. Coda's eyes moved from the doorway to Tex. The other pilot's wide-eyed expression mirrored Coda's. Without another word, Coda pulled a tank top over his head, threw on his socks and boots, and was out the barracks door in less than a minute.

Commander Coleman was already in the ready room by the time Coda arrived. He watched with a grim expression as the pilots filed in and took their seats. Coda grabbed a seat in the second row. Noodle, Tex, and Squawks found seats beside him. Two minutes after the claxons had sounded, Commander Coleman stepped up to the podium.

"At oh one hundred this morning," he began, "the SAS *Jamestown* received an emergency alert from Sol Command. The forward mining operation of Toavis is under heavy Baranyk bombardment. Our fleet, which arrived minutes after the attack began, has been rendered useless by the Baranyk Disrupter, and we have been called in to issue aid."

Excited whispers filled the room as Coda exchanged wide-eyed looks with his friends.

"We picked the wrong night to drink ourselves into a stupor," Squawks said quietly.

Coda chuckled then realized he didn't feel as bad as he'd expected to. Either the alcohol from Squawks's still was some magical concoction that left its drinkers without a hangover, or the additives in their food helped his body metabolize the alcohol quicker than normal.

"This is the real thing," Commander Coleman continued. "This is what we've been training for. Toavis is critical to the fleet's ability to maintain its forward operating bases, and we have over one hundred thousand people on the ground. I don't need to tell you how important it is. I only need to tell you to trust your training. Trust your fellow pilots. Do that, and I have no doubt you'll be victorious."

Commander Coleman hit a button on his tablet, dimming the lights and calling up the display at the front of the room. A moment later, the display showed an updated flight roster of thirty-six pilots.

"We're being called in before your training could be completed, so the final cuts to the squadron never occurred," Commander Coleman said. "For this mission, we will be going with the following flight roster. The first twenty-three pilots here will make up Alpha Squadron." He clicked another button, and a thin red line separated the pilots of Alpha Squadron from the rest. "The next twelve will be standby, loaded up and ready to launch in our extra Nighthawks. The rest of you, stay alert and be ready for additional orders. Any questions?"

Coda had a thousand questions but one in particular. His name wasn't included in either list... neither was Moscow's. He found the other pilot seated in the row in front of him, the same silent question on his lips. Like Coda, though, he seemed to have decided to hold his tongue. This sort of thing was better to talk to the commander about directly.

"Twenty-three pilots, sir?" someone behind Coda asked. "A squadron has twenty-four."

"I'll be leading Alpha Squadron," Commander Coleman said.

"Hell yeah, sir."

"All right," Commander Coleman said. "Your orders have been sent to your tablets. I'll meet you in the hangar once we've arrived. Good luck, godspeed, and let's kill some Baranyk."

Fifty pilots rose as one. Alpha Squadron and the standby pilots made for the adjoining locker room, while the rest waited behind for what would become of them. Though they were part of the first wave, Coda's friends lingered, watching Coda awkwardly and offering sympathetic looks.

"You're the best of us," Noodle said. "You should be out there too."

Coda shrugged, attempting to ignore the terrible feeling of disappointment eating him alive. "Don't worry about me. Just take care of each other and kill some Baranyk for me."

"Oh, we're definitely going to do that," Squawks said, but even his boast fell flat.

With a tight smile, Noodle nodded then turned and strode down the stairs, making for the locker room. Tex and Squawks followed after offering their own disappointed expressions. Coda watched them go, wondering if he should have said something more. They were going to battle, going to war, and there were no guarantees they would come back.

He didn't call out, but he also made sure to watch until they disappeared from view. *Stay safe, guys.*

As soon as they had entered the locker room, Coda dashed down the stairs. He had his own business to attend to. If the commander wasn't following his pilots into the locker room, there was only one place he was going: the *Jamestown* CIC.

Sprinting through the corridors, Coda caught up to the commander before he made it to the bowels of the ship where the commander center was located.

"Sir!" Coda closed the distance between them. "Sir, please."

Commander Coleman stopped and turned to face Coda. "What is it, Coda?"

"It's just that my name wasn't included on the active roster, sir."

"You and Lieutenant Krylov are part of an active investigation, Coda. Why would you expect otherwise?"

"I just thought..."

"No, Coda. We don't have time for this. You and Lieutenant Krylov were left off the flight roster intentionally, and unless some act of God convinces me to change my mind and break all military regulation, it will stay that way. Now if you'll excuse me, I've got a battle to plan."

Commander Coleman strode away, rounding another corner and leaving Coda behind. Coda waited there, lost and, for the first time in a long time, unsure of what to do. He'd had his chance, and he had ruined it. He was a failure. A disgrace. He was just like his father.

41

CIC, SAS Jamestown
  Alpha Centauri System, Proxima B, High Orbit

THE CIC BUZZED WITH ACTIVITY AS COMMANDER COLEMAN strode in. Laid out in a rough circular shape, the CIC was made up of two levels: an outer ring and the pit, which was taken up almost entirely by a three-dimensional hologram that displayed a frozen image of battle. Coleman didn't immediately recognize the image, but he assumed it had been taken from Toavis.

Captain Baez stood in the pit, studying the image. His XO, Commander Zhang, was at his side, receiving a steady flow of information that would help them prepare the ship for the upcoming battle.

"Docking into Jumpgate Centauri-3, sir," a voice said as Commander Coleman made for the pit. "Jump sequence initiating. Jump in two minutes."

"Understood," Captain Baez said, glancing from the

image to one of the officers on the upper ring. The gesture brought his eyes to Coleman. He nodded. "Commander."

"Sir," Coleman said. "The squadron has their orders. They're ready when you are."

"Good," Captain Baez said. "We're going to need them." His attention returned to the battle image. "Another drone jumped in while you briefed them. The battle isn't going well."

Coleman grimaced then studied the image closer. Toavis was a green planet, so rich in color that it almost looked like a gas giant, but underneath a thick atmosphere was a rocky surface rich in nickel, lithium, and other precious metals vital to the Terran manufacturing operations. Stretched out in front of it, however, were six Baranyk carriers.

Like all Baranyk ships, they had an organic appearance, as if they had been born instead of built. The Sol Fleet had recovered more than one ship during the war and had found that the appearance wasn't too far from reality. While not alive as some of the conspiracy theorists on Earth and Mars believed, the ships weren't manufactured in the same way the human ships were either. There were no separate panels fastened together, no rivets, bolts, or rebar. But the results were just as lethal.

The orange, red, and yellowed claw-shaped Baranyk ships were actively engaged with the human vessels, and even outnumbering the Baranyk fleet by two ships, the humans were clearly overmatched. Humanity, it seemed, had come to rely too heavily on the drone attack and had truly forgotten about how deadly the early days of the Baranyk War had been.

"How old is this?" Coleman asked.

"We received the message less than ten minutes ago," Captain Baez said. "But the image itself is over an hour old."

Coleman cursed. An hour old? There was no telling how much damage had been done since the image was taken.

"Recent intel suggests," Captain Baez said, as if reading his mind, "that one of the Baranyk ships has broken away from the larger force and has begun assaulting the planet. The *Virginia* has been called in as well, which should sway the odds back into our favor."

The *Virginia*. Admiral Orlovsky's personal ship was one of the most advanced ships in the entire fleet. If it had been called in, the situation was even direr than Coleman had first thought.

"Docking procedure complete, sir," the same voice from before said. "Initiating jump sequence on your command."

Captain Baez cast Commanders Coleman and Zhang a weary look. "Let's see what we've got." Then to the officer above, he said, "Jump."

"Yes, sir. Initiating jump sequence in five, four, three..."

Coleman studied the map, wondering what they were about to step into, as the odd feeling that always accompanied a jump overcame him. The world seemed to stretch in front of him, his own sense of self and consciousness stretching with it. Gripping the padded rail around the pit, Commander Coleman steadied his breathing, waiting for the sensation to end. When it did, the CIC came alive with fresh activity.

"Arrived at Toavis, sir. Data streaming in now."

The holographic image at the center of the pit had gone dark but was slowly updating as the information, moving at the speed of light from the battle, streamed in. It wasn't a smooth process, however. The images of the ships that had been clear and easily recognizable before had become grainy, as if they had been taken with a low-resolution camera then blown up to a larger size. It was more than enough, though, to see that even the arrival of the famed *Virginia* hadn't been enough to turn the tide of the battle.

All six of the Baranyk carriers still remained, but of the original human ships, only six still offered resistance. The other two were ruined wrecks, slowly descending into Toavis's gravity well. Joining them were hundreds of the inoperable human drones. They were still, lifeless, almost like a school of dead fish floating listlessly on the surface of the ocean. As Captain Baez had indicated, one of the Baranyk ships had begun assaulting the planet's surface without opposition.

"Get to your fighter," Captain Baez said, "and have your pilots provide support to the remaining battle cruisers. Without their combined firepower, we don't stand a chance."

42

Cockpit, Nighthawk
Arradin System, Toavis

COMMANDER COLEMAN CLOSED THE HATCH AND SETTLED INTO the cockpit of his Nighthawk. Going through his preflight routine, he buckled and unbuckled his harness three times then yanked on the straps another three times after it had clicked into place. Satisfied he was strapped in properly, he flipped on the switch to the Shaw Drive thrusters.

To some outside the pilot brotherhood, the preflight routine might look a little obsessive-compulsive, and maybe it was, but Coleman was convinced it kept him alive and one couldn't argue with results.

The final step to his preflight routine was pulling the creased and faded picture from the inside of his G-suit. He hadn't flown in battle since losing his wife and daughter, since his wife had given him the ultimatum: his Nighthawk or them. And Coleman, not knowing that the X-23 program was about to be discontinued, had picked his fighter.

Well, that was only half true. He hadn't necessarily picked his fighter; he just hadn't picked her. Any person who forced another to pick between two things they loved wasn't a person he wanted to spend his life with. It was Aniyah, though, who had suffered the true tragedy. Growing up without her father couldn't have been easy, and had he known his ex-wife would win sole custody of their child then refuse to let him see her, he might have chosen differently.

Stroking the side of his daughter's young face with his thumb, Coleman apologized, uttered a quiet prayer, then set the picture on the instrument panel where it would be on the edges of his vision, just as his family would forever be on the edges of his mind. One day, he would see them again. One day, he would hug his daughter tightly enough to make up for the countless hugs they'd missed over the years. But first, Commander Coleman needed to win the battle.

Being the last to arrive, Coleman was the last pilot loaded into the launch tube. His pilots were antsy, chattering over the comm.

"All right, quiet down," Commander Coleman said. "Launching in one minute. Sound off. Hawk One is a go."

"Hawk Two is a go."

"Hawk Three is a go."

One by one, they sounded off, confirming there were no malfunctions and that they were green to go. When the final confirmation came in, they had twenty seconds to launch.

"Remember," Commander Coleman said, "keep it tight. Fly together. And trust your training."

"We'll do you proud, sir," Squawks said.

"Good to hear it, Squawks. It's my pleasure to fly with each and every one of you. Now settle in. Here we go."

Coleman was thrown back in his seat as his fighter raced

through the launch tube. The pulley screamed, the seat of the Nighthawk vibrated, then... Commander Coleman was hurled into the silent black. The other twenty-three Nighthawks were shot out of the bow in less than four seconds.

"Form up," Commander Coleman ordered. "Delta formations."

Behind him, the rest of the squadron fell into four separate V-shaped formations made up of six fighters apiece. He plotted a course for the nearest human vessel, the SAS *Washington*, which was little more than a black dot against the green of the planet behind it.

"Looks like we've been spotted, sir. I've got five Baranyk fighters closing."

Commander Coleman glanced at his HUD, seeing the red indicators marking the incoming Baranyk fighters. Only five? Against a number five times that?

They think we're drones.

"*Jamestown* actual, this is Commander Coleman. Are you reading the signal of the Baranyk Disrupter?"

"Affirmative, Commander," Captain Baez said. "It appears as if the Baranyk are attempting to use it against you."

"Well, it's good to know it doesn't work on us." Truth be told, Coleman had harbored a nagging concern before their training had ever begun that the Baranyk weapon would fry the Nighthawk computers just as it did the Hornets. "Can you tell where it's coming from?"

"There's a lot of distortion," Captain Baez said. "We're working on it."

"Acknowledged. We have other fish to fry, but if you locate the source of that signal, you let me know."

"Of course, Commander."

"Thank you, sir." Coleman closed the channel then reopened the one with his pilots. "Do not engage the incoming fighters. I repeat, do not engage. Stay on me. Three-quarter thrust."

Punching the throttle, he swerved, plotting a new course that would keep them wide of the incoming fighters. The rest of his squadron followed.

"They're swinging around!" came a panicked voice on the radio. "They're moving onto our six."

They're scared, Commander Coleman realized. *Nervous and not thinking straight.* "They're not in firing range," he said calmly. "Shooting them down might have alerted the enemy that their weapon doesn't work on us. We need to provide support to our ships *before* that happens. Understood?"

"Understood, sir."

"Good, because it looks like we've piqued more interest."

More of the enemy fighters attacking the *Washington* broke off their assault, moving into an attack vector to meet the Forgotten head on. They moved as a single unit, like a flock of birds or school of fish. Early on, Sol Intelligence had thought the Baranyk were a hive mind, not unlike aliens in the popular science fiction novels of the twentieth century, but that wasn't the case at all. Like their human counterparts, the Baranyk were capable of individual thought.

"Prepare to break formation and fire on my mark." Commander Coleman watched as the enemy fighters closed the distance. "Break!"

The human fighters broke formation, twelve pairs shooting off in twelve different directions. Commander Coleman's Nighthawk came alive, vibrating as he opened fire. Two incoming Baranyk fighters broke apart as he zipped through the threshold and into the thick of the battle. It was pure chaos, with ships everywhere, flying at speeds human evolution hadn't yet caught up with.

Alternating between manual guns and computer-aided targeting, Coleman shot down four Baranyk fighters in as many seconds then brought his Nighthawk parallel with the *Washington*, though at a safe distance from its point-defense cannons. Not that there was a true "safe distance," of course, but there were perhaps a hundred Baranyk fighters between him and the *Washington*, and that, at least, gave him the illusion of cover.

The maneuver kept him in prime firing position. He opened fire again. There were more flashes of light as Baranyk mass became space dust. Missiles streaked in from other vectors as more of his pilots came to the *Washington*'s aid.

With the exception of a few enemy fighters, the Baranyk focused all of their effort on the larger capital ship. Seeing the larger vessel up close, Commander Coleman understood why. Gaping holes littered its hull, spewing fire along its length, and fewer than half of its point-defense cannons still appeared operable. The ship was a wounded bird, and the enemy knew it.

"All fighters," Commander Coleman said, "focus on the main contingent. The *Washington* doesn't have long."

Coleman squeezed off several more shots, eliminating three more fighters as the rest of his squadron arrived. Two flights, one beginning at the *Washington*'s bow, the other at the stern, sliced through the enemy like a propeller through water. They mowed down more than half of the enemy's force in a single pass.

The remaining Baranyk fighters broke into two flights of their own as if finally taking the human force seriously. But it was already too late. The next wave of human pilots arrived, flanking them from the *Washington* port side and using it as a backstop. The Forgotten had the remaining Baranyk fighters in a vise, and within moments, they were no more.

Bringing his fighter around, Coleman surveyed the battle. The *Washington* was still engaged with the Baranyk carrier, each ship throwing volley after volley of torpedoes and medium-range artillery at their enemy. In the distance and partially hidden by the curvature of Toavis, the *Virginia*, *Oregon*, and other three human battle cruisers were involved in a similar slugfest with all but one of the remaining Baranyk carriers. The last one was somewhere below the planet's thick atmosphere.

Come on, Baez. Get the Jamestown *into the battle. We won't have numbers for long.*

The human squadron had provided much-needed support and had bought the *Washington* some extra time, but the battle was far from over. And now the enemy knew the human fleet had an advantage of its own. But as severely outnumbered as the human pilots were, would the advantage be enough?

"All fighters form up and prepare for an attack run."

They hadn't gotten to the point in their training that would have focused on bombing runs. As a result, Coleman hadn't ordered the Nighthawks equipped with the heavier artillery used to assault the Baranyk carriers. They'd have to do the job with missiles... and a little bit of luck.

"Two missiles apiece. The *Washington* has done a number on her. We don't need to exhaust our reserves."

Coleman triple-checked that his weapons switch was selected to missiles, then with his pilots forming up behind him, he angled his Nighthawk on a flight path that would have them streak past the center of the enemy carrier in a high-speed pass. The Baranyk carrier, perhaps sensing the danger, shifted focus from the *Washington* to the Forgotten. Point-defense cannons lit up their flight path.

"Evasive maneuvers!" Coleman shouted, throwing his fighter starboard to avoid a stream of incoming projectiles. "And fire!"

Trails of white vapor streaked from the quick-moving fighters toward the massive ship, then a moment later, more than twenty explosions ravaged its hull. Not three seconds after the last explosion lit the void, white-hot fire ballooned out of the center of the Baranyk vessel, splitting it in two and throwing the two ends of the ship in opposite directions. Cheers sounded over the comm as the pilots celebrated their victory.

"Well done," Coleman said. "Prepare for delta formations. We're not done yet. There's still five more of these bastards to go."

43

Ready Room, SAS Jamestown
Arradin System, Toavis

CODA SAT ALONE IN THE READY ROOM, BATHING IN THE battle's radio chatter. He hadn't found a way to tap into the holographic display that they had in the CIC, but he had found a way to pipe into the radio frequencies and play it across the ready room's speakers. It wasn't the same as being in the battle. It wasn't even the same as watching it, but it was the best he had been able to come up with.

He listened with bated breath, often having to remind himself to breathe at all. There had been some panicked chatter at the beginning of the battle then mostly silence as the pilots focused on the task at hand. Now, though, it was beginning again.

"*Jamestown* actual, this is Commander Coleman. Were you able to identify the source of the Baranyk signal?"

"We have, Commander," Captain Baez said. "Sending you the information now. What do you have in mind?"

"With their fighters, they've still got us outnumbered out here," Commander Coleman said. "If we can eliminate the weapon, we eliminate the signal. Then we get full use of our drones and the odds swing back into our favor."

"As long as one of their other ships isn't equipped with the weapon," Captain Baez said.

"Yes," Commander Coleman said. "As long as none of the others are equipped with the weapon."

Coda could almost hear the two men thinking. How much would it cost them to assault one of the Baranyk carriers? Was it worth the risk?

"Make it happen, Commander. The *Washington* and *Jamestown* will provide cover."

"Copy that, sir," Commander Coleman said. "Form up. Our job is to distract the enemy and provide aid for the *Oregon* until the *Jamestown* and *Washington* can arrive. Our target is *this* Baranyk carrier." He must have identified the carrier in question and sent it directly to their onboard computers. "According to the *Jamestown*, this is the ship with the weapon that renders our drones inoperable. We destroy it, and we turn this battle in our favor. Any questions?"

There weren't any.

"All right. Let's do this."

Coda leaned forward in his seat. Something told him that the next battle wouldn't go as smoothly as the last. From the sound of things, the Baranyk hadn't thought the new human fighters were much of a threat, but they wouldn't make that mistake a second time.

Come on, guys. You can do this.

So focused on the sounds of the battle, Coda almost didn't hear the door to the ready room slide open. Moscow stepped inside then, spotting Coda, froze. He clearly hadn't expected company.

"Here they come," Commander Coleman said over the speakers. "Forty contacts, positive-Z six degrees, one hundred thousand meters and closing. Break in three, two, one. Break!"

Moscow's eyes slid from Coda's to the walls of the ready room, no doubt looking for the speakers, then still refusing to look in Coda's direction, he made his way across the ready room and took a seat on a far chair.

Screams and panicked voices filled the room.

"They're everywhere!"

"There's too many of them!"

"I lost sight of Hawk Twelve!"

"He's on my six! Bear, you see them?"

"Where's my wingman? Where's Hawk Four?"

"Hard left! Hard left! Bring it around. I've got them."

"I can't shake them!"

"Break right and two degrees negative-Z. Now!"

"Mayday! Mayday! Hawk Six is down. I repeat, Hawk Six is down."

Coda tried to remember who Hawk Six was. Dot? Burn? Baldy? And who were Hawks Twelve and Four? He hadn't studied the flight roster closely enough to remember. He listened, half hoping to hear one of his friends over the radio. That would mean they were in trouble, but it would also mean they were alive.

"Damn it!"

"Keep it level. That's it. Two sec—"

"Ahhh!"

"Hawk Fourteen is down."

Coda flinched with every confirmation of another human death. They were getting cut to shreds out there.

"I'm hit! I'm hit!"

"*Jamestown* actual," Commander Coleman bellowed, "where the hell are you?"

"Sixty seconds, Commander."

"You're going to have to do better than that." Commander Coleman's voice was more concerned than Coda had ever heard it. "We don't have sixty seconds."

"Negative, Commander. If we increase thrust any more, we won't be able to slow down in time."

"Then jump!"

Silence.

"What are they waiting for?" Moscow asked, speaking for the first time. He was looking in Coda's direction, his eyes wide.

"Probably seeing if it's doable," Coda said.

"Of course it's doable," Moscow said. "The Shaw Drive can't make galactic jumps, but intersolar jumps are... bah, you already know all that."

"The *Jamestown* is a defensive ship around a quiet mining colony," Coda said. "Captain Baez probably hasn't ever seen real action, let alone made a quantum jump mid battle. And you and I know how difficult those are to plot. One tiny mistake, and they'll jump into the planet's core."

"Doesn't matter," Moscow said. "Captain Baez needs to do something. We're getting destroyed out there."

Coda couldn't argue with that. If the battle was even half as bad as it sounded, the squadron couldn't hold out much longer.

"Commander, *Jamestown* actual. Jump coordinates sent to your computer. Avoid the area at all costs."

"Copy that," Commander Coleman said. "All pilots fall back. The *Jamestown* is jumping in. Let's see if we can draw a few of these fighters away from the rest in the meantime."

"He's dividing their forces," Moscow said.

Coda nodded.

"We should be out there," Moscow added. "Not locked in here."

They weren't technically locked in the ready room, but Coda knew what Moscow was getting at. "Yeah, well, we sure did a damn good job of messing that up."

"Yeah..." Moscow's voice was tinged with regret. "You think we'll ever fly again?"

Coda blew out a long breath. "No idea." He toyed with the idea of telling Moscow of his exchange with Commander Coleman in the corridor but decided it wouldn't make either of them feel any better. "Thanks for putting in a good word, by the way. You know, during the review."

The last step in the investigation had been for Coda to review all statements and offer a counter or clarification statement of his own. In doing so, he'd been privy to all statements made about him and had been surprised to see that Moscow had come to his defense, going so far as to say that he believed the squadron was better off, and its pilots safer, with Coda in it.

Moscow shrugged. "It's true."

"Well, I still apprecia—"

The world stretched in front of Coda. The *Jamestown* initiated its jump. Coda held his breath, wondering if it would be his last, then let it out as the world snapped back to normal, the jump completed.

"All pilots," Commander Coleman's voice boomed over the radio, "reverse course and engage. Use the *Jamestown* to your advantage. Smash them like a bug under your foot."

Coda tried to picture the battle outside, only dimly aware that he and Moscow were now a part of it. The *Jamestown* would have likely arrived parallel to the Baranyk carrier, with the *Oregon* flanking it from the other side. The distant rumble of cannon fire vibrated through the floor of the ready room as the *Jamestown* opened its main batteries. With it, the radio chatter changed pitch again, becoming more encouraging.

"Here we go!"

"Nice shot!"

"Take it! Take it!"

"Bingo!"

The chatter brought a smile to his face. Even tucked away in the relative safety of the *Jamestown*, Coda felt as though he were playing a role in their success. Those were his wingmen out there. His friends. He rubbed his hands together as if washing them, his eyes drifting back to Moscow.

"For what it's worth, I feel the same way. You're a damn good pilot, Moscow. And if I'm allowed back into the squadron, I want you there with me."

"Thanks, Coda." It was the first time Coda could remember Moscow calling him by his call sign instead of his last name. "I never said that, you know, after the accident. I never said thank you."

It was Coda's turn to shrug, though in truth, he didn't want the conversation to end. For the first time he thought he and Moscow were really getting somewhere. "You didn't have to. I didn't save you for any other reason than because I'd want someone to do it for me. Golden rule and all that crap, you know?"

Moscow grinned. It was a small thing but further proof that the ice was thawing between them. "Either way, I was an ass. You tried to talk to me, tried to be the better man, and well, I didn't help things."

"I just wanted to keep flying," Coda said with a knowing grin.

Ha! Well, I should have followed your example. Instead, I let my emotions get the best of me. If I had, we'd be out there right now. You're not a bad guy, Coda. You're not your... You're not your father. Whatever happens, I want you to know that."

Coda fought back a strange swell of emotion, biting the inside of his cheeks to distract him from the lump in his chest. "I appreciate that," he said softly. "You have no idea how much I appreciate that."

Moscow made a satisfied face and nodded.

"You know," Coda said, "when this is all over, we need to grab a drink. Clear the air. Completely. With us on the same side, nothing stands a chance."

"Hell yeah," Moscow said. "There's only one problem: there's no alcohol on board."

"That's where you're wrong."

"Yeah?"

"Yeah."

"Screw it, then," Moscow said. "It's a deal."

44

Cockpit, Nighthawk
  Arradin System, Toavis

"GIVE IT EVERYTHING YOU'VE GOT," COLEMAN SAID OVER THE comm. "Press the advantage."

He didn't receive a reply, though he wasn't expecting one, either. His pilots had other things to worry about—things like the hundred or so Baranyk fighters that they had drawn away from the carrier before the *Jamestown* had jumped in. The vessel was now in a pitched battle, flanking the Baranyk capital ship and laying into it with heavy close-range fire. The rest of the pilots were still focused on the single-manned Baranyk fighters, though the point-defense cannons on the *Jamestown*'s starboard side aided them.

Like the rest of his pilots, Coleman had taken longer than he would have liked to settle into the rhythm of the battle. They had never experienced it, and he hadn't in years. But things were different now. Things felt good. Things felt *right*.

He pulled a high-g turn, caught an enemy fighter with cannon fire as it streaked past in pursuit of one of his squad mates, spun out of its expanding debris field, then pushed the stick forward, diving below the Z-axis of the battle plane. Another short burst later, another Baranyk fighter was gone. Spinning again, he pulled back up then leveled out, cutting a path along the top of the *Jamestown* and laying waste to the fighters attacking it.

But despite how well the squadron was faring, they were still facing a significant numbers disadvantage. The worst of the battle was still ahead.

Strafing across the stern of the *Jamestown*, Commander Coleman flipped, preparing for another pass. Rather than flying toward the bow, he veered starboard, turning back into the thick of the battle. He targeted the nearest friendly fighters and provided aid to those with enemy tails. He could continue to pick off unsuspecting fighters almost at will, but unless some of his pilots were left to assist, it would all be in vain.

He juked, janked, shifted, dove, and climbed, moving with the never-ending music of battle. It was a silent battle, of course. The sounds of gunfire, missile launches, and ship explosions had no way of traveling across the vacuum of space, but the music was in his head. All he had to do was write it down.

Coleman was about to request a status of the Baranyk vessel when a terrible, white-hot explosion erupted from the *Oregon*.

"What the hell was that?" someone shouted over the comm.

"No!"

Coleman watched in horror as additional explosions ravaged what was left of the *Oregon*. In seconds, what had been the pinnacle of human ingenuity and invention was nothing more than an expanding debris cloud.

"Someone get me the goddamned status of that enemy vessel," Coleman bellowed into the comm.

"We're showing significant damage along its port and starboard sides," a female voice replied. "If we'd had another twenty seconds, it would have been slag. Without the *Oregon*..."

Coleman hated the tone of her voice. She sounded defeated. *Goddamn it, the battle isn't over. Not yet.*

"Launch all remaining fighters," Coleman said. "I repeat, launch all remaining fighters. We *have* to destroy that ship." He didn't get a reply, but a few moments later, twelve more fighters shot out of the *Jamestown* in rapid succession. "All right, *Jamestown*. Keep up the attack. We'll provide the extra firepower."

"What are you doing, Commander?" It was Captain Baez again.

"What we were trained to do, sir," Coleman said. "We're going to unload everything we have on that ship. When we're done, it'll be nothing but slag."

"And so will you."

"No faith, sir." Coleman tried to keep his voice light-hearted. "Either way, with that ship gone, the Baranyks' advantage is gone too. Our drone reinforcements can do their job."

There was a slight pause, followed by "Get it done."

"With pleasure, sir." Coleman switched back to his squadron's frequency. "Take heart, pilots. The men and women of the *Oregon* honored your sacrifice. Now it's time to honor theirs. Prepare for an attack run. It's time we reminded everyone why we're here."

Bringing his fighter around in what would become its attack vector, Coleman watched as the rest of his squadron broke off their attacks and fell into a loose formation behind him. The remaining Baranyk fighters saw the sudden change and moved to press the advantage. Their pursuit didn't go unnoticed by the other pilots of the Forgotten, and Coleman could hear his pilots' concern. It was evident in the way their breathing increased, the way they cursed under their breath, forgetting that everyone else in the squadron could hear them.

Coleman ignored all of it, keeping one eye on the path in front of him, the other on the pursuing fighters behind. The attack vector would bring them around the stern of the *Jamestown* and slightly above the Baranyk vessel in what would allow them to devastate the entire length of the enemy ship. But they weren't there yet, and the enemy fighters were nearing missile range.

Close enough.

"Release your chaff," Coleman ordered.

Flying in formation, the pilots had little concern of hitting their friendly fighters behind them, and almost as one, the pilots dropped their chaff. Moments later, the canisters detonated, creating clouds of expanding sand particles. At the high velocity, individual grains would be more than enough to wreak havoc on the pursuing fighters, but as close as they were, the fighters entered a thick cloud of it. The pursuing force was decimated, only a handful of the remaining Baranyk fighters able to successfully navigate the debris cloud.

"Good headwork, sir," Noodle said over the radio.

"We're not done yet," Coleman said. "Switch to missiles, and lock onto the enemy craft. Fire everything you have. We *have* to take out that ship."

Coleman crested the bow of the *Jamestown* then brought his fighter around for his attack run. *We can do this.*

Coleman unloaded his entire arsenal. And so did his pilots. In one glorious moment, nearly one hundred missiles streaked toward the enemy vessel. With its point-defense cannons focusing on the *Jamestown*, the missiles wreaked havoc across its hull. Explosions—more than he could count—riddled the enemy ship, and as he streaked past the bow of the ship, he brought his fighter around, watching, waiting for some sign that the attack had been enough.

It started with what looked like a normal explosion. And then there was a second gout of flame. Then a third. Before he knew it, the entire ship was coming apart.

Coleman screamed into the radio, his voice mixing with the voices of the remaining fighters. They had done it. It had cost them the *Oregon* and nearly a quarter of their squadron, but they had destroyed the enemy vessel armed with the Baranyk weapon. Toavis had a chance.

"*Jamestown,*" Coleman said triumphantly, keying the entire squadron into the communication. "Prepare to launch drone fighters, and instruct the rest of the fleet to do the same."

No answer came.

"*Jamestown*, acknowledge."

Still no answer.

"Did the explosion knock out their communications?" one of his pilots offered.

Maybe. But the uneasy feeling seeping into his gut suggested otherwise.

"*Jamestown* actual, this is Commander Coleman. Release all drone fighters. Acknowledge."

"Negative, Commander," Captain Baez said. His voice was low, breathless. Defeated.

"Why not, sir?" Coleman said. "We just watched the Baranyk ship turn to slag. It's time to press the advantage."

"Because, Commander. That ship wasn't the only one equipped with the weapon."

"Say again, sir?" There had to be a mistake. They had unloaded everything they had on the ship. They didn't have anything left.

"I said that ship wasn't the only one equipped with the weapon. We're still registering the Baranyk signal from at least one other source. Our drones are useless. It's just us."

It's just us. But that won't be enough.

Coleman's reply died on his lips.

45

Ready Room, SAS Jamestown
  Arradin System, Toavis

"WE'RE STILL REGISTERING THE BARANYK SIGNAL FROM AT least one other source," Captain Baez said. "Our drones are useless. It's just us."

Coda saw Moscow looking at him out of the corner of his eye. He ignored him, trying to focus on what Captain Baez had just said. Another signal? Commander Coleman had just bet everything on the fact that the Baranyk ship they just destroyed was the only one equipped with the Disrupter. How could they repel the Baranyk forces now?

"Don't do it," Moscow said. "Don't do it."

"Don't do what?" Coda asked.

"The commander's going to order an assault on the other Baranyk carrier."

Coda thought for a moment, trying to come up with another option. There wasn't one. "He doesn't have a choice."

"Sure he does," Moscow said. "Order the remaining fighters back to base for rearmament. It took every missile we had to destroy that carrier, and that was after it was already heavily damaged."

"There's not enough time. Even ten years ago, it took twenty minutes to rearm a single Nighthawk and re-launch. And that was when the crews were well versed in the process. How long would it take now? Thirty minutes? Forty? The battle will be over by then."

"Then do it in waves," Moscow said. "Ten fighters at a time."

Coda thought for a moment. That made more sense, but he still didn't think it would work. And the commander didn't, either.

"*All fighters,*" Commander Coleman said. "Prepare to assault the second Baranyk carrier."

"I knew it!" Moscow shouted. "Damn it, this isn't a battle we can win."

"He has to try," Coda said. "That's his job. That's *our* job."

"Fine," Moscow said, casting him a frustrated look. "But he can't win this way. He has to think outside the box, the same way he did when he used chaff against the incoming fighters."

"What, though?"

"I don't know." Moscow pinched his forehead as if attempting to massage an idea into being. "I don't know. But sometimes it's not about sheer force. It's about getting creative. Have you ever heard of a Molotov cocktail?"

"Of course," Coda said. "They were used during World War II to help fight tanks."

"Not exactly," Moscow said. "They were actually created before then and gained notoriety when the Soviet Union invaded Finland. Molotov, who was the Foreign Minister of the Soviet Union and involved in the invasion, said that he was just providing aid to the starving Finns. The Finns knew it was a lie, of course, and attacked the invading tanks with what they called 'Molotov bread baskets.' The weapons worked so well, the Finns began mass-producing them, and the Molotov Bread Baskets became Molotov Cocktails. Point is, even the underequipped and outnumbered Finns were able to repel Soviet tanks with little more than glass jars filled with gasoline. That's what we need."

"Flaming jars of gas?"

"Something that turns a weakness into a strength," Moscow said. "Or a strength into a weakness. The Molotov cocktail didn't work because it was powerful. It worked because it exploited the tanks' weaknesses."

"The Baranyk carriers don't have a weakness," Coda said. "That's the problem."

"No," Moscow said. "Everything has a weakness. But that's not what I was thinking. What's *our* biggest weakness?"

"Numbers," Coda said slowly. "Numbers because our drones are inoperable."

"Exactly."

"Holy shit!" Coda said, finally understanding Moscow's train of thought. "Moscow, that's genius!" He jumped to his feet, rushing to the terminal on the wall of the ready room. Unlike his personal tablet, it was linked to the *Jamestown*'s shipboard communication.

"What are you doing?" Moscow asked.

Coda ignored him, punching in the correct frequency. When he had it correctly inputted, he opened the channel. "Commander Coleman? Commander Coleman, do you copy?"

"Who is this?" Commander Coleman asked.

Coda shot a look toward Moscow, whose eyes were wide with disbelief. "It's Coda, sir. We have—"

"Coda, this is a private—"

"Sir, please—"

"—channel. You are to confine yourself—"

"Moscow and I know how to defeat the Baranyk."

There was a slight pause.

"Out with it then, Lieutenant."

"The drones, sir," Coda said.

Commander Coleman cursed. "The drones are inoperable. Now remove your—"

"No," Coda said. "The drones are not inoperable. We just can't navigate them once they're outside our hull. But this is space, sir. Nothing can stop them once they're *moving*."

"You're not making any sense, Lieutenant. You have three seconds."

"We launch the drones *at* the ship, sir. They're kamikazes. Space-age Molotov cocktails. And they'll inflict just as much damage as our missiles. Maybe more, depending how much kinetic energy we can create."

Coda held his breath. One second. Two. Four. He looked at Moscow helplessly. It was their best idea. Their *only* idea. If Commander Coleman didn't use it, if he didn't appreciate Coda's butting in, then Coda was sure he had just doomed any chance he would have at ever piloting a Nighthawk again.

"Captain Baez," Commander Coleman said. "Are you listening to this?"

"I am, Commander."

"How many drones do we have on board?"

"Two squadrons of pilots," Captain Baez said. "With twice as many drones."

Two squadrons. Forty-eight pilots. Ninety-six drones.

And that was just aboard the *Jamestown*. Coda's heart lurched in his chest. They had more than enough drones. They had hope. They could win.

"Make it happen, Lieutenant," Commander Coleman said.

Coda beamed. "Yes, sir."

"We're counting on you, Lieutenant. You understand?"

"I understand, sir."

"Good. Get down to the Drone Operation Center, and radio me when you're set."

"Yes, sir." Coda ended the transmission then turned to face Moscow, who was wearing a grin of his own. "We did it."

"Not yet," Moscow said. "But we gave ourselves a chance."

46

Drone Operation Center, SAS Jamestown
   Arradin System, Toavis

THE DRONE OPERATION CENTER REMINDED CODA OF THE
Coliseum back at the Terran Fleet Academy. Rows of steep
stadium seating circled a three-dimensional imaging
display. Only here, there were no spectators. Coda and
Moscow had arrived only moments before, finding the
display already showing the battle and the drone pilots
plugged in.

The *Jamestown* continued to defend itself against the
enemy fighters that remained from the destroyed Baranyk
carrier, but it was otherwise on the outskirts of the battle.
Nearer to the planet, the remains of the human fleet were
engaged with three Baranyk carriers in orbit, and even with
numbers squarely on their side, they were showing signs of
losing the battle. The human ships took heavy fire, burning
in multiple locations, their once-pristine hulls pocked and

damaged, smoke spewing from them like steam from a kettle.

Coda and Moscow remained on a platform at the base of the image, the seating spiraling up around them. Unlike the Nighthawks, which had to be manually loaded into the launch tubes, the drones were already preloaded, their activation handled by their pilots remotely.

As the last of the pilots settled into their seats, Coda began his briefing. "We don't have a lot of time, and our mission, as simple as it may be, is critical to the success of this battle. As we speak, the *Jamestown* is navigating toward the Baranyk ship equipped with the Disrupter. Once in position, we will launch our drones, piloting them at full thrust into a collision course with the Baranyk carrier itself."

"Won't the weapon render all controls useless?" one of the drone pilots asked.

Unable to tell which pilot had asked the question, Coda looked in the general direction of the voice. "Yes, but the Baranyk signal isn't omnidirectional. It needs to be pointed at its target. That will give us the precious time needed to plot our course of attack. Any other questions?"

"How long are we talking?"

"From the moment our drones are spotted? Two to three seconds. Maybe. We can't count on more than five from the moment our drones leave the launch tubes."

Hushed voices filled the large space as the pilots muttered their disbelief.

"Fortunately," Coda said above the din, "our target is huge and vulnerable. We're not fighter pilots here. We're shooting a gun. Just point it at its target, and let it fly."

There were no further questions after that, and Coda sat down at his own station beside Moscow. "You ready to do this?"

"Just like our days back at the academy."

"Only now, we're on the same side," Coda said.

"I can hear the Baranyk crying for mercy already."

The world as Coda saw it disappeared as he slid on his VR helmet. Gone was the Drone Operation Center, replaced by the first-person view of the inside of a drone cockpit. After spending so much time in the Nighthawk, Coda needed several moments to refamiliarize himself with the view. He brought his drone online then activated his radio, patching in the rest of the drone pilots into Commander Coleman's squadron's line.

"Coda to Commander Coleman. We're ready, sir."

"Excellent," Commander Coleman said. "Prepare to launch on my mark."

Coda shifted in his seat, listening to the accompanying radio chatter. Commander Coleman and Captain Baez were working through the intricacies of the plan, moving the *Jamestown* into position.

For the first time since radioing the commander, nerves fluttered in his stomach. His arms and legs felt weak, and he felt like he needed to throw up, piss, or both. Steadying his breathing, he put himself through a quick relaxing exercise.

The thought of sitting in that office back at the academy brought a smile to his lips. So much had changed since those days, not the least of which was his relationship with Moscow. Things had been bad then had become worse, and now they sat side by side, having come up with a battle plan that would save the other members of their squadron.

"Still with me, Coda?" Commander Coleman asked.

"Still here, sir. Waiting for your order."

"Show them what you've got," Commander Coleman said. "Mark!"

Someone other than Coda handled the launch, but at

the commander's order, the launch tube became a blur, and at one-sixteenth-of-a-second intervals, he and the rest of the forty-nine pilots were hurled into the black.

There was no time for formations, no time to form up. As soon as Coda's drone was beyond the *Jamestown*, he directed it at the Baranyk carrier. At the distance, it was nearly invisible, so he relied on the *Jamestown*'s computer to target it and plot a collision course. Once it was within his sights, Coda punched it, accelerating the drone to full throttle. Aside from the ever-increasing speedometer and the subtle shift of space, there was no way to tell if the drone had responded to his command or not. No accompanying g-forces. No sudden weight on his chest. Nothing.

"Hornet One is a go and on course," Coda said.

"Hornet Two is a go," Moscow echoed then gave an enthusiastic hoot.

More pilots announced their successful course.

Coda tried to determine how much time had passed since his launch. Three seconds? Four? He would lose operational control at any moment. Spinning around, he saw nearly two full squadrons of drones racing through the black. It was a beautiful sight. One he had dreamed about during his early days at the academy.

... and then it disappeared.

The Baranyk had hit them with their weapon.

47

Cockpit, Nighthawk
 Arradin System, Toavis

"Hawk One, this is Hornet One," Coda said over the radio. "We have lost control. I repeat, the Baranyk have targeted our drones and we have lost navigation."

Coleman let the words wash over him. The drone pilots had launched only seconds ago. Had they had enough time?

"Captain Baez," Coleman asked, "how many drones were able to successfully plot a collision course?"

"Looks like forty-three, Commander."

"Copy that," Coleman said.

Forty-three out of an even fifty. That number was remarkable, considering the small window they'd been given to work with. Commander Coleman had often discounted the drone piloting program. In his opinion, flying what amounted to a glorified paper airplane wasn't flying. But there was little doubt that their pilots were good at what they did.

I'll have to go easier on them in the future.

As expected, a number of Baranyk fighters broke away from the battle, moving to intercept the incoming drones. They would make short order of the human attack force if it had no backup.

"All right, ladies and gentlemen," Coleman said. "The drones are away. Time to make sure they find their target. Let's go. Time to plow the road!"

He punched the throttle, rocketing toward the battle and Baranyk vessels. Positioned as they were, the Nighthawks were a full two seconds ahead of the drones and approaching the incoming enemy from their flank. The Baranyk flew in a tight formation, which was a mistake, given that Coleman and the rest of his fighters were out of missiles.

As the first fighter came into range, Coleman opened fire, squeezing the trigger in short, controlled bursts. He shot down two fighters before the rest of his squadron opened fire. Within moments, a dozen more became space dust. With the smaller human force the larger immediate threat, the Baranyk fighters altered course, moving to engage the Forgotten. Coleman hooted as the drone ships zipped past unmolested, their path to the capital ship clear.

Then the dogfight began. He swerved, avoiding an incoming Baranyk fighter, opened fire, and shot down a second. Then he veered, peppering a third while bringing the capital ship back into view. Its point-defense cannons shot down many of the incoming drones, but dozens of explosions erupted against its hull. Terrible gouts of flame inflicted more damage than anything his missiles had been able to accomplish.

Coda had been right.

But would it be enough? Coleman longed to have more

kamikaze drones, but they had purposely left the second squadron aboard the *Jamestown*. The Baranyk weapon would be pointing in the *Jamestown*'s direction already, further shortening the drones' operational window. More importantly, if their attack succeeded in destroying the Disrupter, the remaining drones would become fully operational and able to enter the battle. For that same reason, they had reserved the drones on the other ships as well. They would need them. Because god be damned, they were going to succeed.

Coleman went positive-Z. The Baranyk ship disappeared from view just as more explosions riddled its hull. The sudden change of course was the only thing that saved Coleman's eyes. A triumphant explosion lit up the black as the second Baranyk carrier erupted into flames.

Jubilant shouts filled the radio.

"Captain Baez," Coleman said as he shot down another Baranyk fighter. "Tell me that did it. Tell me we've eliminated the Baranyk signal."

The radio remained silent as the *Jamestown* was no doubt running the diagnostics. Coleman spun then pulled a tight, high-g turn, catching another fighter in his sights. But he wasn't done. He shot down two more before Captain Baez's voice came on the radio.

"All ships, this is Captain Baez. The Baranyk signal has been eliminated. Launch all drones. I repeat, launch all drones."

More triumphant cheers echoed across the line.

Coleman opened a private channel. "Sir, what if there's a third signal? We just committed every drone in our fleet."

"This battle is over, either way, Commander," Captain Baez said. "Either the signal is destroyed and our drones can engage, or it's not, and we're forced to retreat."

"Forced to retreat?" Coleman repeated. "The strategy worked. If there's another ship with the weapon, we can—"

"The Baranyk will just shoot down the next wave of drones. The strategy could only work once. And my intel shows me that nearly all of your fighters are down to their last ten percent of ammunition. You are ordered to return to base."

Coleman wanted to argue. He wasn't done. He'd waited years to get back into the cockpit, to get back into battle, and he wasn't ready to give that up. But he'd been given a direct order, and besides that, Captain Baez was right. They were all dangerously low on ammunition.

"Acknowledged." Coleman switched to his pilots' channel. "All fighters, this is the commander. Good work. We've done our jobs and given the fleet a chance. RTB for rearmament and await further instruction."

Coleman shot down another Baranyk fighter before flipping around and blazing a trail back to the *Jamestown*. He passed the *Jamestown* drones headed to battle, and something told him that Coda and Moscow, who had led the previous assault, wouldn't have given up their place in the squadron. Despite everything that had happened, they would get their chance to fight after all.

Do your squad mates proud, gentlemen. You've already earned my admiration.

48

Drone Operation Center, SAS Jamestown
   Arradin System, Toavis

It was joy. Pure, unbridled, glorious, never-felt-before joy.

Tucked away in the safety of the drone fighter pod in the Drone Operation Center, Coda grinned as his drone belched fire and death, tearing through Baranyk fighters with reckless abandon. He zigged and zagged, through and around, above and below hordes of Baranyk fighters still taking part in the battle. Even after the destruction of the second Baranyk carrier, they showed no signs of giving up. Their carriers and the remaining vessels from the Sol Fleet duked it out about Toavis like heavyweight boxers trading haymakers. Hornet drones poured from the human carriers, assaulting the Baranyk carriers like swarms of angry bees.

Moscow was on his wing the entire time, mirroring Coda's flight when Coda wasn't mirroring his. Coda had spent so much time studying his former rival that Moscow's flight strategy was as familiar as his own, and together, they created a true fighter pair. They cut through the Baranyk droves like a knife through water. Coda had already lost count of how many fighters he had shot down, but he was sure it was over twenty.

This is what the commander meant, Coda realized. *This is what he meant when he said that a pilot needed to know everything about his wingmen. If the entire squadron was this comfortable with each other, nothing could stop us.*

"Coda, you've got one on your tail. Drop negative-Z, twenty degrees, and loop right in three, two, one, break!"

Trusting Moscow completely, Coda dove below the battle plane and pulled his drone around in what would have been an excessive high-g maneuver capable of causing blackout. Separated from the stresses of spaceflight, Coda took out another pair of fighters while Moscow cleared his tail.

"Thank you," Coda said, meaning every word. Though he was safely tucked away in the bowels of the *Jamestown*, they had expended their extra drones in the process of destroying the Baranyk carrier. If his drone was shot down, he would be out of the battle.

"Does that make us even?" Moscow said.

"Even?" Coda barked a laugh. "For that? Yeah, right! I saved your ass from becoming a new crater on Theseus. You've got a long way to go."

"You never know 'til you ask."

Coda laughed then squeezed off another burst, taking down two more fighters. Moscow's drone appeared beside Coda's, and together, they performed a gentle turn, bringing the heart of the battle into view. The remaining Baranyk carriers were flanked on both sides by their human counterparts, taking heavy fire. The various drone squadrons attacked in coordinated wave after coordinated wave.

"All *Jamestown* drone pilots, this is Captain Baez. You are to join ranks with the drone squadrons from the *Virginia*, *Oregon*, and *Edmonton* and focus all your efforts on the carrier assaulting the Toavis installation."

A sudden, blinding explosion punctuated the captain's words as another of the Baranyk carriers exploded.

Three down. How much longer will they hold out?

"Let's go," Coda said. "They're on the run now."

"Right behind you," Moscow said.

Coda darted below the battle plane, plotting a course through the Toavis atmosphere toward the Baranyk carrier. He and Moscow flew with hundreds of Hornets, each on its own slightly different course. Having never flown in a proper Hornet squadron before, Coda and Moscow had fallen back to their Nighthawk training, flying as a fighter pair and leaving the formations to their counterparts.

Atmospheric flight was entirely different from space flight. It was slower, with more drag, and under the constant effect of gravity. In space, the drones could flip and reverse course in less time than it took to say the words, but atmospheric attacks were closer to bombing exercises—something they hadn't been trained in.

We'll have to make do.

Dropping his speed, Coda brought his drone behind the *Jamestown*'s Coyote Squadron and prepared for his attack run. The battle had been so thick with Baranyk fighters that he hadn't needed to use his missiles and had instead relied heavily on his cannons. He flipped the switch on his stick to missiles then targeted multiple points along the Baranyk carrier's length. Zooming into position, he squeezed, and two missiles launched away in rapid fire.

Coda spun, watching the missiles streak toward their mark. Accompanying them were hundreds of additional bands of white vapor cutting across the Toavis atmosphere, ending in explosions that tore into the organic Baranyk hull.

As a single unit, the Hornet drones looped around, preparing for their next run. Baranyk point-defense weapons cut through their ranks but not before more missiles found their target. More explosions tore through the hull. Some, Coda noticed, came from *inside* the ship. The Baranyk ship suddenly careened, smoke billowing from thousands of impact holes, and began to lose altitude.

"One more," Coda said, digging himself deeper into his seat. "One more."

And as if they could hear him, the drone squadron leaders brought their fighters around for a final pass. Coda, who only had two missiles remaining, targeted two more points on the Baranyk vessel and squeezed the trigger. His missiles joined ranks with another volley, and a moment later, a terrible explosion lit up the Toavis sky.

Boom. Coda watched as the Baranyk ship disintegrated, falling to the planet's surface. It was a beautiful sight.

"*Jamestown* pilots, this is Captain Baez. It's time to come home. The remaining Baranyk carriers are bugging out."

Cheers echoed across the line and through the Drone Operation Center. Coda added his to the mix.

49

Drone Operation Center, SAS Jamestown
   Arradin System, Toavis

CODA REMOVED HIS HELMET AND PLACED IT ON THE HOOK inside the drone operation pod. The Drone Operation Center vibrated with the sounds of pilots cheering. There were screams and hoots, trash talk, and hugging. Victory had never sounded so sweet.

Someone grabbed him under his arms, yanking him to his feet. It was Moscow. He yelled victoriously, hugged Coda tightly, then gave him a vicious shove.

"We did it!" he shouted. "We sent them back to their hole!"

Coda grinned, excited and proud. But something was off. He wasn't as excited as he had expected to be.

Moscow saw it, his own smile faltering. "Are you all right?"

"Yeah." Coda didn't know how else to respond. He didn't know what was wrong. Didn't know how he felt.

"Bullshit," Moscow said. "I know you well enough to know to know something's up."

"I don't know how to describe it," Coda said. "I just feel... *relieved*. It's stupid, I know."

"Your idea just saved a lot of lives, Coda."

"It was your idea, not mine."

"No." Moscow shook his head. "I only knew *something* needed to be done. Not *what*. That was you."

Coda wasn't buying it. Moscow was just trying to cheer him up. "And I wouldn't have thought of it without you."

"Fine," Moscow said. "We came up with it together."

The door to the Drone Operation Center slid open, interrupting their argument. The remains of the Forgotten streamed in, their cheers adding to the rest, making the celebration damn near deafening. Squawks and Noodle saw Coda and broke into a sprint that covered the distance between them in a blink.

Squawks crashed into Coda, nearly sending them both to the deck. "You crazy son of a bitch! You've got some balls on you, you know that? Barging into the commander's communications like that. What the hell got into you?"

Coda laughed and pushed Squawks off him. "I channeled my inner Squawks, that's all."

"What does that mean?"

"It means that I had something to say, and I wanted everyone to hear it."

Squawks thought about the words for a moment. "So if I'm hearing you right," he said slowly, "you're saying that without me, you never would have told the commander your plan."

"I guess so," Coda said.

"Then I'm a hero." Squawks turned to Noodle, giving

him a playful shove. "You hear that, twig? I'm a hero. I'm a goddamned hero!"

"Someone stop him," Noodle said, failing to hold back a smile. "Please."

But Coda was too busy laughing. It felt too good to have all of his friends back together again.

Except...

"Where's Tex?" Coda asked.

Noodle's smile disappeared, and he looked to Squawks, whose own jubilant attitude faltered.

"What?" Coda already knew the answer but needed confirmation. "What happened?"

"It was hell out there for a while," Squawks said, his voice haunted. "He... He didn't make it."

Coda shook his head, refusing to believe it, refusing to let himself be consumed by his emotions again. Tex was gone. Coda would never laugh at one of his ridiculous sayings again... or be put at ease by his genuine concern. It was almost unthinkable. And Tex wasn't the only one. The squadron had suffered major losses. How many other pilots would never return home? Would never see their loved ones again? The celebration in the room suddenly felt very wrong.

"He died doing what he loved," Noodle said. "He wanted to fly a Nighthawk so bad, he joined the program twice. And you know what? His family told him he wouldn't live to see thirty-six, and he proved them wrong, didn't he?"

"That, he did." Coda swallowed the lump in his throat. "That, he did."

The intense feelings of reflection returned. It was in that moment that he finally understood the true meaning of the name Commander Coleman had chosen for his squadron.

Thinking of his friends and follow wingmen, everyone who had joined the program with them, Coda made them a promise.

You won't be forgotten.

50

Commander Coleman's Quarters, SAS Jamestown
Arradin System, Toavis

COMMANDER COLEMAN HAD HIS BACK TO CODA AS HE STEPPED into the commander's personal quarters. Even after a decisive victory, it seemed the commander still couldn't get an office worthy of his station.

"Have a seat, Lieutenant," Commander Coleman said.

Coda did as instructed, watching as the commander turned to him, holding a pair of glasses. This time they were both filled with a brown liquid. He handed one to Coda then sat down opposite him.

"Thank you, sir," Coda said.

"Falcon Rare," Commander Coleman said, nodding at the glass.

That obviously meant something to Commander Coleman, something Coda didn't understand. He sniffed the alcohol then took a sip. It tasted the same as any other whiskey he'd ever drank, but the commander obviously thought highly of it, so he wasn't going to argue.

"So how does it feel to be a hero, Coda?"

Coda shifted in his seat. Squawks had taken no issue with calling himself a hero and shouting it for the entire world to hear, but the idea that Coda was one made him uncomfortable. "I'm not sure I'm a hero, sir."

"That's how it always works, Coda. You never *feel* like a hero, just like a villain never feels like a bad guy. But make no mistake, you and Lieutenant Krylov are to be commended." Commander Coleman took a sip, watching Coda over the rim of his glass. "Your father would be proud."

Coda stirred again. If being called a hero was enough to make him uncomfortable, then being called a hero in the same sentence as his father was damn near unsettling. But Coda had learned something in the three days since the battle.

"Permission to speak freely, sir?"

"Granted."

"You once said that my father cast a huge shadow over my life. And you were right. When I was a kid, my father was a decorated war veteran, one of the best fighter pilots in the fleet. Then as I got older, his mistakes overshadowed me. For the longest time, all I've thought about was making my own way, earning my own glory, and using that to restore honor to my family name. But you know what I realized? I've been lying to myself, sir, and I don't even know for how long.

"I realized after the accident that I haven't wanted to bring honor back to my family name for *me*. I want to do it for *him*. It's clear to me now. I loved my father, and it's terrible to say, but I was angrier at him for leaving me than I was for what he did. And as much as I try to act like I don't, I miss him. Restoring honor to his family name is the single greatest gift I could ever give to him. It's the only way I can truly undo what he did. It's the only way he can ever truly rest. So that's what this has been all about. I didn't do it for me. I did it for him."

Coda took a deep, shuddering breath then a sip from the glass, letting the alcohol burn away the emotion in his throat. The words were finally out. He'd been wrestling with them for a lifetime, trying to comprehend them, accept them, and put them into action.

"Your father was a good man," Commander Coleman finally said. "I know I've said that, but it's true. And it's a shame things turned out as they did."

"You were there, weren't you, sir? Everything about that mission is classified, but... I know it. I can see it in your eyes. You were there. You know what happened."

Commander Coleman's eyes fell from Coda to his glass. He stared into its contents and licked his lips. "I was there."

"What happened, sir?" Coda knew that he was breaking a thousand military regulations and putting the commander in an uncomfortable spot on top of it, but he couldn't hold back. He had to know the truth.

Commander Coleman looked up from his glass with a sad expression. Whether it was from the memory or what he was about to say, Coda couldn't tell. "One of these days, Coda, I'll tell you. But now is not the time."

Coda let out a disappointed breath. He hadn't expected the commander to answer, but he hadn't been able to keep himself from hoping, either. Fighting every urge to ask again, to press the commander into action, Coda nodded. He could live with getting answers someday in the future, as long as he knew he would get them.

Commander Coleman took another sip. "I also thought

you'd like to know that the results of your review have come back."

"The review?" The last three days had been such a whirlwind that he'd completely forgotten about the review. Apparently, their victory at Toavis hadn't settled that. Coda couldn't help but feel as though he'd been thrown from one inferno to the next.

"Cleared of all transgressions."

Coda blinked. "Just like that?"

"Just like that."

"I'm not going to lie, sir," Coda said, letting himself smile. "That's the best news I've heard in a while."

Commander Coleman smiled back. "I'm sure it is, Coda. It also means there's a place within my squadron if you want it. We could use you, Coda. Command is creating an entire fighter group. Ten squadrons. Your former school is being retrofitted to train future Nighthawk pilots until the Baranyk Disrupter can be countered. Even then, I'm not convinced they'll discontinue the program altogether. The Nighthawks and Hornets made a hell of a one-two punch."

Coda studied the commander. There was something in his eyes. Something that told him that, just like when he'd agreed to compete for a spot among the Forgotten, this might be one of the most important decisions of his life. And just as he'd felt back at the academy, he had no way of turning the opportunity down.

"What about Moscow, sir?"

"Lieutenant Krylov? What about him?"

"Will he be a part of your squadron?"

"Your newfound friendship continues, I take it?" Commander Coleman gave him a sarcastic smirk. "That's good to know. Lieutenant Krylov accepted his position twenty minutes ago. He will be a member of the Forgotten."

Coda smiled again. For the first time since Joseph O'Neil's treasonous actions, Coda felt as though he belonged. That his life was finally *his*. The world might not know it yet, but the O'Neil family name once again had honor.

"Then I accept, sir. It would be an honor to fly with you."

If you liked *Wings of Honor*, please consider leaving a review on Amazon. Aside from purchasing a book or recommending it to other readers, leaving a review is the single most helpful thing you can do for an author and I'd be incredibly grateful.

If you want to know the moment *Wings of Mourning*, Book 2 of the Forgotten Fleet is released and get an exclusive fan discount, please sign up for the mailing list!

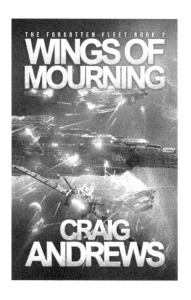

AUTHOR'S NOTE

This book exists for two very specific reasons: because I've been dreaming about X-Wings since the first time I saw Star Wars, and because my oldest son is named after the title character in my favorite book of all time, *Ender's Game*.

So when my youngest son was old enough to realize that his brother had a book of his own and he didn't, I decided that I would write one for him. Dusting off an old idea, I set out to write the awesomest, geekiest book I could write, filling pages with my version of epic X-Wing battles, and writing a character my son could look up to, just as my son Ender can look up to Ender Wiggin.

I hope you enjoyed reading it, and I hope Callan does too (when he's old enough), because I had a blast writing it.

ABOUT THE AUTHOR

Craig Andrews graduated from Portland State University with a Bachelors of Arts in English. Growing up on a healthy diet of fantasy and science fiction, some of his favorite memories include being traumatized by the TV shows Unsolved Mysteries and The X-Files. He currently lives in a small town outside of Portland, Oregon with his wife and two boys.

Craig Andrews Mailing List

craigandrewsauthor@yahoo.com

http://www.craigandrewsauthor.com

Milton Keynes UK
Ingram Content Group UK Ltd.
UKHW012336270224
438567UK00016B/376

9 780999 178423